NO HARD FEELINGS

NO HARD FEELINGS

AN AUGUST RIORDAN MYSTERY

MARK COGGINS

Down & Out Books
3959 Van Dyke Rd, Ste. 265
Lutz, FL 33558
www.DownAndOutBooks.com

Design by Michael Kellner
Photography by Mark Coggins

ISBN-10: 1937495914
ISBN-13: 978-1-937495-91-6

For M.R. Ballou

"No hard feelings, I hope."

"No feelings at all, Captain. No feelings at all."

—RAYMOND CHANDLER, *The Long Goodbye*

CHAPTER 1

Winnie

WHEN SHE GOT TO SAN FRANCISCO and found that August Riordan wasn't there, she decided to kill herself. She took a cab from downtown to the Presidio and walked out on the Golden Gate Bridge. She went past the historical marker placed by the Native Sons of the Golden West, past the section of the walkway bordered by a chain-link fence, and onto the part where the only barrier between pedestrians and a two-hundred-fifty-foot drop was a chest-high railing.

At midspan she stopped to contemplate the lumpy ocean below. Although it was summer, the weather was miserable. Wind shrieked in her ears, and heavy mist coated her face. The oppressive rumble of the traffic behind her—punctuated by tires bumping over the steel joints in the roadway—was nearly as unpleasant. This was not the romantic, graceful end she had imagined.

But how long would she retain this final freedom, the freedom to take her own life? Today she was able to walk. Today she was able to move her arms and hands, to interact with the physical world nearly as well as an undamaged person—instead of the quadriplegic that she was. Being able to do that tomorrow or the next day was no longer certain.

The experimental technology that had restored her mobility was failing. The Winemaker, the man who stole the technology from her husband, murdered him, and sent mercenaries to kill or capture her, was closing in. And now, after months of struggle, she learned that August Riordan, her only living ally, had left San Francisco.

She put her hands on the railing, thinking about what it was going to be like when she hit the water. There almost certainly wouldn't be any pain: after all, she had no feeling below her neck. With any luck, she would plunge straight into the water, drown or die from the impact, and be swept out to sea. It wouldn't be so bad…

Suddenly, she laughed aloud. She probably would die in the Bay, but if she lived—as some few did—she might actually make things worse by severing her spine in a new place, rendering the technology useless. She would be paralyzed once more, the thing she feared the most. And there was more. Whether she lived or died, the Winemaker would very likely get possession of her body and harvest the last few secrets of the technology. She couldn't let that happen.

She stepped back. She had to reframe the decision. Killing herself meant doing it right: a gun to the brain or a razor to the wrist. None of this romantic soaring into the golden afterlife bullshit. And she would have to do it alone, in a place where her body would never be found. Not killing herself meant fighting through the episodes of intermittent paralysis and continuing her search for Riordan. And maybe, just maybe, stopping the Winemaker and avenging her dead husband.

She trudged back to the Presidio parking lot, where she found the taxi driver who had brought her here munching on a Chinese pork bun. He drove her down the Peninsula to the San Francisco Airport—and after two hours of staring at airplanes taxiing on the runway—she felt a renewed resolution to go forward.

Riordan, she had been told, had moved to Palm Springs. It was a long way to travel in her vulnerable state. If she flew, she risked losing her ability to move while surrounded by a plane full of people. That in itself wasn't dangerous, but the hoopla of an onboard medical emergency would draw attention to her, especially if it was reported in the news. She knew from firsthand experience that the Winemaker's people were watching for ER patients with sudden unexplained paralysis.

If she rented a car, she risked losing control of it on the freeway. While she knew that could mean death or serious injury, she decided it was better than being captured by the Winemaker's thugs. She gave Hertz a credit card and a license with a fake name and in return received a Lincoln sedan, which she pointed south down Highway 101.

Inside her purse, which was lying beside her on the passenger seat, was an electronic device about the size and shape of a pack of cigarettes. Its inventor called it a neuromuscular transceiver. She called it a garage-door opener, not because it had anything to do with opening garage doors, but because she had found that it was the best way to explain its presence in her bag.

The transceiver's real purpose was to capture and retransmit impulses from her brain through a set of surgically implanted neurostimulators on either side of the break in her spine. It served, in effect, as a kind of wireless jumper cable for her motor impulses. But it only worked in one direction. It enabled her brain to tell her muscles how to move, but it didn't allow her body from the base of her neck down to tell her brain what she was sensing.

She was used to the one-way nature of the system. She'd been living with it for ten years, ever since she had been selected as a subject for an experimental system intended to aid spinal-cord-injury victims. What she was not used to was having it fail. The transceiver had failed abruptly twice in the last month, depriving her of movement, depriving her of control. The first time she had been jogging, with the transceiver strapped around her arm as if it were an MP3 player. It cut out on her in midstride and she collapsed like she'd been shot. That time, the transceiver resumed functioning almost as soon as she hit the ground. The next time she was not so fortunate.

She'd been in a hotel bed with the transceiver in her purse on the nightstand. She had reached for her cell phone and accidently knocked the purse off the stand. The transceiver had shut off, and her outstretched arm overbalanced her, causing her to tumble from the bed.

She lay with her nose buried in the carpet, thirsty, nearly suffocated, the scratchy fibers of the carpet irritating her skin, until 1:08 p.m. the next day when a knock had sounded on the door and someone had mumbled, "Housekeeping," from the other side. She had cried out for help, the door opened, and a stout Latina woman in a hotel uniform ran to her side.

"I fainted," she had lied to the maid. "Would you help me roll over?"

The maid had dropped to the floor, shoveled the purse and its spilled contents out of the way, and grasped her by the shoulder to turn her face up. Then, just as abruptly as it had cut out, the "nerve tone" to her lower extremities had returned. She sprung to a sitting position.

"Thank you," she had told the startled woman at her side. "I feel much better already."

She decided that the transceiver had a loose connection since each breakdown and restoration had been accompanied by a jolt or a sudden movement of the device. She thought about taking the box apart to check, but she quickly rejected the idea. She lacked the manual dexterity for one thing, and she was terrified of making things worse. She settled for wrapping the device in a sheath of foam rubber to protect it against shocks. A more permanent fix would have to wait for Riordan. Everything now depended on finding him in Palm Springs.

The first four hundred miles or so of the drive passed without event. She endured the boring passage down Highway 5 to Los Angeles, fought LA traffic to Highway 10, and approached the western edge of the Sonoran Desert where Palm Springs lay. Near a dusty little town by the name of Banning, she stopped at a Sinclair station to fill the thirsty Lincoln's tank for what seemed like the twentieth time. She was pumping gas, watching the late afternoon sun sink behind the station's big green dinosaur sign, when a 1969 Chevy Chevelle rumbled up.

Its rear tires were jacked up and its dual exhaust pipes were crimped in the shape of the Chevy logo. The driver's and passenger's doors opened simultaneously and two men in cowboy boots and jeans tumbled out. The driver was taller and wore a bandanna—a do-rag—with an American flag pattern. The passenger was fatter and dumber looking—if that was possible—and wore a T-shirt with the message THERE WILL BE NO QUITTERS UNTIL WE KILL ALL THE CRITTERS across the front.

Both men checked her out in an obvious way. The fatter one

elbowed the other and made a comment in an undertone. The only word she caught over the whine of a passing semi was "tits." She impulsively raised her left hand with her middle finger extended. She didn't want to call attention to herself unnecessarily, but she knew the Winemaker would never employ a pair of bottom-feeders like these. And she was long past the point where she was going to put up with shit from anyone in their pay grade.

The men laughed. "It ain't polite to eavesdrop," said the driver. "Shrake's observation about your fun bags was for my private consumption."

The Lincoln was a good five gallons from the fill line, but she figured she had enough gas to make it to Palm Springs. She clicked off the pump, shoved the nozzle back into its holster, and screwed on the gas cap. "Mouth off to me again," she said, after she pulled open the door to the Lincoln, "and you'll have the toe of my boot for your private consumption."

The retort caught the men flatfooted. She was behind the wheel of the Lincoln with the door partway closed by the time they answered. "Don't go away mad," yelled the fat one. "You haven't heard what I was going to say about your ass…"

She drove through lengthening shadows until she came to a sign for an upcoming rest stop. It reminded her that she had left the service station without going to the bathroom. Since she was unable to feel the pressure of a full bladder or bowels, she compensated by making frequent trips to the toilet. She pulled into the rest stop and parked directly in front of the women's restroom. There were no other cars in the lot.

She ran in and quickly did her business. She returned to the Lincoln and angled across the lot, heading for the exit. It was then that she hit a seam in the pavement that had been obscured by shadows. The car jolted across the gap, and she made the mistake of hitting the brakes. The Lincoln lurched to a stop, and her purse spilled forward on the passenger seat. Until that point, she had always belted it in after a stop, but in her hurry she'd been careless.

The transceiver shut down, and she slumped against the door, pulling the wheel to the right as her hands fell away. Her foot slid off the brake, releasing the car to proscribe a lazy arc back toward the rest-stop buildings. There was another lurch when the front wheel hit the curb. Without a foot on the throttle, the car wasn't going fast enough to propel it onto the sidewalk, so the Lincoln remained wedged there, idling as if she were waiting for someone.

She lay with her cheek pressed against the sticky glass of the window, willing herself not to panic. This wasn't as bad as the time in the hotel room, she told herself. Someone would come along soon and help. She would think of an excuse to get him or her to rummage through her purse—perhaps by asking for pills to help with her "condition"—and in the process the transceiver would get jostled and kick in.

She was right about the first part: a car pulled up beside her in less than ten minutes. Unfortunately, it was the Chevy Chevelle from the gas station.

Tweedledee and Tweedledumber slithered out of the muscle car, grinning with big yellow teeth. "Lookie here, Shrake," she heard the one with the do-rag say through the glass. "It's her. Our girlfriend from the filling station."

The pair walked over to the Lincoln and bent down to stare at her face mashed against the driver's window. "Huh," said Shrake. "Is she sleeping?"

"No, you idiot," said Do-Rag. "Her eyes are open."

"Then let's see if she wants to come out and play." Shrake popped the door. She spilled out against his legs, forcing him to catch her by the shoulders.

"Leave me alone," she bleated, sounding impotent even to herself.

"What's wrong with her?" said Shrake. "Why isn't she moving?"

"Maybe she's playing possum," said Do-Rag. "Let's find out." He squatted beside her and put a grease-stained hand on each breast, kneading them like so much dough. When she did nothing but curse him, he laughed. "Must be an epileptic."

"What's that mean?"

"It means she's having a spaz attack. She's lost control of her body." A beat went by. "Let's take her behind the men's room."

"Ya think?"

"Yeah, I think."

She stared at a gold-capped incisor in Do-Rag's fetid smile. "Don't," she said. "I'm a cop."

Shrake laughed. "A cop? Nice try, bitch."

"Look in my purse. You'll find a shiny gold badge. I'm a lieutenant with the LAPD."

Do-Rag glanced up at Shrake, the slightest bit of doubt on his face. He straightened and ambled over to the passenger door, yanking it open. He snatched the purse from the seat and began rummaging through it. When he didn't immediately find a badge, he upended the bag and shook out all the contents. "I knew it," he said, after sorting through the detritus. "You're bluffing. Shrake, pull her out of there."

Nerve tone to her extremities had returned as soon as the transceiver had hit the seat, but she waited to make her move until Shrake pulled her limp body from the car and was hauling her toward the men's room. She twisted out of his grasp and stepped back to deliver a kick to his midsection. He bent over the blow with a surprised grunt. She kneed him in the face then came forward to cradle his head in her stomach. She yanked his jaw up while twisting the back of his head over. *Snap* was too clean a word for the grinding, popping sound his neck made as it broke. She let his body drop to the asphalt with a rubbery thump, not giving a passing thought to the irony of the manner in which she had dispatched him.

Do-Rag rushed her, taking her down with a chest-high tackle. He didn't realize it, but it was the worst mistake he could have made. The transceiver system slowed her reactions, so she was not as effective in a stand-up fight where there was a need to parry or dodge blows. Wrestling was another matter. Since she never felt fatigue in her muscles, she trained relentlessly with weights and cardio exercises, often as much as six hours a day. Her hand, arm, and leg strength were off the scales for a woman, and she had practiced self-defense techniques to channel that strength in the most effective manner.

Do-Rag got on top of her and locked his hands around her throat, squeezing while he called her a "psycho skank." She watched him with clinical dispassion then reached up to take the index finger of his right hand, bending it as if it were a pipe cleaner. He howled in pain, his grip on her neck slackening. She rose to head butt him and then slapped both of his ears with her open palms. She scrambled out from beneath him and took hold of the knot at the base of his do-rag. She slammed his forehead into the edge of the curb. After the first impact, he slumped to the asphalt. After the second, his legs convulsed, and his hands twitched open and closed. After the third, he voided his bowels and lay still.

She stood to survey the wreckage. She would have shuddered if she were able to. The Winemaker had done this to her, the Winemaker and the horse-riding accident that had severed her spine when she was fourteen. The accident had stolen her adolescence, her puberty, the chance to have any sort of a real relationship with a man.

Being selected as the guinea pig for the neurostimulator technology offered salvation. It held out the promise of a normal life; it led to an unhoped-for marriage with charismatic Ted Valmont, the venture capitalist who had founded the company to commercialize the technology. But the Winemaker had snatched it all away. He had ambushed and killed Ted, and sent her on the run. Her grief and rage at Ted's murder—and her subsequent struggle to avoid capture—had ground the humanity out of her.

She stepped over Do-Rag to the Lincoln, dropping into the seat to put the shifter in reverse before she pulled the door closed. She backed away from the buildings and sped out onto the highway, not sparing a glance at the rearview mirror.

CHAPTER 2

Winnie

SHE FOUND RIORDAN IN A TRAILER PARK in the northwest corner of the city, nestled at the base of Mount San Jacinto. His trailer had started life as a single-wide, but at some point had been encased in wooden sheathing that extended from both sides like wings to form a pair of carports. It was better than some in the park, but worse than most. The sheathing and the trailer itself were painted pink, and the concrete in the carports was stained forest green. The "lawn" in front consisted of a semicircle of dirt that extended out from the dented aluminum skirt of the trailer. River rocks, weeds, and a half-buried truck tire were the only things that broke the chalklike surface of the dry desert soil.

Riordan stood beneath a floodlight in the carport on the right. Around him was a mismatched collection of dumbbells and barbells and a wobbly-looking bench and power rack. He loitered shirtless in cut-off sweatpants and tennis shoes by a table with a bottle of whiskey and six shot glasses. Invisible in the gloom across the street, she watched as he threw back a shot then got down to work on the bench to press what looked to her practiced eye to be around 350 pounds.

He did five reps with relative ease, but strained to finish a sixth, grunting and tensing the muscles in his neck as he barely managed to bring the barbell into the holders at the top of the uprights. He lay on the bench for a moment to catch his breath then levered himself upright and shambled back to the table, where he downed another shot.

Once again, she reassessed her decision to seek him out. Her late husband had thought him a drunken buffoon. Riordan took stupid risks, was a complete Luddite—he didn't even own a cell phone when she had known him—and he ran his mouth when he shouldn't. He wasn't even a good detective in the conventional sense. Yet somehow this buffoon made things happen and, more important, he had saved all of their lives.

Standing in the dark by a palm tree, she shrugged. She shrugged even though no one could see her and even though shrugging required a level of conscious thought from her way beyond what most people gave it. She knew she really didn't have a choice. She knew she needed his help, and she knew she owed him. If she didn't warn him, the Winemaker's thugs would find him as surely as she had. And if there was one person the Winemaker hated more than her, it was August Riordan.

As she crossed the street, he returned to the bench and maneuvered his torso under the barbell. He lifted it from the uprights and let it drop to his chest. He worked to complete a shaky repetition—just barely finding the strength to lock his elbows—and hesitated with the weight balanced above him. Just when she was certain he would realize it was time to call it quits, she heard him say, "Fuck it," and he let the bar down again.

She stepped into the circle of light and approached the bench from behind. Riordan's face was contorted under the barbell, but she could see that he had aged. Wings of gray sprouted from his temples, and the scar at the corner of his mouth seemed deeper and more pronounced. The skin at his throat had lost elasticity.

She watched as the bar dropped lower. Riordan groaned and squeezed his eyes closed, unaware of her presence. In another moment, he risked fracturing his sternum—or worse, choking himself to death.

She reached a hand between the uprights and took hold of the barbell at a spot between his grip. She pulled. He seemed not to understand what was happening at first, but eventually he opened his eyes and strained his head back to see above and behind him.

"You," she said, as she yanked the barbell onto the uprights, "need a spotter."

CHAPTER 3

Riordan

I SLID OFF THE BENCH and stood at the end, taking in the attractive woman who materialized out of nowhere to save me from wearing a 360-pound bow tie. "A spotter?" I said. "What do you mean? I had it under control."

"Sure you did. You had it under control the way the French had the blitzkrieg under control."

I grinned and nodded, suddenly very self-conscious that I was shirtless. "You live around here?"

"I save you from bench-press suicide, and now you're trying to chat me up? You don't recognize me, do you?"

I squinted at her through the glare of the floodlight. She wore a dark tracksuit over a body that managed to be curvy and muscular at the same time. If you told me she was an elite-level sprinter, or even a competitor in a field event like discus, I would have believed you. Her skin was pale with peach undertones, her eyes a startling green. Her jet-black hair didn't seem to go with her complexion, so I put it down for a dye job.

I snapped my fingers like I'd figured it out. "Of course, you're my third ex-wife."

"There's no way you convinced three women to marry you. Here's a hint—think Napa Valley."

I thought about Napa Valley, and I thought about all the bad associations the place had for me. Then the dime dropped. Her hair used to be longer and strawberry colored—and she had bulked up considerably—but it was the same woman. She had been a human guinea pig for a device to help people with spinal-cord injuries walk again, but some bad guys had tried to steal the technology from the start-up where it was being developed. The final showdown cost me a two-month stay in the hospital—and two life sentences for the bad guys.

"Jesus," I said. "Last I heard you got married to your venture-capitalist friend and were living happily ever after. What are you doing here?"

She took hold of one of the hundred-pound plates on the barbell and spun it idly. "Did you read about our company going public?"

"No, but I don't follow that kind of stuff."

"How about how our technology was improving the lives of thousands of spinal-cord patients?"

"No, I didn't. To tell you the truth, that whole episode was like a bad dream to me. There were times I couldn't believe it really happened. That a technology could really do—could do what it does for you. I didn't go looking for further developments."

"If you had, you wouldn't have found them. The company never got off the ground. We were never able to replicate the success I had with the prototype device." She gave the plate on the barbell a final, violent spin. "And then the Winemaker broke out of prison."

"He couldn't have got very far."

"Think again. He got clean away—and now he's out for revenge."

I walked over to the table where I'd laid out a half-dozen shots of whiskey and picked one up. I offered it to her, but she waved me off, so I tilted my head back and threw it down the hatch. I snagged my shirt from the carport floor, pulled it on, then turned to face her. "Who'd he get? That geeky mad scientist guy who invented the technology? What's his name, Niebuhr?"

"Dead."

I hesitated. "Valmont? I mean, Ted—your husband?"

"Dead."

"Jesus, I'm—"

She waved me off again, seemingly no more affected than when she passed on the whiskey. "Keep the party going. Who else?"

"His brother?"

"Dead."

"There's no one else but you and me."

"He also killed Breen, his old partner, who was imprisoned in another state."

I took a moment to absorb all of this. "Why hasn't he come after us?"

"They've sent five teams after me so far. I think they want to take me alive, but I've never been able to confirm it. None of them lived long enough for me to question them. On the other hand, I think he just hasn't found you yet—or possibly he's saving you for something special."

"Special? I only met the man once."

"But, oh, what a meeting. You put a knife through the throat of his employee and then shot and beat him senseless with a phone book. It tends to make an impression."

"I suppose it does." I gunned the final whiskey shot, not bothering to offer it to her. I remembered now that she couldn't drink: Alcohol scrambled the signals from the device to her central nervous system. "You're here to warn me, then. I appreciate it, but you didn't have to come personally. A phone call or a letter would have sufficed."

"That's vintage. I could never tell whether you were stupid or just saw an advantage to acting that way. No, I'm not here to warn you. I'm here to get your help. If we don't hang together, we'll hang separately. A saying from one of your Founding Fathers."

I nodded, remembering that she was British, although there was nothing left of her accent. "Yeah, Ben Franklin. Where'd you park?"

"Where'd I park?"

"If you parked in the carport by the front gate, you're gonna get towed. May already be towed. That's for residents only. Mrs. Grenshaw watches those spots with an eagle eye and calls the wrecker whenever she sees a car she doesn't recognize."

"That's where I parked."

"Give me your keys. The trailer's open. Wait in there and we'll concoct our plan for world domination when I come back."

She looked at me like I was trying to pull a fast one.

"I'm not going to steal your car. You'll never find the visitor lot. It's way in the back and it's not even lit."

"Okay," she said, and pulled a set of rental-car keys from the pocket of her warm-up. "It's a black Lincoln."

"Pretty cushy for you."

She passed over the keys and I started toward the front gate. "Hey,"

I said, turning back to her. "What do you call yourself these days?" She had a phony name when I had met her, and I'd never learned her real one.

She smiled for the first time, and pronounced dimples appeared in her cheeks. I remembered those, too.

"Winnie," she said.

"Winnie? As in *Winnie-the-Pooh?*"

"No, not as in Winnie-the-fucking-anything. Just Winnie."

It was my turn to grin. "Winnie. How sweet."

I found the Lincoln at the front of the complex as advertised. I glanced over at Mrs. Grenshaw's trailer and saw her face pasted to the glass of her kitchen window, hand cupped against the glare. I was half convinced that she received kickbacks from the towing company, and the nasty look she gave me as I opened the door of the Lincoln did nothing to change my mind.

I started the car and pointed it toward the back of the trailer park, mulling over Winnie's story as I navigated the labyrinth of streets. I decided it was mostly bullshit. I didn't doubt that her company had failed, but the business about the Winemaker's escape from prison and his subsequent efforts to get revenge was hard to believe. Maybe her husband had left her—maybe he had actually died. The story had to be a deluded coping mechanism.

That a person in her position could come unhinged didn't surprise me. She was like the operator of a construction crane. She sat atop an elaborate machine, controlling it without any direct connection to or feedback from the mechanism. She was estranged and isolated from the physical world in ways I would never understand.

I parked the Lincoln next to a white van in the visitor's lot. Three-quarters of the park residents had left to spend the summer away from the 110-degree heat, so I was mildly surprised to find even one other car there. I trudged back to my humble abode. A block from my place, I cut through the yard of a neighbor I knew was in Minnesota and came out across the street from my trailer. Two guys were standing in front. One was pulling up the cover on my vintage 1968 Galaxie 500 to look at the license plate, and the other was watching him do it. My pulse jumped up a notch. Maybe Winnie was onto something after all.

The interlopers heard the crunch of gravel from my footsteps and turned to look at me.

"Hello," said the one who wasn't monkeying with the cover, a Lurch-like giant whose bald head gleamed dully.

"Hi there," I said. "You a friend of August's?"

"Yes, we are. We didn't get an answer when we knocked and we wanted to make sure this was his place. Have you seen him around?"

"I saw him earlier in the day. We made a date to work out together." I gestured at my attire and then at the bench press, where I noticed something puzzling. "But I'm a little late."

The guy by the car let go of the cover and straightened up. He was short and sleek, and was wearing too many clothes for the desert. "Is Winnie visiting him?" he asked.

"Winnie?" I said, in what I hoped was a puzzled tone.

"His old girlfriend."

I started across the street. "He never mentioned her. How do you guys know him? Fraternity brothers?"

A pause. "That's right."

I came to a stop in front of them, standing slightly closer to the larger one. I had moved the Lincoln key to my left hand, positioning the notchless shank between the fingers of my closed fist like a tiny dagger. I smiled. "So the frat publishes the license plates of its members, does it?"

Lurch started to smile back, but realized halfway through that I was calling their bluff. Whatever expression he would have assumed next was lost when I hit him in the mouth.

I felt the key lacerate his cheek and he fell against the trailer, reaching instinctively to staunch the blood that was already spurting from the wound. I turned to face the short guy just as he fumbled a police Taser from the pocket of his windbreaker.

He jerked his arm up, the laser sight glowed red, and there was a pop like a lightbulb exploding. One of the two Taser probes bit into my thigh. The other spooled past me, the copper wire that ran from it to the gun shimmering with reflected light. I heard the rapid-fire crackle of voltage being sent down the wires, but with the second probe lying on the cement behind me, very little juice was being conducted across the gap.

I rushed the short man, threading my way past his outstretched arm to bring the heel of my palm square into his nose. It spread like Smucker's boysenberry jam. I helped him into a back dive, and he went reeling into the Galaxie. The crown of his head caught the rear bumper and he crumpled to the ground and lay still.

If I thought Lurch was out of the fight, I was in for a surprise. I heard a grunt and twisted back just in time to take a roundhouse kick from him in the gut. Twisting avoided a blow to the ribs and a debilitating fracture, but as I folded over his shin and flopped to the ground, it was hard to gauge the immediate benefit. Lurch jumped forward and began aiming further kicks at my head.

I brought my arms up to protect my skull and tried to roll out of range. His partner's prone body stopped my progress. Lurch skipped in for the kill. He feinted at my stomach then aimed the toe of his wingtip straight at my throat. I barely managed to block it with my hands, but it stung like hell and I knew his next kick would find its mark.

Except there wasn't one. I heard a sickening thump, and Lurch collapsed to the ground like a rope ladder. A split second later, one of the twenty-five-pound plates from my bench press came clattering down beside him. It rolled on its edge for a foot or so, imprinting a trail of red blood behind it, and then went into a flat spin like a quarter tossed on a bar.

I scrambled to a sitting position. My heart slammed kettle-drum beats. I looked at the plate, I looked at Lurch, and I looked at the deserted street in front of my trailer. "What the fuck?" I said in summary.

"Up here."

Winnie stood on the roof of my trailer, arms akimbo, staring down at me.

"What are you doing up there?"

"That's kind of a stupid question, isn't it? You just saw what I was doing up here."

I eased to my feet, holding my bruised stomach muscles with one hand while I tried to detach the Taser wire with the other. "I meant, why did you go up there in the first place? I told you to wait in the trailer."

"How did I know you weren't working for them? That you hadn't gone to call them?"

She had a point. I was too busy doubting her story to think about how it looked from her perspective. "Okay," I said finally. "Then the plate from the bench press..."

"Was intended for you. I brought two of them since I know you have a hard head."

"Thank you for that. But if you had two, why didn't you use one a little sooner?"

"Let me answer that question with another. Why, after convincing them you were a neighbor, did you walk right up and let them know you were onto their game? I thought you had something better in mind."

"Oh."

Winnie dropped to her haunches, turned, and lowered herself over the side of the trailer. She hung from the edge of the roof for a moment then let herself fall to the ground. Her landing was a bit wobbly, but no one observing her would guess that she was a quadriplegic. She went past me to squat by the short guy. She peeled back an eyelid to check his pupil then pressed hard on one of his nail beds. She did the same for Lurch. "Dead," she concluded. "Both of them."

"Terrific."

"Far from it. I needed—correction, *we* needed—to question them." She came up to stand beside me. "Now *we* need to get rid of the bodies."

CHAPTER 4

Winnie

Winnie helped Riordan pull the bodies from the front of the trailer to a dark corner of the second carport behind the covered auto. They searched both men, finding a set of rental-car keys on the shorter one and another Taser and a 9mm automatic on the taller. Neither had a wallet or ID of any sort.

"What's with all the Tasers?" asked Riordan, holding the stubby weapon to the light.

"They have their reasons. One I already told you—they want me alive. Also, guns aren't the best thing to use against me unless you get a head shot. I don't feel the shock and pain of being hit, so I might just keep coming at you until I bleed out."

"Glad you can be so dispassionate about it."

She ignored his comment. "And although I've never been jolted with one, I'm sure a Taser would completely scramble the signals from the transceiver. It would probably affect me more than it would a normal person."

Riordan shrugged and flipped the Taser onto the stomach of the shorter man. He nudged the body with his toe. "And you were planning on getting rid of them how?"

"You're the local."

"Yes, I'm the local. That means I can tell you where to get a tasty margarita or a good deal on tires. It doesn't mean I am familiar with popular body-dumping grounds."

"Get creative. Exercise your right brain a little."

"Let me see the car keys." She passed them over, and Riordan examined the handwritten tag from the rental-car company. "Okay. Come with me. I'll bet I know where they're parked."

"Your famous visitor's lot?"

"You got it."

She followed him on a circuitous route through the trailer park, sometimes crunching through the gravel yards of other residents, sometimes walking along darkened streets. The place seemed almost completely deserted. At the back of the complex, a road descended to a swale of unpaved desert with a few parking places marked with white rocks. Her Lincoln was there, lodged in front of a saguaro cactus that had been maimed repeatedly with a .22 rifle. Beside the Lincoln was a white van.

Riordan pressed the clicker on the key fob. The van chirped in response and its door locks flicked open. "Open sesame," he said.

Standing at his shoulder, she watched as he pulled the driver's door open and looked inside. There was nothing remarkable in the passenger area, but when they walked around to the back and opened the cargo door, they found a mattress on the floor and two pairs of handcuffs locked around metal tie-down loops.

"Your intended home away from home," he said.

She nodded then reached to take hold of a large duffel bag that was lying on top of the mattress. She pulled it in range and yanked down the zipper. Inside, she found two pump-action shotguns, another 9mm automatic, ammunition for both, duct tape, several sets of PlastiCuffs, two pairs of military-grade night-vision goggles, two body-armor vests, and still more Tasers. There was also a leather case containing three hypodermic syringes loaded with a cloudy liquid.

Riordan whistled. "All the party fixins," he said, scratching his armpit reflectively. "Wonder what the hypos are loaded with."

"Probably some kind of horse tranquilizer." Winnie picked up one of the automatics and squinted at the markings on the slide. "Numbers have been filed off."

He took the gun from her and checked the other places where the serial number would be stamped. "Yeah, every one of them." He returned it and fished out a vest, holding it out for them to examine. "Hmm, what's that say?"

She leaned in. She could barely make out an insignia printed in gold ink: a tiny fortress with text jutting over the top. "Praetorian."

"Sounds familiar. Ring any bells for you?"

It *did* sound familiar, but apart from the association with ancient Rome, Winnie couldn't place it either. "No," she snapped. "And I don't care if it says Fisher-Price toys. We can use it. All of it."

"Use it how? To start World War III?"

"If we have to. Now, what was your idea with the van? We put the bodies in the back, and..."

He threw down the vest. "And drive it to the north forty of the long-term parking lot at the airport. They won't open it for weeks, and if we're careful about wiping everything down, they won't be able to tie it to us when they do."

"You almost sound like you've done this before."

"No comment."

Riordan got behind the wheel of the van and Winnie got in the Lincoln. They drove to his trailer, where he backed the van up close to the bumper of his old car to block the view from the street. They loaded the bodies in the cargo area, wiped the van down, and stowed the duffel bag in the trunk of his car. Then they caravanned out to the airport, where she waited in the cell-phone lot while Riordan went to the long-term one. Before leaving the trailer, he had put on a baseball cap and pulled a hoodie over it. She realized he was worried about cameras at the entrance of the long-term lot and was pleasantly surprised that he'd had the presence of mind to obscure his appearance.

Winnie had been waiting in the cell-phone lot for less than twenty minutes when she saw him ambling through the forest of sodium-vapor lamps in the lot like an overgrown gangbanger. He nodded at her when he saw the car and went around to the passenger door.

"Any problems?" she asked, once he was seated beside her.

He shook his head and pulled off the long rubber gloves he'd been wearing. "Except the damn gloves. They stink of Lysol."

She laughed. "If you were a proper criminal, you wouldn't have to make do with the gloves you use to clean the toilet."

"I'll take that as a compliment. You hungry? I never had dinner, and we can talk while we eat."

She realized she hadn't eaten herself since breakfast. She glanced at the Lincoln's dashboard clock. It was 11:20. "I'm game. Is there anything open? Or are you proposing to cook something?"

"I'm proposing to let a guy named Denny cook something. He works 24/7."

"Delightful."

He directed her to a Denny's about three miles west of the airport. They got a booth in the back and ordered from a gum-chewing waitress who appeared to be obscuring a tattoo on her neck with heavy makeup. Riordan ordered a chicken-fried steak. Hoping for the best, Winnie got something called Tilapia Ranchero. She knew it was crazy to order fish at a Denny's this far inland, but she was careful about what she ate and didn't want to pollute her body with red meat or fried food.

Riordan had pulled the hoodie off his head. Now he removed the baseball cap and took off the sweatshirt. After brushing his hair back in place, he leaned back in the booth and regarded her. He wasn't an entirely unattractive man—not that his looks had anything to do with what they had to do next.

"You said you came to me for help," he started. "Then you mentioned something about starting a war with that cache of weapons we found. What exactly do you have in mind?"

She snorted. "Isn't it obvious after tonight? We need to help each other stay alive and keep out of the backs of vans."

"Okay, but I get the definite sense you have something more offensive than defensive in mind. We could stay alive by moving to Tahiti."

"If that's a proposition, I'll pass. Yes, I need your help with more than just running away. The first thing is something that has to do with me—with my particular situation." She explained about the problems she'd been having with the transceiver. "I need a way to get it fixed, but I can't risk making the problem worse or breaking the transceiver entirely."

"That is a problem. But you don't expect me to open it up and attempt surgery, do you? I can barely replace the battery on my cell phone."

Winnie did have some idea that Riordan could at least take a peek inside to look for obvious loose wires. She brought her hand to the back of her neck and squeezed. It was one of the few places in her body where she had any sensation and the muscles were tied in knots. "I at least need you to pull guard duty while somebody else looks at it. I can't risk losing my ability to move without a protector."

"Sure."

"And how about helping me find someone to look at it?"

Riordan hunched over his water glass, jockeying the ice cubes in the glass with his knife. "What sort of person do we need? A digital computer expert? Palm Springs isn't exactly Silicon Valley, you know."

"Thanks for the geography lesson. There is a computer chip with specialized firmware in the device, but it also contains a radio receiver and transmitter. I guess you could say it's a mix of digital and analog. Humans are analog, after all, and the transceiver's ultimate purpose is to relay nerve impulses from my brain to my spine."

He set the knife back on the table and looked up at her. An impish smile came over his face, erasing about ten years' worth of mileage. "Hey," he said, "I know just the guy."

CHAPTER 5

Winnie

RIORDAN REFUSED TO SAY ANYTHING ELSE about "the guy" except that they should go to see him immediately. He hurried them through the meal, dodging any conversation about long-term plans. She let him drive the Lincoln back to the trailer park, where once again he parked it next to the saguaro in the visitor's lot. He led them down a street that fronted the outermost ring of trailers, to a double-wide that was lit up like a government building, if the government had double-wide trailers crudely painted to look like UFOs. Beside the trailer was a fifty-foot tower with a many-masted radio antenna at the top.

"It's past midnight," she said, as they went up the walk to the front door. "Are you sure he'll still be up?"

"If it's past midnight here, it's early evening in the South Pole. He'll be up."

Riordan knocked sharply on the door and then yelled, "Hey, Ray, open up. It's me."

A moment later the door was opened by a stooped old man with a Santa Claus beard. Earphones flopped around his neck and he pointed the jack for them at Riordan like an accusing finger. "What do you want now? I had Jessica from Palmer Station on the line."

Riordan turned to Winnie. "He's a ham radio operator. This Jessica is the only woman on staff at a scientific research station in the Antarctic. He figures he's got better odds with a woman stuck at the bottom of the world with nothing but penguins to keep her company."

"But what about the men at the station?" she asked.

"They're not twenty-something actors like me who are about to hit the big time in Hollywood," said Ray.

"Really? I would have guessed you were a young-looking forty instead of a twenty-something."

"I'm eighty-two. But she doesn't need to know that."

"Let us in," said Riordan. "We've got something serious we need your help with."

The old man waved them into the living room, where they sat on a couch draped with a Navajo rug. He went to sit in a wooden swivel chair near a hutch along the back wall. Floor-to-ceiling electronics covered the wall, and a large bullet-shaped microphone sat near a radio with a glowing dial.

"Ray," said Riordan, "this is Winnie. Winnie, this is Ray."

Ray looked at her with obvious fascination and practically licked his lips. "Pleased to meet ya," he managed.

"Charmed," she said, and turned to Riordan. "Are you sure this is a good idea?" If she met him on the street, she wouldn't trust the crazy geezer to give directions to the library, much less diagnose and repair problems with complex electronics.

"Relax," said Riordan. "Ray was an engineer at McDonnell Douglas. He designed the avionics for the F-something-or-other fighter aircraft."

"F-4E Phantom II," corrected Ray. "And I was the chief engineer on the project."

"When was this?" asked Winnie.

"1960."

Winnie lowered her head to massage the muscles in her neck once more. She waved at Riordan to get on with it.

"Now, Ray," he began, "I'm going to tell you a story that will sound a little fantastic, but stay with me. It's all true and you need the background before I explain where you come in." Riordan began to describe the start-up company Winnie's husband had founded to help patients with spinal-cord injuries, but Ray quickly interrupted.

"Sure, NeuroStimix. I read about it. Never really went anywhere, did it?"

Riordan looked at Winnie from under his brows. *I told you so.* "That's the company, Ray, but it turns out that they had a prototype that worked very well. The prototype is Winnie here."

"You mean you have a spinal-cord injury?" asked Ray.

"I'm a quadriplegic," said Winnie.

Ray took the headphones from around his neck and set them down next to the radio. He stood and walked over to Winnie. "You have some sort of neurostimulator implant?"

Winnie got to her feet and turned her back to him. She lifted her hair off her neck and yanked down her shirt collar. "I have two implants. One just above the C7 vertebra to transmit motor signals from my brain to a transceiver, and a stimulator below the break to relay the signals from the transceiver to my body." She felt his finger run over the first implant and presumably continuing down to touch the second.

"My God," said Ray. "Your movements are so natural. What's this transceiver you're talking about?"

She retrieved it from her purse. She pulled it from the crude protective sheath she'd fashioned and held it up. "Here. Like I said, it relays motor signals from my brain to the stimulator. It's also programmed to send ancillary signals independently. Subtle movements to help me maintain my balance or keep a natural gait while walking."

"Amazing."

"Yeah, but not so amazing just at this moment. It's broken."

"Broken how?"

She explained about the intermittent failures, seemingly caused by jolts or vibrations to the circuitry inside the box. "I thought it might be a loose wire."

Ray laughed. "Now who's talking about 1960s technology. It's probably a cracked solder joint."

"Can you fix it?"

"Sure."

She locked her eyes on his to emphasize the serious of the matter. Ray's seemed to gleam with amusement, which only served to agitate her further. "You understand this is very important to me," she said. "If you screw this up, I'll be paralyzed again. I'd rather die."

The old man frowned then brought his hand up to stroke his beard. "If you're so worried about it, why don't you take it back to the NeuroStimix folks for a tune-up?"

She started to respond, but Riordan beat her to the punch. "That's not an option, Ray," he said. "Bridges have been burned."

"All right, then you'll have to put your faith in Uncle Ray. If I get the box open and decide it's something I can't handle, I'll close it right back up. But I doubt that'll happen. The innards of this thing can't be any more complicated than your typical garage-door opener."

She smiled in spite of herself at the mention of garage-door openers. "Okay, how do we do this?"

"Let's go to the lab."

The "lab" proved to be a bedroom with a long wooden table shoved against the far wall. Scattered across the table were a smorgasbord of electronic components and circuit boards in various stages of assembly. There was also a lighted magnifier on a goose neck, test equipment of various sorts, and two soldering irons resting on stands. Holes burned in the table and the carpet beneath gave evidence of wayward solder. Winnie took particular note of the magnifier and thought of a dentist she had as a child who required special glasses to continue to work as he got older. She remembered the painful jabs he gave her when his hands slipped, and she bit her lip. She hoped Ray had it more together.

She handed him the transceiver. "Will you need to disconnect the battery?"

"Yes," he said. "You can't test or solder with juice going through the circuit."

"I'm going to lie on the floor, then. I need to be in a safe position when you pull the plug."

"Wouldn't it be more comfortable if you used the couch in the living room?" asked Riordan.

"More comfortable for what? My head? The rest of me can't tell the difference. Besides, there's no way the patient is leaving the room during the operation." She lowered herself to the floor and lay on her back, staring at the ceiling. "Let's get this over with."

Ray nodded and pulled up a chair by the table. He set the transceiver beneath the magnifier and used a screwdriver to loosen the pair of screws that held the cover—then he promptly flipped it into the air. It bounced off the rim of the magnifier and cartwheeled down to a spot a foot from her head.

"Jesus," she said. "You're not exactly building my confidence here."

"Sorry. I only meant to use the edge of the screwdriver to pop the lid off."

"You popped it pretty good."

Riordan picked the cover off the floor and put it back on the table. "Steady on, Ray. What's next?"

"Gotta pull the battery."

"All right with you, Winnie?" said Riordan.

"Yes, yes, get on with it."

Ray fished the battery out of its cradle and disconnected it. The nerve tone to her lower extremities cut off immediately. *Paralyzed.* It was such an ugly word. She realized with a start that she might never get off this floor under her own power. She bit her lip once more and squeezed her eyes closed.

She heard Riordan moving beside her. When she opened her eyes, she found him sitting next to her, holding her hand. "You know I can't feel that," she said, but she was pleasantly surprised by the gesture.

"That's okay. I can."

She nodded and looked up at Ray. He was holding the transceiver close under the magnifier, turning it this way and that under the light. He set it back on the table and probed its guts with a needlelike instrument, checking the reading on an attached meter each time he touched the probe to the circuitry. It wasn't so very different than the dentist probing for cavities, Winnie thought glumly.

When she couldn't bear to look anymore, she turned back to the ceiling. She distracted herself by watching the broken threads of a spiderweb hover in the ambient breeze. Then she heard Ray grunt.

"What?" she and Riordan said in unison.

"The solder on one of the component leads is bad."

"So you were right," said Riordan.

"Yep. And you were, too. This is definitely a prototype unit. The components on the circuit board are through-hole mounted rather than surface mounted—which is preferred for production designs— and it's clear the leads were hand soldered."

"So what's all that mean?"

"It's good news as far as repairing. It's much harder to fix surface-mounted boards that are wave soldered." He reached for the soldering iron closest to him and turned it on. The smell of hot metal filled the room.

Ray repositioned the magnifier to give himself some maneuvering room beneath it and then brought the iron and a length of solder wire down to the transceiver. A thin stream of smoke issued from the box. After a moment, he lifted out the wire, followed shortly by the iron. "Done," he said.

"That's it?" said Riordan. "That's all you've got to do?"

"Yep. The hard part is figuring out where the fault is. It's nothing to fix. Give it a minute to cool and we can put the battery back in and test it."

Winnie spent more time with the spiderweb, waiting until Ray pronounced the transceiver ready. He picked the battery off the table and reconnected it. Her nerve tone snapped on immediately. She gave Riordan's hand a hard squeeze and he yelped in response, yanking his tenderized fingers out of her grasp.

"Glad you're back to your old self," he said.

She rose from the floor and walked over to Ray. She watched as he reattached the transceiver cover, but she shook her head when he moved to return the box.

"No," she said. "We don't know for sure that you've fixed it. We just know that you haven't made it any worse."

Ray frowned. "I take your point. It's possible I soldered the wrong lead or even that there were two bad leads. But the only way to find out is to subject the box to the same sort of jolts or vibrations that provoked the problem before."

"Exactly."

"That's fine in theory. The problem is this thing really isn't built to absorb shock. If I give it a whack or drop it on the floor, it may damage something else and we'll be back to square one."

Riordan joined them at the table. "Could you put it in some sort of packaging to handle shock better? You're the military electronics expert. Don't tell me that the electronics on your 4-F fighter stopped working everytime somebody had a hard landing."

"F-4E Phantom II," corrected Ray.

"What you said. How about it? Can you do something?"

Ray eyed the small box in his hands and nodded. "Sure, I'll need to get the right materials, but I can make it more shock resistant."

"That's great, but I still want to test if the original problem is fixed," said Winnie. "Let's take it back to the living room and drop it on the couch. If it still works after that, then you can do all the armor plating you want.

Ray snorted and pushed his chair back. "You're the boss."

They trooped back to the living room, where Winnie braced herself at one end of the couch in case the transceiver failed again. Ray stood at the other and held the box about six inches above the fabric of the Navajo rug. He let it go. It bounced slightly on impact and came to a stop.

"How's that," he said.

"Fine," she said. "But that's not high enough. Drop it from three or four feet."

Ray gave an exasperated sigh and picked up the transceiver again. He was just lining up another drop from a yard or so above the couch when the doorbell rang.

The three of them eyed one another as if they'd been caught in the middle of a burglary. Winnie jumped to her feet and herded Ray and Riordan to the far corner of the room.

"Who would be knocking on your door at two in the morning?" she asked in an undertone.

"No one," said Ray. "Except maybe him." He nodded at Riordan.

"Well, we know it ain't me," Riordan said. He lifted his shirt and drew an old automatic from under his waistband at the small of his back. She recognized the gun as a Luger and realized he must have secreted it there before they left for the airport. "It'd be swell if it was Jessica from Palmer Station." He pulled the toggle action on the weapon to bring a round into the chamber. "But somehow I kinda doubt it."

CHAPTER 6

Riordan

I GESTURED WITH THE LUGER toward the front door. "Go ahead and answer it, Ray," I said in an undertone. "These trailers open with a sneeze—they wouldn't be knocking if they wanted to play rough. Just remember, you don't know anything about Winnie and I'm not here."

Ray grunted and handed me the transceiver, which I put in the pocket of my hoodie. "Okay," he said. "But you two have some explaining to do."

Winnie crouched behind a half-wall that partitioned the kitchen from the living room. I moved to the hinged side of the door and pressed myself against the wall. Ray put the chain on the door and opened it a crack. Light from the porch flooded across the living-room floor.

"Kinda late to be calling, isn't it?" said Ray through the opening.

"Our apologies, sir," said an officious voice from the other side.

"We're with Southern California Edison. We're investigating an urgent issue with the smart meters in the complex."

"Smart meters?"

"Yes, sir. As you may know, smart meters transmit usage data via radio to the utility. They were recently installed in the complex and now we are experiencing interference with our signal."

"What's that got to do with me?"

The guy with the officious voice chuckled in a phony way. "Well, sir, we couldn't help but notice the large antenna outside your house, the creative paint job...and the fact that there's a transmission at the same frequency coming from the vicinity."

"How do you know that?"

"Trust us, sir. It's our job to detect transmissions that might interfere with our meters."

"Well. I know a little something about electronics, and—"

"The device my coworker is holding is a sniffer we use for this purpose. The needle on the proximity meter is pegged right now."

Ray took a step back from the door and combed his fingers through his beard. "What frequency?"

"2.4 gigahertz."

"Okay. I know what's going on." He shoved the door closed.

"Wait—sir," pleaded the now-muffled voice. "We're not finished here."

"Hold your horses," said Ray, loud enough to be heard on the other side. To me he whispered, "They're tracking Winnie's transceiver. I'll get something to confuse them, but you've got to take the cover of the transceiver off and be ready to pull the battery."

"When?" I said.

"You'll know."

The guy outside pounded on the door. "Sir, we need to talk with you."

"Give me a minute. I'll be right back," yelled Ray, and he trotted off like a demented elf toward his bedroom.

I hustled over to Winnie and told her to lie on the floor behind the partition. When I pulled the battery, she needed to be prone like before. She hissed something about "letting the geezer order us around," but I didn't stay long enough to hear her out. I hurried back to the lab, grabbed the screwdriver, and removed the pair of screws to the transceiver cover.

I nearly collided with Ray when I returned to the front room. He was carrying, of all things, a model airplane and a remote controller. "We'll tell them the signal is coming from my remote control," he whispered, as I resumed my station.

Ray put his airplane down on the carpet where they could see it when he reopened the door. I put my Luger on the carpet, too, and got ready to pull the battery on the transceiver. By now, I had a pretty good idea of what Ray was planning.

"Here I am," he said, as he pulled the door open, holding the remote controller in front of him. He took a sudden step back, and I saw surprise on his face. "Whoa, he said, "what's that for?"

A beat went by. "I'm sorry, sir," said the guy with the officious voice. "We were afraid you might have gone to get a firearm."

"But what are *you* doing with a gun?"

"It's not a gun. It's a Taser. We are authorized to carry them. Unfortunately, some of our customers have had very strong reactions to the smart-meter program."

"If you say so."

"There, I've put it away. Please accept our apologies. What is that?"

"It's the remote control for my model airplane." Ray pointed at the plane behind him. I could tell he was making sure to stay in my line of sight. "It must be the source for the interference you measured."

"What frequency is it transmitting on?"

"2.4 gigahertz—same as you said."

"I see. But that's not a frequency that's typically used for RC planes, is it?"

Ray dipped his head. "No, it's not. I built the remote control myself. As I said, I'm an electrical engineer. In fact, I built the avionics for several aircraft. The F-4—"

"That's great, sir. Are you transmitting now?"

"Yes, I was checking the trim on the ailerons before the plane's maiden flight tomorrow."

"Very exciting. Can you turn off the remote controller so we can verify that it is the source of the signal we're detecting?"

"Sure."

This was my cue. As Ray went through the motions of flicking a switch on the controller, I fumbled the battery out of the transceiver. I heard a new voice from outside say, "That's got it. Signal's gone."

"Sir," said Mr. Officious. "Would you turn it on again, just to be certain."

Ray nodded and went through the motions of turning the switch back on. I had more trouble getting the leads attached to the battery than I had pulling them off, and even after I got them attached, I was worried that I hadn't made good contact.

After several wrenching moments where nothing was said, the other guy on the porch pitched in, "On again. The needle's pegged."

"See," said Ray. "I told you."

"You did indeed. I'm glad we found the source of the interference.

May I suggest that you switch to a different frequency so you don't interfere with the smart meters?"

"Happy to. I'll just change out the crystal." Ray smiled and pointed back to his plane. "Since you're here, would you like to see me put my baby through its paces? On the ground, of course—have to wait until tomorrow to get it airborne."

"No, thank you, sir. We'll let you get back to your preflight prep. One last question—have you seen any other visitors at the trailer park recently? Two men in a white van?"

Ray brought his hand up to comb his beard again. "No, summer's the slow season. All the snow birds are gone. Hardly anybody here right now."

"Okay, we'll let you go now. Thank you again. Good night."

"'Nite."

Ray pushed the door closed and grinned at me as we listened to two pairs of feet going down the steps to the porch.

"'Would you like to see me put my baby through its paces?'" I mimicked in an undertone.

"What?" he said. "You think I was gilding the lily?"

Winnie stood up behind the partition. "Shellacking the turd would be more accurate."

CHAPTER 7

Riordan

WE DECIDED IT WAS TOO RISKY to leave the trailer before daylight since we had no way of knowing if the two "Southern California Edison" employees were waiting in ambush. I sacked out on the floor and Winnie slept on the couch even though she insisted it didn't matter where she slept as long as she had a pillow. Ray also offered her his bed, but she flatly refused that comfort, muttering something about bedbugs and BO when he was out of earshot.

Despite her continued hostility toward him, Ray got up early the next morning and cooked us all pancakes using a mold in the shape of an airplane. We sat around the tiny hutch in the kitchen and watched while Ray drowned his squadron of buckwheat aircraft in a gallon of syrup. I made do with a half squadron and nearly as much syrup, while Winnie nibbled on one lonely pancake and chugged a glass of milk and a raw egg.

I pointed at the nose of one of the planes on my plate. "Is this an F-4 Phantom, Ray?"

"No," he said, not even bothering to chide me for abbreviating the name. "Jets don't have propellers. I know what you're doing."

"What am I doing?"

"You're trying to distract me from asking about what's going on. Well, it's not going to work. What the hell is going on?"

Winnie and I looked at each other across the table. I inclined my head her direction. "I hate to steal your thunder."

"All right," she said, without enthusiasm, and then launched into a condensed version of the story she had told me earlier.

Watching her talk, I realized that her body language was subtly different than that of a normal person. She rarely gestured with her hands, crossed her arms in front of her when she was disengaged, or leaned into a conversation when she was interested. Perhaps she felt the effort to mimic these usually unconscious movements and postures was wasted. Only her face gave any indication of her emotional state, and I noticed that she often went out of the way to keep her expression neutral. Now she sat with her arms at her sides, face blank, talking in a monotone as she explained to Ray how her husband and coworkers had been murdered, how their company had been destroyed, and how she had been hunted across the country by the Winemaker's thugs.

By the time she finished her story, Ray had long since stopped eating. He pushed back his plate and pointed at me with his fork. "And what does he have to do with this mess?"

"He's the one who maimed the Winemaker and sent him to Corcoran."

"Corcoran State Prison?"

"Yes, why?"

Ray got up and retrieved the morning paper from where he had left it in the living room. He held up the front page.

Explosion at Corcoran State Prison Fifty Inmates Killed,
George Donovan Escapes

"That's why."

Winnie jumped up from the table and snatched the paper out of Ray's hands. She scanned the article then slapped the paper back into Ray's gut. "He's settling more scores," she said.

"Scores?" I said. "What did those fifty inmates do to him?"

Winnie bit her lip and looked away from me. It was one of the few physical displays of emotion I'd seen her give. "You understand what *you* did to him, right?"

"Yes, I understand. I shot him in the back—after he fucking broke my teeth and kneecap."

"You shot him in the back and *paralyzed* him from the waist down. He went to prison in a wheelchair. It won't surprise you to learn that he wasn't popular there. From what I heard, he got on the wrong side of one of the gangs. They used him."

"Does that mean what I think it does?"

"Yeah. They beat and gang raped him. Tied his arms behind his back and suspended him from the ceiling. Then they—"

"That's enough." I choked back a taste of bile, feeling like the airplane pancakes in my gut were getting ready to take flight. "Jesus. I'm not saying he didn't deserve it, but Jesus. How did he even survive?"

"They made sure he did. They dumped him outside the infirmary when they were done. They wanted him broken, not dead. But they miscalculated. He was so badly injured they had to move him to a hospital in Fresno. It was child's play to bust him out of there. When he recovered, he started his rampage."

"How do you know all this?"

"I went down to Fresno to interview the hospital staff. They gave me the whole story."

"But where's this Donovan character fit in?" asked Ray. "The article says he escaped in a helicopter."

Winnie laughed and looked over at me. "Now we know why the insignia on the vests seemed familiar."

"We do?"

"George Donovan was a high muckety-muck at Praetorian, which—as you will now recall—was a private security firm hired to protect U.S. embassy employees during the Iraq War. He was jailed for machine-gunning civilians while leading a team of contractors in Baghdad."

I groaned. I did remember. Donovan was an ex-Navy SEAL, and Praetorian was staffed with others just like him: Special Forces operatives, soldiers, and retired law enforcement agents. "Are you saying the Winemaker is in league with Donovan? With all of Praetorian?"

"I'm saying it explains where the Winemaker got the teams of men to send after me. I doubt it's all of Praetorian. Just some hot numbers from Donovan's Rolodex."

I nodded. "But what's in it for Donovan? His own people could have arranged the prison break. Why throw in with the Winemaker?"

Suddenly, for no reason I could see, she got angry. "You of all people should understand. How did the Winemaker break your teeth and kneecap? He ran you into a brick wall. The version of the technology I have enables me to control my own body with my own thoughts. He is using it to control *other* people—to turn them into electronic slaves. Think of the military applications—shock troops, kamikaze warriors. God knows what else." She yanked the paper out from Ray's grasp once more and held it under my nose. "This is serious—deadly serious—and you don't seem to get that. It's more than just you and me. It's fucking geopolitical. We shouldn't have sent those guys away last night with an idiotic story about toy airplanes. We should have captured them and tortured them until they told us where to find the Winemaker."

She threw down the paper. "Is any of this sinking in? We can't afford to play a waiting game. We've got to fix the mistake the gang made at Corcoran."

CHAPTER 8

Riordan

I PUSHED MY PLATE ASIDE and stood, looking at Ray to avoid blowing my top at Winnie.

"What are you looking at me for?" he asked. "I wasn't the one questioning your, ah, grasp of the situation."

"No, you weren't. Nor were you the one who advocated torturing people to death."

"Not to death," said Winnie, who had picked up the paper from where she'd thrown it and was now—in a gesture that conveyed the slightest bit of contrition—folding it neatly into quarters. "Just until they talked."

"And what do we do then? Buy them a bus ticket home?"

She opened her mouth to respond, but I cut her off. "Don't answer that. You say we need information. Okay, we need information. But we're going to get it my way."

"There's no one to get it from. They're long gone."

"No, they're not. They're not leaving until they find the other two... which won't be for a while."

"What other two?" asked Ray.

I brought my hand up to massage my temples, avoiding his gaze.

"Fine," he said. "I'll just occupy myself washing up and avoid an indictment for conspiracy to kidnap or murder or God knows what." He stacked the plates from the table and carried them to the sink.

"So how are you going to find them?" asked Winnie.

I hadn't a clue. "I've got my ways," I said to her, "but it's going to take some planning."

She snorted and dropped the paper onto the couch. "Right. While you exercise your big brain on that assignment, I'm going to get a more traditional workout at your posh home fitness center—and then clean up. Is it foolish to hope your shower isn't completely encrusted with mold like Ray's?"

"I heard that," called Ray over his shoulder.

"Good, you were meant to."

"The shower's fine," I said. "I want to talk some things over with Ray, but I'll walk you back to my place first."

"Worried those guys are still outside?"

I shrugged. "Not really, but it would make finding them a lot easier."

I told Ray I'd be back shortly and made Winnie wait by the door while I slipped out to make a quick patrol of the area, holding the Luger in a tight grip at my side the whole time. The only thing I found was one of the semiferal cats that infested the complex gnawing on the tail of a lizard. I couldn't tell whether the remainder of the lizard had made its escape or was in the belly of the beast.

I fetched Winnie, and we detoured by the visitor's lot to collect a roller bag from her car before taking the now-well-beaten path back to my place. I unlocked the trunk of the Galaxie when we arrived and retrieved a 9mm automatic from the duffel we had liberated from the van. I set the gun on the table next to the weights, then watched as Winnie proceeded to load up the bench press with as nearly as many plates as I used. "Now who needs a spotter?" I said.

"Not me," said Winnie. "This is just to warm up. Anyway, it looks like you are leaving Mr. Glock there to keep me company."

"Yeah. I think we both need to carry from now on. I've got a shoulder rig we can fit you with later."

She smiled as she settled herself beneath the bar. "Thanks, old man. I appreciate the concern, but I've gone up against these guys more times than you have. I'm 5–0 on my own. Not to mention that I'm not very good with handguns. The shotgun would have been more my speed."

"That's a little showy for my front porch. Be careful—with both the weights and the bad guys. I'll be back in a few."

"Ciao," she said, and snatched the bar off the uprights.

Trundling back to Ray's, I couldn't help but wonder—once again— what the hell I'd gotten myself into. There was no disputing that Winnie and I were in danger. The part that was less obvious was the appropriate response. Going after the Winemaker with guns blazing didn't seem like the brightest idea, especially given what Winnie had said about his intentions for the technology. And then there was the *generalissima* herself. I wasn't used to a woman being more macho than me, and I certainly wasn't used to thinking of myself as the levelheaded one.

When I got back to Ray's trailer, I found him on the stoop, painting a foul-smelling lacquer on the stick-and-tissue-paper wings of another model airplane. "Jesus," I said. "How can you breathe that stuff? You gotta be bumping off a million brain cells a minute."

He made a careful pass over a seam on one of the wing tips and looked up at me. "I still have enough brain cells left to know you shouldn't be involved with that girl."

"Did you hear me talking to myself on the way over? I agree, but I don't think I have a choice."

"You always have a choice." He set the brush down on the edge of the stoop and then secured the wing to a wooden stand I'd seen him use before. "Hope you're doing her at least."

"No, I'm not 'doing her.' It's not that kind of deal."

"What kind of deal is it?"

I cleared my throat. "I'm not sure, exactly. We're like two people in a life raft trying to fight off a shark. We didn't ask to be in the raft together, and we didn't ask for the shark, but we have to make the best of the situation and protect ourselves."

"Well, that certainly clears things up." Ray made a face as he screwed on the lid to the lacquer jar. "Whew. You're right about the fumes. I need to start paying the neighbor kid to do this."

"You wouldn't trust him to do it right."

"Probably not. Now, what did you want to talk about? And it better not involve anything illegal."

"I wanted to ask about something you told the Cal Ed guys last night," I said, making little quote marks in the air as I pronounced the name of the power company.

"Shoot."

"You said you could change the frequency of your remote controller. Can you do that for Winnie instead?"

"Change the frequency she transmits on so they can't track her?"

"That's right."

He shook his head. "Have to be a surgeon to do it. It's not just a matter of changing the transceiver box. You'd also have to change the implants in her neck."

"Nuts."

"But I could stop the signal from being detected."

"How?"

"It's called RF shielding. You use a barrier made of conductive or magnetic materials to block the radio waves from getting out."

"Wouldn't that also prevent the signal from being relayed to and from the transceiver?"

"As long as the transceiver and implants are all under the shield, everything will work fine. The system will be closed and isolated."

I rubbed my knuckles over the stubble on my jawline. It didn't sound very comfortable. "Does that mean she'll have to go around in some kind of giant soup can?"

Ray laughed. "Yeah, she'll be like Joan of Arc in a suit of white iron. You can be her trusty but dim-witted squire."

"Very funny. I take it there's an alternative."

"Yeah. There's a fabric with a layer of conductive material made of nickel, silver, and copper. It's flexible enough to wear under a turtleneck or something similar, and no one would be the wiser."

"Swell. Where do we get some?"

Ray held his hands out and bowed his head as if acknowledging applause. "Uncle Ray comes to the rescue again. I've got a whole bolt of it in the lab. Swiped it from McDonnell Douglas before I retired."

I reached over and gave him an affectionate thump on the shoulder, surprised at how bony his arm felt under the T-shirt. "Tremendous. When can I bring Joan of Arc by for her chain-mail shirt?"

Ray's eyes got a faraway look to them, and he brought his fingers up to comb through his beard. "What?" he said finally.

"I said when can I bring Winnie over for a fitting?"

"Anytime. And I'll go you one better."

"I don't think she'd be interested in pants."

"Not pants, you idiot. A decoy. How useful would it be to have a dummy box that transmitted on the same signal?"

I considered the idea for a moment, and for the first time I had the vaguest notion of how to ensnare the ersatz utility employees. "Very useful," I said. "In fact, I'll take two."

CHAPTER 9

The Winemaker

I FIRST STARTED THESE NOTES in Corcoran State Prison, writing in pencil on a Big Chief tablet I purchased from the commissary. The tablet cost six dollars for forty-eight sheets, and I had filled out twenty-one of those when Brian "Earwig" Killen caught me in the prison library and made me eat my words—all twenty-one sheets plus the cardboard cover with the picture of the Indian wearing a headdress.

Mr. Killen is, or was, the leader of the Aryan Brotherhood in Corcoran. He earned his colorful sobriquet by jamming a shiv through the ear of a member of the Black Guerrilla Family while serving a stint in San Quentin. As I am neither black nor Mexican nor Native American, you may wonder how I came to be on the wrong side of Earwig. Put simply, it was my own fault. I could have avoided all the trouble if I'd kept my head down, my eyes averted, and eaten my meals at the far end of the table away from the members of the Brotherhood. Instead, I elected to debate them.

You see, *I* am no racist. I know that we are all descended from the same tremulous puddle of African monkey spunk. No man can claim to be better than any other on the basis of race. We are all programmed with the same code: the same selfish genes are inside us, guiding our behavior, controlling our physical characteristics and capabilities for the sole purpose of propagating a copy of themselves in the next generation.

Likewise, I am no theist. In fact, it would be more accurate to call me an antitheist. I know there is no God. And I know that many, if not most, of the misguided, deluded, and outright pernicious things in the world come from religion—particularly Islam.

Although Earwig and his brethren would hardly have characterized themselves as practicing Christians, they were clear about what they were not: Jews. Hearing from me that Christians were no better than Jews—that both were worse than atheists and that whites were no better than blacks—did not endear me to them. They expressed their disagreement through intimidation, beatings, and sexual assault. I settled the debate by blowing them to bits with 2,080 sticks of C-4 explosive, ending their genes' chances of infecting future generations.

My point is this: I am a man of principle. And I am willing and ready to act upon those principles, even at high personal cost.

My time at Corcoran was not all pain and tribulation. In addition to making the acquaintance of Earwig, I met George Donovan. He has proved invaluable from a recruiting perspective. He shares my views on the danger of Islam and, just as important, understands that we won't defeat it with one hand tied behind our backs. At the time I met him, Donovan was fond of quoting a line from a movie that I hadn't seen and can't be bothered to watch now. "You can't handle the truth!" the line goes. This is apparently shouted by a military commander to a courtroom of people who have no appreciation of the extremes required to defeat an enemy.

In Donovan's retelling, the dramatization seems puerile, but there is no denying the underlying message. We must always be prepared to match and then exceed the enemy's tactics to defeat him. We can't let squeamishness prevent us from doing what is necessary. The ends truly justify the means.

Are you surprised to see it stated so baldy? You shouldn't be. Do you think that natural selection would stop at anything, *anything at all,* to ensure propagation of genes from one generation to the next?

Charles Darwin famously lost his faith in an omnipotent god when he came across the suffering caused by the ichneumon wasp, which uses a chemical to paralyze a caterpillar and then lays its eggs inside the host for its young to devour. And scientists have discovered a fungus that infects the brains of ants, turning them into zombies that are controlled by the fungus to position themselves to infect still more ants. In both these examples, natural selection has taken the gloves off. The selfish genes in the wasp and the fungus care nothing for the suffering they inflict in other species as long as they survive to the next generation.

When I watch the decapitation videos posted by Islamist fundamentalists, I am outraged. I want to decapitate the decapitators. But that would only be aping their tactics. On the other hand, when I think of the example of the fungus and the ant, and how it might be applied to the colony of Islamist zealots that infests the world, I am comforted and see a way forward.

CHAPTER 10

Riordan

RAY MADE WINNIE A HIGH-COLLARED VEST out of the conductive material. We put the transceiver in a shoulder holster intended for one of the automatics, strapped the holster underneath the vest, and then covered the whole arrangement with a windbreaker of Ray's that zipped to the chin. It wasn't the most stylish thing she'd ever worn, but the windbreaker hid the bulge from the transceiver and covered the fabric of the RF shield.

Ray checked the shield out with a sniffer device of his own, walking toward Winnie from a spot about thirty yards down the street while she waited on the stoop. He held his thumb up as he walked until he got within about three feet of her, then he shrugged and shook his head.

"There's a tiny bit of leakage," he told her, "but the bad guys would have to be right on top of you to detect it."

"If someone gets that close to me without figuring it out, they are going to have other things to worry about."

"What about the decoys?" I asked.

"Done and done." Ray stepped into the trailer and came back a minute later carrying a pair of metal boxes with toggle switches on the sides. "All you need to do is flick it to the on position and you'll be sending out a signal on the same frequency as Winnie's transceiver. They're powered with a single nine-volt battery and should transmit for at least twenty-four hours before you need to swap it out."

"How close would you need to be to detect the signal?"

"A half mile or so. I'm guessing that's about the same range as Winnie's radio."

I clapped my hands together. "Very good, Q. You've done it again."

"Q?" asked Ray.

Winnie laughed. "He *is* like Q. But now he should warn us to take good care of the equipment and harrumph about the cost to the British taxpayer."

Ray looked back and forth between us. "I've no idea what you two are running on about."

"Never mind," said Winnie. "You did good."

She smiled and Ray just about melted into a puddle despite all the tough talk earlier.

"We should go," I said. "It's going to be dark in an hour."

"All right," said Winnie. "You do your motels and I'll do mine, but if you find them first, you better call me."

"I will. This is definitely a team effort."

Winnie nodded and slipped behind the wheel of her Lincoln, which was parked in front of my Galaxie in Ray's driveway. She started the car and backed out, waving to us before she put it in drive and powered down the street.

Ray watched her round the corner then shook his head. "I shouldn't have to say this, but be careful, will you?"

I was nodding before he finished speaking. "Yeah, yeah. My turn—don't answer the door for anyone, keep the shotgun handy, and call the cops if you don't hear from me by midnight."

"Roger that. Good luck, then."

"Thanks."

I got into the Galaxie and muscled it out of the drive and down the street after Winnie. We had made a list of hotels and motels where the Winemaker's thugs could be staying and divided it between us. The idea was to cruise each of them, looking for white vans like the other team had been driving. If one of us found a likely van, or actually ID'd the creeps based on the description Ray had given us, we would alert the other. Then we would put into play the more imaginative part of my plan. Winnie wasn't a terribly big fan of it, but at least it didn't involve torture and murder.

Winnie had the longer list of hotels because I had a detour to make before I started. It involved a delivery to a home in a moneyed old neighborhood of Palm Springs called Deepwell, possibly best known as the subdivision where William Holden owned a property. The place I was looking for was on Driftwood Drive, and while it probably wasn't as fancy as Holden's old house, it had to be worth more than twenty times what my trailer would fetch.

It was built in a style of architecture I recognized as Desert Modern. Long and low with a wide overhang, the front of the boxy building was nearly all glass. The roof was flat and painted white to reflect the heat of the sun, as a lot of roofs in the Springs are. But the only architectural detail I really cared about was the stubby brick chimney on the end. That was where I hoped to make my delivery.

I parked the Galaxie a half block away in front of another low bunkerlike house that had a line of fifty-foot palms guarding the front yard. I spent a minute in the car tying a length of twine to one of Ray's decoy transmitters. Then I sauntered back like I belonged in the neighborhood. Fortunately, there wasn't anyone around to see the act. It was still too hot to be outside unless you had good reason.

I couldn't tell if anyone was home at the target house, but I knew for a fact that it had a sophisticated alarm system. I just hoped they hadn't bothered to wire up the roof. When I reached the property line, I stepped onto the well-tended lawn and strode back to an overgrown banana tree by the cinder-block fence dividing the front yard from the back. I bushwhacked my way past banana fronds to the fence and leaped up to grasp the top of it.

I wedged my toe into a seam between the blocks and pulled, kicked, and squirmed my way to a sitting position astride the fence. The gutter of the roof was at eye level, just inches away. I reached a hand over to test the temperature of the roof. It was warm all right, but not warm enough to burn. Bracing myself on the overhang, I got my feet under me and half flopped, half climbed onto the roof. I fell forward as I came, landing on my shoulder with a thud. I lay on the roof looking up at the sky, waiting to hear the front door swing open, followed by steps pounding down the sidewalk as the occupant hurried out to see what had crash-landed on the house. Nobody obliged me.

I rolled onto my hands and knees, and crawled to the chimney. There was a cap over the opening, but it was an older style without a screen, so there was still a three- or four-inch hole through which I could thread the transmitter. I flicked the switch on, pushed the transmitter through the gap, and lowered it down the chimney by the cord like I was lowering bait down an ice-fishing hole. When I felt the transmitter hit bottom, I pulled it back a few inches and then tied it off on one of the metal posts of the chimney cap. Although the brick of the chimney would reduce the range, Ray had assured me that the signal would be detectable to someone standing outside the house with a sniffer.

I was crawling back to the edge of the roof when my phone rang. I recognized the number as Winnie's, but I was in no position to talk and—in my panic—couldn't remember how to turn the damn thing off. I shoved it deep into my pants pocket and dangled my foot off the roof, groping for the edge of the cinder-block wall as the barely muffled strains of the *Jeopardy!* theme song—my ring tone—filled the air. Eventually, I got a toehold and slithered off the roof. Then I hoisted myself over the edge of the wall and dropped back among the banana tree fronds.

I quickstepped it off the property and hurried down the street, counting the cuts, scrapes, and bruises on my hands and arms as I went. As I got close to the Galaxie, the phone rang again. This time I punched the answer button.

"What?" I demanded. "What do you want?"

"Just calling to coordinate with my partner as agreed," said Winnie. "What got up your nose?"

"Sorry. Your first call rang at an inopportune time."

"I'm not able to take advantage of the feature myself, but I understand people with feeling in their lower extremities put their phones on vibrate in similar circumstances."

"I'll keep that in mind."

I'd keep it in mind as soon as I could figure out how to do it.

"Did you drop off the transmitter?"

I unlocked the Galaxie and slumped behind the wheel. "Yes, mission accomplished. How about with you? Any luck so far?"

Winnie chuckled. "You could say that. I'm in the parking lot of the Denny's we ate in last night, watching our two smart-meter guys ordering dinner from the same waitress."

"You're kidding."

"No."

"How do you know it's them?"

"I started with motels near the airport. I found a white van at a dump called the Painted Sands Inn, and before I could even park the car, these two jokers walked out of adjoining rooms and piled into the van. I followed them to the Denny's, which is about three blocks from the motel. They're exactly as Ray described—a beefy Latino guy and a smaller guy with red hair."

"Huh. That actually makes sense. They probably picked you up with the sniffer last night when we ate there and then tracked us back to the complex."

"That's what I figured. You got a plan?"

I shoved the key into the ignition and started the Galaxie. "Yeah, number one—wait for me. I'm only three miles away. Number two, call up the Denny's and order takeout."

"Nobody orders fucking takeout from a Denny's."

"Sure they do. Try the Tilapia Ranchero. I hear it's good."

"All right. I see where you're going with this, but hurry the fuck up."

"On my way."

I made the trip from the Deepwell neighborhood to the Denny's in about ten minutes and pulled into a parking spot a few cars down from Winnie's Lincoln. I slunk across to her car and slipped in the passenger door. Winnie watched me settle in with an expression on her face that was half amusement, half poorly suppressed exasperation.

"I got fries," she said. "They take less time. They already brought the order up to the register."

"Good thinking. Where are the boys sitting?"

"Over there in the booth underneath the clock. The big guy has his back to you, but you can see the redhead chowing down on nachos."

I looked at the men Winnie had indicated through Denny's big plate-glass window. They were both in dress shirts, and the redhead was wearing glasses with thick black rims. They definitely had the look of ex-military, and from what I could see of them, they seemed to fit Ray's description. "Were they carrying anything that looked like a sniffer?"

"The redhead has some kind of man purse he keeps looking into. It could be in that."

"Guess we'll find out soon enough. So, go in, get the fries, and get out. They won't try anything in a public place, and they are going to have to pay before leaving. That'll give you enough of a head start."

"That assumes they even notice me. They won't have a good view of the front from where they're sitting, and they may not check the sniffer immediately."

"All right. Go ahead and turn on Ray's decoy box now. We'll give 'em a little early warning."

Winnie unzipped the pocket of her windbreaker and flicked the switch on the second of Ray's decoys. "Bombs away," she said.

"You got the address of the house?"

"Already plugged it into the GPS. And before you ask, the shotgun is right here." She patted the friction-tape-wrapped grip of one of the shotguns we'd taken from the duffel bag. I'd cut down the stock and barrel to make it easier for her to handle, and she had it crammed in the door pocket of the Lincoln.

"Good. But that's only for plan B."

"Just like the birth control pill. Only after we're fucked."

"Ah, right. Okay, here we go." I slipped out of the Lincoln and took a post loitering by the newspaper boxes near the front door. I wanted to be close if I was wrong about the Winemaker's employees not getting physical in public.

Winnie got out of the car at a more leisurely pace, walked past me without a glance, and went into the Denny's. I watched as she talked to the hostess and pointed at the bag of fries under the heat lamps near the register. The hostess passed them over and rang up the sale. Winnie paid and turned to go out the door. That was when things got interesting. The redhead appeared at the end of the lunch counter, holding a metal box in his hands. He tracked Winnie out the door and then pivoted to go back to his booth.

"They're coming," I said to Winnie in an undertone as she went by. She didn't acknowledge the comment but sailed serenely on to her car. She got behind the wheel, backed out, and was well down Palm Canyon Drive—the street in front of Denny's—before the ersatz power-company employees made it through the door.

I kept my nose in one of the newspaper machines as they went by and waited until they, too, had pulled out onto Palm Canyon before I returned to the Galaxie. Once I got it started and pointed in the same direction as the other cars, I called Winnie. She answered on the second ring.

"They are about two minutes behind," I said.

"Good. How soon before I turn off the box?"

"I'd wait until you are parked. Ray said they can't triangulate directly on your position. They can only tell if the source of the signal is closer or farther. I'm worried that if you cut your signal off too soon they won't pick up the weaker one at the house."

"Okay. I'm going to go a little faster, then. I don't want them coming up on me in traffic."

"Just don't get pulled over by a cop."

"How did I know you were going to say that?"

We drove with the line open, not speaking, for a tense five minutes. Then she broke the silence. "I'm here. I'm shutting off the transmitter and getting out of the car. I'll meet you at the corner."

"I'm on my way."

Now I drove faster than *I* should have through a yellow light at West Ramon and down to East Mesquite, the street that led back into the neighborhood. I found Winnie on the corner where we agreed, huddled beneath a palo verde whose branches were drooping out into the roadway.

As she slid across the bench seat of the Galaxie, I reached over to squeeze her arm. "I'm glad to see you."

"I'm glad to see you, too. But you keep forgetting I can't feel that."

"Oh, yeah. Sorry."

"It's the thought that counts." She pointed with her chin in the direction of the house where I'd planted the transmitter. "What now?"

"The safe way to play it is to go directly to their motel and hope that things develop as planned. Worst case, we'll have a few hours while they're occupied trying to figure out where the signal went."

"What's the risky way to play it?"

"As if you didn't know. Stake out the house and watch."

"I like the risky approach."

I sighed. I pulled the shift indicator back into drive and eased my foot off the brake. It was a few minutes past eight and the sun had already set, so lights would normally be in order, but I left them off as I oozed down the street to the target house. At just about the spot I'd parked on my first visit, we found the white van. Its lights were off, too, and nobody appeared to be inside. I swung around and parked on the other side of the street, facing the house.

"That seems like a good sign," I said.

"You sure you don't want to get a little closer?"

"Yes. I'm sure I don't want to get any closer."

She wrinkled her nose at me. "Chicken."

"One-hundred-percent leghorn."

She looked out the window then snapped her gaze back to me. "Let me ask you a question. The whole point of this scheme is to avoid hurting people, right?"

"That's the idea."

"What about the owner of the house? Or worse, his family?"

"He doesn't have any family. He's, ah, gay."

"Really? How about a boyfriend?"

"I don't know, but even if he does, I'm hoping the boyfriend is with him tonight."

"Which is not at the house, apparently."

"No, he's receiving an award in LA for Latino Law Enforcement Officer of the Year."

Just about that time, red and blue flashing lights blossomed in the rearview mirror. A pair of patrol cars surged past us without sirens and pulled to a stop in front of the chief's house. Four cops with riot guns jumped out.

Winnie wasn't satisfied with the view from the car. She threw open the door and darted partway up the street. I ran after her to tug her by her windbreaker to a slightly less conspicuous location on the sidewalk. We watched as the cops charged the house, made quick work of the front door, and flooded through. Lights snapped on in rapid succession throughout the building, and I heard shouts but no gunfire.

Two more cars materialized at the far end of the block and sealed it off. Officers stood at the back of the vehicles, brandishing more riot guns and talking on microphones.

Finally, a familiar figure in a dress shirt and black-rimmed glasses was disgorged from the house, led from behind in handcuffs by one of the cops. His beefier buddy followed next, and both were quickly situated in the back of a patrol car and locked inside.

Winnie turned to me. "I got to hand it to you," she said. "That was *nearly* worth the trouble we took to make it happen."

CHAPTER 11

Winnie

WINNIE DECIDED RIORDAN WAS RIGHT about one thing: It hadn't been the best idea in the world to watch the proceedings at the house, especially from the sidewalk across the street. She heard the scuff of shoe leather on pavement and turned to find a police officer coming up behind them with a flashlight. He had the burly but corpulent look of a college football player gone to seed.

"Good evening, folks. Are you from the neighborhood?"

"Yes, from nearby," said Winnie, trying her damnedest to sound nonchalant and credible at the same time.

"May I ask what you're doing?"

"My dad and I were out for a walk when we saw the police cars go by. We were curious, so we came up to see what was happening." Riordan had turned to greet the officer with a friendly look on his face, but she saw his jaw clench when she dropped the D word.

"Did you see anyone else while you were out?"

"No," said Riordan. "We've been all by our lonesome. What's going on? Domestic dispute?"

"I can't discuss it, sir." The cop took a half step back and pointed down the sidewalk with his flashlight. "If you don't mind, I'll ask you to detour around the block. We need to keep the area clear."

Riordan shrugged and stepped around the patrolman. Winnie followed and they walked in silence past Riordan's old car all the way to the end of the block where they turned right onto a busier street.

When they were well out of range, Riordan wheeled on her. "Your dad?" he demanded. "How did you come up with that one?"

She grinned at him. It was so easy to push his buttons. "Nothing else is credible. A hot twenty-something like me out with an old fifty-something like you. What else could I say?"

"'What else could I say?'" he mimicked her. "Not trophy wife because you're no trophy."

"Ouch."

"And FYI, I'm only fifty-two."

"I was just winding you up. I'm actually thirty-two.."

"All right. You see what the up-close-and-personal view cost us. Now we've got to wait until they leave to retrieve the car."

"Relax. There can't be much left for them to do. Let's walk to the next light and turn around. I bet they'll be gone by the time we get back."

Riordan grunted.

Cars surged past them in the darkness. A mourning dove cooed on a wire above. The smell of creosote wafted from the bushes that grew in the no-man's-land between the sidewalk and the high cinder-block walls of the properties that lined the road. They walked to the stoplight and Riordan made a point of tagging it ceremoniously before starting back. "Hope you're enjoying your little tour of Palm Springs," he said.

Something that had been bothering Winnie pushed to the front of her consciousness. "You never said why you came."

"Where?"

"To here, Palm Springs."

"No, I never did."

"It probably saved your life. If the Winemaker had found you in San Francisco as easily as I found your old office, he would have killed you."

"I'm not sure I would have cared."

She glanced over at him, trying to gauge his seriousness. "What's that supposed to mean?"

"It means what it means. When I left the city, I was at an all-time low."

"Why?"

He shook his head. "Next topic."

"All right. But why come here?"

"A silly reason. Although I never knew him, my father lived here—in the trailer I'm in now. He was a friend of Ray's."

She laughed.

"What's funny?"

"I was just thinking that Ray is the father you never had."

"Now you've crossed the line." Riordan reached over to tweak the tip of her nose. "And, yes, I got you there so you'd feel it."

"Duly noted. But while you were abusing crippled girls half your age, a cop car pulled out of our street. I bet the coast is clear."

"Let's hoof it, then."

They hurried back to the police chief's street. It was dark and quiet, and all the patrol cars appeared to be gone.

"Nuts," said Riordan. "They towed the van."

"Does that surprise you?"

"No," he said, holding open the passenger door of his Ford for her. "Not really. But I hoped we'd have a crack at it."

"A waste of time," she said, after he got in beside her. "Nothing for us except another duffel bag full of guns and drugs."

"Maybe. But that just leaves the hotel. The Painted Sands, you said?"

She nodded. "Rooms 127 and 129. I just hope they're not—"

"Yeah, yeah, don't say it. A waste of time, too."

They drove to the motel and parked in a spot between the two rooms. Riordan got out and hurried around to the trunk, where he retrieved a flexible metal rod with several sharp bends in it. A thin cord dangled from one end.

"What in the hell is that?" she asked.

"Our door key."

"I thought you said you had lock picks."

"I do, but they're no good on hotel locks that use magnetic swipe cards."

She frowned. "You mean we're dependent on your ability to open the doors with *that*? It looks like something you'd order on late-night TV."

He came up to her. "Look, I'm a private detective. I break into hotel rooms all the time. This looks goofy, but it works. You slip it under the door and maneuver it up to hook the door handle from inside—then pull. The door pops open. Now, why don't you play lookout while I do the first one?" He passed her one of the 9mm automatics.

"Go" was all she said.

He walked up to room 104 and knocked. When no one answered, he dropped to his knees and slipped the metal rod under the door.

He twisted it with one hand while he tugged on the cord with the other. She heard a faint clanging noise from the inside, and seemingly without any further precipitating action, the door slid open. Riordan scrambled to his feet, pulling his Luger from the small of his back as he rose. "Come on," he urged.

She darted past him into the room, flicking on the light as she passed. No one was in the bedroom, and when she checked the bathroom and the closet, she found them empty as well. Unfortunately, there didn't appear to be much in the way of luggage or computer equipment, either—things that she and Riordan had hoped would provide clues to the Winemaker's whereabouts.

Riordan retrieved his gizmo from the door handle and pulled the door closed. "Well?" he asked.

"Good job on getting us in, but the pickings look slim."

He shrugged. "I'll take the bathroom if you want out here."

"Fine."

Winnie started with the dresser, opening the drawers from the bottom like a burglar to minimize shifting. Whoever had left his clothes in the room was neat—and traveling light. She found two pairs of carefully folded underwear, two polo shirts, two pairs of socks, and a rolled-up web belt like you might wear with khaki pants. The closet netted the expected pants, a blue poplin dress shirt, and a navy blazer. There was also a pair of Nike running shoes and a completely empty roll-aboard. Winnie triple-searched the luggage for a tag or any sort of identification, but there was none.

She was lifting the Gideon Bible out of an otherwise empty desk drawer when Riordan returned from the bathroom.

"Any luck?" he asked.

"Nada. How about you?"

"Apart from learning the guy uses Minoxidil on a bald spot and wants softer stools, no."

"That's more than I needed to know. What do you think? Should we tear up the place looking for hidden stuff?"

"We should go next door first. We can toss the rooms if it comes to it, but I'm a little worried about the cops paying a visit. Better to see what we can see quickly."

"Okay. Just let me get this vest off before we tackle the next room. I'm burning up." Winnie stripped off the windbreaker and tugged at Ray's RF shield. When it cleared her head, she found that she'd drawn the fabric of her T-shirt clear over her chest. Riordan stood rooted, leering at her breasts in her sports bra. She yanked her shirt down and waggled her finger at him. "These aren't the droids you're looking for."

Riordan reddened. "Sorry," he mumbled. He jerked open the door and strode over to room 103, where he knelt once again with his gadget.

If anything, he opened the door more quickly this time, and something of immediate interest appeared inside. A four-foot case with a hinged lid stood open in the middle of the floor. Winnie reached to turn on the light—and Riordan gasped.

"What?"

"I swear I saw something inside move—something like an arm."

Winnie couldn't make herself be surprised. She knew that prosthetic limbs were a possibility. She raised her right arm again, holding it above her head. An answering movement came from inside the case, an aluminum and gray plastic wrist and hand hovering above the edge. She balled her hand into a fist and the metal hand followed her. She relaxed her fist and rifled her fingers. It mimicked her—a creepy game of Simon Says.

"Stop that," said Riordan, pushing her arm down so that the metal one disappeared. "What is going on?"

"It's a prosthetic. They have it paired to my transceiver. All my arm movements are played on it in stereo." She paused and then laughed. "I guess my mention of droids was more appropriate than I realized."

"Enough with the droids." Riordan yanked the door closed and took a step forward to peer over the edge of the crate. "What's the point? Why make a mechanical arm to copy your movements, and why bring it to Palm Springs?"

"I can't say for sure, but I bet it's tied to their reason for wanting me alive. Our company was never able to replicate the success we had with my prototype device, and I wonder if the Winemaker has run into similar roadblocks."

"Yeah, but what's that have to do with a mechanical arm?"

She blew air through her nose. He could be so single-minded. "I said I don't really know. It might be something to do with testing out my transceiver if they managed to get hold of it."

"Okay," said Riordan. He peered farther over the edge of the crate. "I can see a big orange power button. Okay if I turn it off?"

"Be my guest."

He leaned down into the crate, but before he could put his fingers to the switch, she pantomimed reaching up and grabbing his wrist. The prosthetic arm rose like an Indian cobra and made a clumsy pass at him. He yelped and danced out of the way. "That's not funny," he said.

Winnie snorted and came up to the crate. Holding her right arm still by her side, she leaned down with her left and flipped the switch. The prosthetic dropped. "I guess they thought they were going to get some action tonight or they wouldn't have powered it up."

"I guess. What are *we* going to do with it?"

"Smash it or take it with us. But I'm hoping there's more of interest than this. We still need some clue about where the Winemaker is holed up."

Riordan nodded to the bathroom. "I'll search the bathroom. You can have all the fake limbs you find out here."

She started with the dresser like before. This guy was less prissy about his clothes, but he was traveling just as light. She pulled out a New York Fire Department shirt and held it up, angry. The asshole didn't deserve to wear this.

"Winnie," said Riordan, a strain in his voice. "You better come back here."

She threw down the shirt and stepped into the bathroom. Riordan was on his knees by the tub. He'd unrolled a small towel on the floor, revealing the surgical kit wrapped inside. Scalpels, gloves, bandages, needles, and syringes were all in the inventory. He was gripping a laminated card, making a face while he read it.

She took hold of it and tugged. "Nothing is going to shock me at this point," she said, when he resisted letting go. It was a step-by-step *Surgery for Dummies* to remove the implants from the back of her neck. It went into gruesome detail about dealing with any scar tissue that might have formed around the devices and made it clear that under no circumstances were the implants to be jeopardized for the patient's sake. It also described how the implants and the transceiver should be packed up for transport after they were harvested, and only then did it bother to give any suggestions about dressing wounds.

She threw the card back down and brought her hand up to massage her temples. "Thoughtful of the Winemaker to laminate his instructions to avoid bloodstains, wasn't it?"

Riordan stood up beside her, looking distinctly unsettled. "Yeah."

"What's wrong with you? I'm the one they were going to cut up."

"That doesn't make it better," he snapped. Riordan paused. "Torture or any kind of abuse of medical technology just freaks me out."

They were silent for a moment, looking down at the glint of the scalpel under the bathroom light. "It confirms why they are after me," she said finally. "But it doesn't help with their location. We still don't have a fucking clue where they are."

Riordan shook his head. He leaned down to take the towel by a corner, dumping all the surgical paraphernalia to the floor. He held it so she could see the words and logo embroidered along the bottom. The logo looked like a bit for a horse, and the words confirmed it: BRIDLE BIT RANCH.

"So?" she said.

"It's a golf towel. Businesses give them out as promotional items."

"And?"

"I've got a pretty good idea where that business is."

CHAPTER 12

The Winemaker

ROI. RETURN ON INVESTMENT. The benefit an investor receives for the capital or know-how he supplies an enterprise. A simple enough concept, but many people struggle with its application, particularly the *return* part.

Some years ago, a venture capitalist friend of mine asked me to make an investment in a medical-devices fund he was putting together. At the time, I had no particular interest in medical devices, but I wanted to diversify and the VC firm had a good track record, so I agreed to put in $100 million. After the fund closed, Ted Valmont, a flamboyant young partner in the firm, took some of the money and put it in a start-up called NeuroStimix. NeuroStimix's business plan called for the commercialization of a technology intended to restore mobility in patients with spinal-cord injuries. The research behind the technology had been done in a university setting by a scientist named Warren Niebuhr, and Niebuhr was joining the company to take it to the next level. Total market size for the product was estimated at half a billion, and profitability for the company was projected at year three. So far, so good.

Three years came and went, and the company had no viable product, much less a revenue stream. The concept was still compelling, but Valmont had botched the execution. I had also realized that there were many more uses for the technology than the narrow application Valmont envisaged and was now more motivated than ever to have it succeed. To turn things around, I approached Niebuhr for a separate effort, rewarding and incentivizing him as Valmont had never done, and also sweeping away the regulatory roadblocks that had been retarding progress.

Chief among those roadblocks was approval for a human trial. My agents in England found the ideal candidate in a young woman named Winnie, who had been paralyzed in a horse-riding accident. We brought her to my estate in Napa where Niebuhr implanted a set of prototype neurostimulators and equipped her with a portable transceiver to relay motor impulses around the break in her spine. The results far exceeded our expectations. I then directed Niebuhr to develop variants of the technology for use with individuals who were not paralyzed. They, too, performed admirably, although more work was required for the military and industrial applications I had in mind.

At this point, I had invested a great deal more than my original $100 million, but I was satisfied with the progress and was looking forward to the benefits I and the world at large would accrue. I hadn't reckoned on Valmont's sense of entitlement. He claimed the moral high ground, but his betrayal was motivated by greed. He wanted sole control of the technology and he hired a detective named Riordan to help him. I can't bring myself to fully describe the set of circumstances that resulted in my being maimed, convicted of multiple felonies, and imprisoned in Corcoran. It is enough to say that it involved freakish bad luck and the invulnerability of idiots.

Whatever the judgment of society, there was no question in my mind that I owned the technology. My money paid for its development. My involvement accelerated its evolution. I was due a return. After my release from prison, I set about collecting it.

I cashiered Niebuhr, who had allied himself with Valmont again—but only after we extracted every bit of information from him about the technology. We then went after Valmont, catching him with Winnie in the parking lot of their company. I wanted them alive. What I got was Valmont dead from a sniper's bullet and Winnie on the run, very much alerted to the threat. It wasn't exactly the sort of performance I expected from former Navy SEALs, and I let Donovan know that even as he moldered in Corcoran awaiting his own release.

For her part, Winnie continues to surprise and infuriate. Niebuhr could not fully explain why her version of the stimulator technology is so much better than the others. Perhaps it is the design of the implants. Perhaps it is the programming of the transceiver. It could even be some unique aspect of her physiology. We'll know soon enough. Sometimes you have to break a thing to understand it.

That leaves only Riordan. We have reason to believe that Winnie has sought him out again. She couldn't have picked a worse partner. He will only drag her down. And Riordan, in particular, has a long fall ahead of him.

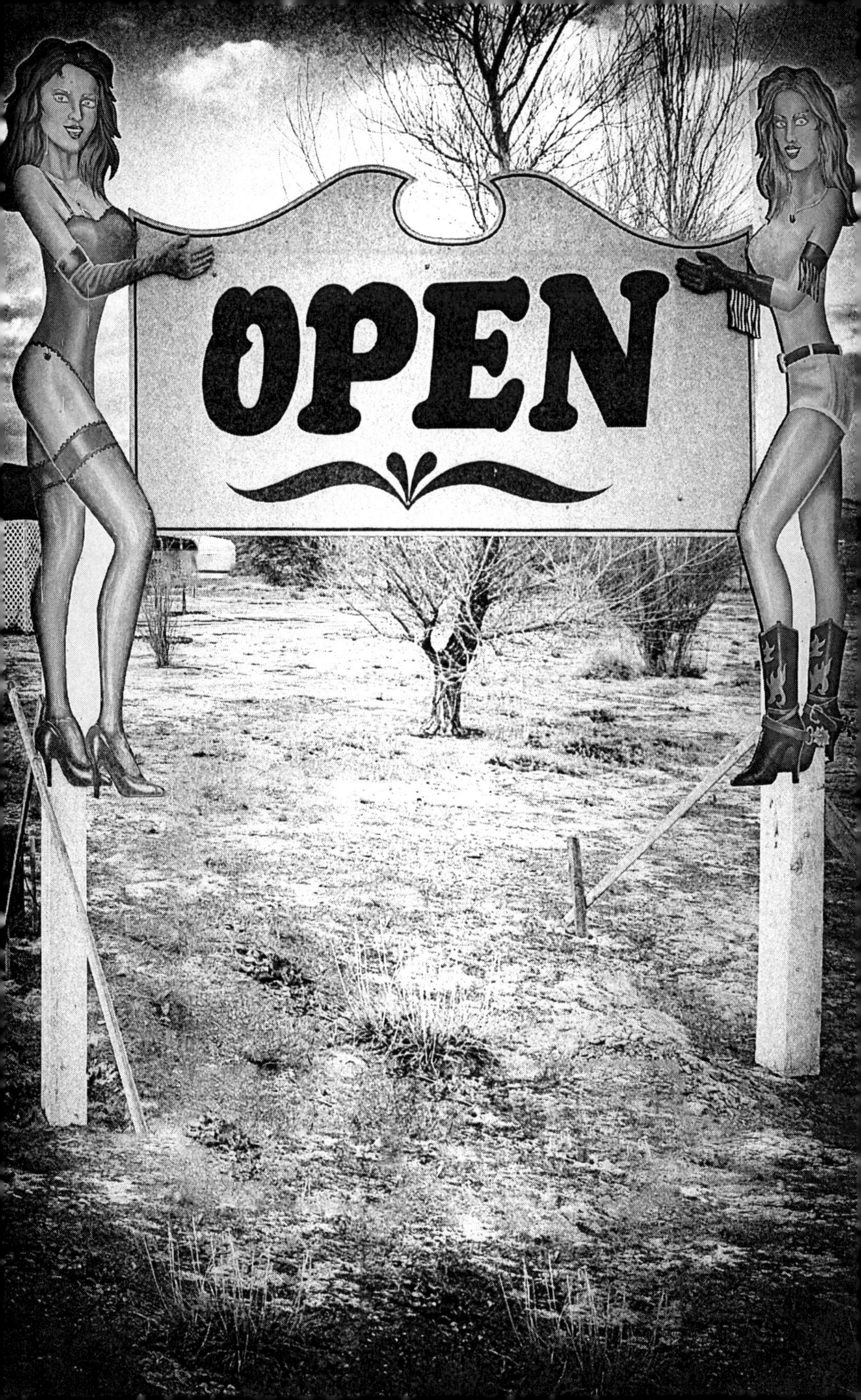
OPEN

CHAPTER 13

Riordan

WE SETTLED ON WINNIE'S LINCOLN for the trip. It wasn't the least conspicuous car on the road, but it stuck out less than my Galaxie and was presumably more reliable. I did the driving—and I did it in one gulp.

We started at six in the morning two days after our adventure at the hotel, taking the duffel bag of weapons and drugs we'd confiscated from the Winemaker's men, Ray's RF shield and decoy transmitter, and a final bit of electronic wizardry he had cooked up for us when it became clear where we were going and what we might find. "Electronic countermeasures," he called it. To me and every other schmo without a PhD in electrical engineering, it looked like an old-school flip phone made for senior citizens or people uncomfortable with technology. It looked exactly like mine, in fact.

We took I-10 out of town and latched on to U.S. 395, the road that would take us through the Sierra Nevada over some of the highest passes in California to our stopping point for the night, Reno. Winnie showed little interest in conversation or the spectacular scenery, opting instead to spend her time building hand strength and dexterity by working obsessively with a set of space-age exercisers the likes of which I'd never seen. The strangest one was a kind of half glove with retractable cords that sprouted from the palm and went to each finger to exercise the muscles that opened the hand rather than closed it.

Around Mono Lake, Winnie finally set her collection of torture devices aside and turned to look at me.

"What?" I said, more than a little perturbed by the sudden attention.

"How did you know that the Bridle Bit Ranch was a whorehouse?"

It was a question I'd been dreading ever since we'd confirmed my hunch by googling the name on Ray's computer. I'd hoped the excitement of the discovery was enough to push any curiosity about the source out of her mind. "It's not a whorehouse, exactly," I said. "It's a legally licensed brothel."

"You know what I mean. How did you know it was a place where men go to pay for sex?"

"I've never been there."

"The question stands."

I pressed the accelerator to pass a wheezing VW microbus I'd been content to follow up until now, but it was easier to run away from the bus than the question. "Look," I said, "I might possibly have made a trip to the area to patronize a similar establishment. And during that trip, I might possibly have heard about the Bridle Bit."

"You and Ray went, didn't you?"

"I'd rather not say."

"You don't need to, the way he turned beet red when the topic came up."

"He has problems with flushing."

"The hell he does. What did you hear about this place?"

I squeezed the wheel. This was exactly the line of questioning I wanted to avoid. "Not a lot. I talked about it with a guy I met at the bar of the other establishment. He said the Bridle Bit girls were very attractive—and that they were very expensive. More than double the going rate. He also said that..."

"What?"

"Well, I didn't understand it at the time, but he said that while the girls seemed very enthusiastic about their work their, ah, performance was a bit scripted. In fact, he went back a second time and asked for the same girl. She didn't recognize him from before and said almost exactly the same things. It was almost like she was—"

"Programmed?"

"Yeah, that was the word he used."

She picked up one of her hand grips and snapped it closed a few inches from my face. "It's not so hard to understand now, is it?"

"No, I guess not."

I tried to steer the conversation to the Winemaker and whether we were going to find him at the brothel, but she wasn't having it. She screwed the earbuds of an MP3 player into her head and went back to her exercises.

Stopping only for lunch at Astorga's in Bishop—and several times to fill up the thirsty Lincoln—we covered the distance to Reno in a little more than twelve hours. Winnie maintained strict radio silence the whole way. By the time we passed the famous neon sign at the entrance to downtown, I was so tired of stewing in my own juices that I tried to kick-start things by reading the sign aloud. "Reno," I announced, "'the biggest little city in the world.'"

Winnie snorted. "'The biggest little boil on the ass of the world' is more like it."

"Are you going to be like this from now on?"

"Like what? This is me. Get over it."

"I think you're still pissed about the brothel business. I'm sorry, but we wouldn't know about the Bridle Bit if I hadn't happened to do some firsthand research."

"First of all, I don't give a flying fuck what you do in your personal life. We aren't going to the senior prom; we're trying to stop the Winemaker. Second, we found out what we needed to know from frigging Google. So even if we didn't have the benefit of your so-called research, we would still be exactly where we are now."

"Whatever," I said, and gestured at the pile of 1970s concrete to my right. "Circus Circus okay with you? It's cheap and the rooms are clean."

"Why not? Clown partner, clown hotel."

I made a growling noise in my throat and started to say something really nasty. I settled for "It's a pleasure working with you, too."

We checked into rooms on the same floor, and I proceeded downstairs for the $13.99 prime-rib dinner and a fifty-dollar fleecing at the casino blackjack tables. Winnie informed me in monosyllables that we would meet at ten the following morning and chose to dine alone in her room.

Later, as I lay in bed thinking about our plans for the next day, I realized that she was probably just as angry about what I was *going* to do tomorrow as she was about what I had already done.

We got underway around eleven, driving east out of town through Reno's sister city of Sparks along Interstate 80 for about fifteen miles until we found the exit for Cottonwood Canyon Road. There weren't any cottonwoods around that I could see—just a lot of red dirt and high-desert scrub. The road led to the base of some red-dirt foothills where the Bridle Bit Ranch was nestled in a U-shaped notch in the terrain. But before we got onto the grounds, we had to pass through a gate with a guardhouse.

The guard was a lean, ropy-looking guy with a cowboy hat and a horseshoe mustache. He poked his head out of the guardhouse, taking in me and the car. Winnie he would have needed X-ray vision to take in because she was hidden in the trunk, wearing Ray's RF shield and packing the sawed-off shotgun and two of the 9mm automatics. She might have had one of the Tasers, too.

"Picking up?" said the guard.

"Excuse me?"

"Are you here to pick up someone?"

"Oh," I said. "You mean because of the Lincoln. No, I'm here for myself."

The guard gave me a wide if completely phony grin. "Well, have a good time, then. Please park near the entrance in one of the designated spots. Starlet will meet you at the door."

I nodded and pulled the car forward across a surprisingly ample (and nearly empty) parking lot to the main building. It looked like an overgrown Motel 6 trying hard to be an Italian villa, but there was a limit to what pink stucco and red roof tile could accomplish. The structure was T-shaped and, we knew from Google Maps, had a pool and an outbuilding in back. We also knew that there was another gate barring access to the rear, so for all practical purposes the front door was our only way in.

I parked as close to the entrance as possible to minimize the ground Winnie had to cover when she emerged from the trunk. *My* presence

had obviously been telegraphed to the inhabitants by the guard, because a blonde woman wearing leopard-skin hot pants and a gauzy
black blouse greeted me the moment I walked through the door.

"Hello, cowboy," she said, "I'm—"

"Starlet," I suggested.

She giggled. "Yes, that's right. Welcome to the Bridle Bit Ranch.
I've got some friends who are dying to meet you."

This, I knew from previous experience, was the preamble for the
lineup, a ritual where all the available girls in the house were paraded
in front of a customer for him to select one or—if he was so inclined—
more. The first and only other time I'd been to a brothel, Ray had told
me not to make a selection during the lineup. "If you jump at a girl
then," he counseled, "it makes it twice as hard to negotiate price. Have
a drink at the bar first and spend some time getting to know the girls.
Then pick one. You'll be bargaining from a stronger position."

While Ray's advice might have been sage under normal circumstances, I wasn't at all eager to prolong the process today—particularly
with Winnie baking away in the trunk. I let Starlet lead me over to
a leather wingback chair in the center of the room, just in front of a
little stage or platform. A rustic-looking bar was off to the left, and
behind it stood a guy with his hair slicked back and parted in the
middle. He wore an old-timey bartender's getup, right down to the
vest and arm garters. He smiled and nodded at me while rubbing a
beer glass with a rag.

There wasn't anyone else in the room. The customers who came in
the few cars in the lot must have made their selections and moved to
the back. That much of our plan was working: Winnie and I hoped
by coming early we would limit the number of civilians caught in
the crossfire.

Starlet clapped her hands. A curtain at the right parted and an obvious bouncer stepped through and held the red velvet back with a clublike arm. Following him was a line of women who could have come straight from the stage of the Miss Universe Contest. They were all different races and had different hair colors, skin tones, and heights, but they were all arrestingly beautiful. The women in the first brothel I visited had been attractive enough, but theirs was a pedestrian kind of beauty. If you'd seen the same group in green aprons working behind the counter at Starbucks, you wouldn't have given them a second thought. If I'd seen even one of these women at a Starbucks, I'd have made it my mission to camp out at the store ordering double espressos for as long as she was on shift.

They were different in other respects, too. The women at the first brothel were looser and more outgoing, winking and flipping their hair when they came up to us, infusing their speech with innuendo and invitation. As these women filed onto the little platform to introduce themselves, they were poised and formal, almost as if they were competing in a beauty contest. Each held her face in a fixed smile, and each limited her greeting to a solemn and toneless, "Hello, I'm so-and-so."

When all of them had their turn on the platform and had assembled off to the side in a too-perfect line, Starlet came up to caress the back of my neck and purr, "Well, partner, who do you like?"

While I didn't want to linger on the decision for all sorts of reasons, I realized in a panic that I didn't have any basis for making it. Picking the one I liked best would be the worst thing to do. It was wildly inappropriate, and it would only piss off Winnie more. Then it dawned on me that it didn't matter. Winnie would assume I had picked my favorite whomever I chose. "The first," I blurted. At least I could blame my selection on the random order of the lineup.

"You mean Destiny," said Starlet.

"Yes, I guess I do."

Destiny had short black hair cut in a bob that curled just under her chin. Her eyes were dark and rimmed with kohl, and her skin had a hint of olive to it, making me think she was at least part Middle Eastern. She didn't acknowledge her selection but walked serenely off to the left down a corridor that opened beside the bar. The other women retraced their steps through the curtained doorway.

"Isn't she going to wait for me?" I asked.

"We do things a little differently at the Bridle Bit," said Starlet. "We don't like to burden our girls with the business side of things. You and I are going to an anteroom where we can talk service and price, and get you checked out. Destiny will be getting ready to show you a wonderful time."

She beamed down at me, apparently waiting for me to acknowledge the information. "That's swell," I said, sounding like a perfect moron even to myself.

Starlet led me down the same corridor that Destiny had taken and pulled open the second door on the left. Inside was a small room with a gold-trimmed daybed and a chair that was done up with statues, paintings, and gold-trimmed curtains like Donald Trump's version of Julius Caesar's mudroom. A closed door that presumably led to the bedroom was at the back. Starlet gestured for me to sit on the daybed and pulled the chair up just a few inches away. Floral perfume that was about as subtle as a roach bomb wafted over me.

She crossed her legs and tugged at the hems of her hot pants, complaining, "These things are always creeping up around your waist." She winked and relaxed back into her chair. "So, what kind of party did you have in mind?"

I cleared my throat. "I'm a simple guy. I'm just looking for plain vanilla sex."

"Just an old-fashioned screw, eh? No problem. Destiny can scratch that itch for you." Starlet tittered then stopped abruptly. "That'll run you $1,200 for thirty minutes."

"$1,200?" I wasn't here to bargain, but I doubted anyone paid that without at least a little push back.

Starlet's voice lost the facade of forced cheeriness. "Listen, cowboy, the Bridle Bit is a special place. The girls are the most beautiful in Nevada—in the world, maybe. And quality costs." She put a bit of honey back into her voice. "But I think you'll find it's worth it."

I nodded. "Okay."

"Excellent. Cash or credit card?"

I had two thousand bucks in a money clip in my front pocket next to Ray's phony cell phone. I pulled out the clip and counted off the bills.

Starlet snatched them up and walked them over to a small desk, where she fed them into a slit in a heavy metal box in a lower drawer. From another drawer she took a pair of rubber gloves and tugged them on. She turned back to me when she was ready and held her arms open wide. "All right. Time for the pecker check. Stand and drop your pants, big boy."

I knew this was coming, but that didn't make it any less humiliating. A visual inspection for sexually transmitted diseases was standard procedure at Nevada brothels. While I couldn't argue with the rationale for the policy, it had been the thing that made me swear off brothels forever after my last trip. The whole experience was tawdry enough without including a USDA sausage inspection.

I stood and dropped trou. Starlet approached and gave me a

thorough once-over, pinching and pulling at will. "Oh," she cooed, "you're going to make a certain someone very happy."

If Winnie and I were right about the Bridle Bit, that was certainly true. But not in the way Starlet meant. "I bet you say that to all the boys," I told her.

"Naw. You've got a great package." She tapped me on the hip and started pulling off the gloves. "You can zip up. But one last thing. No weapons of any sort are allowed in the boudoir, including knives. You look like you are traveling light, but I have to check. This is Nevada, after all."

I was traveling light—just jeans and a T-shirt. I yanked up my pants and then turned out my hip pockets, displaying the meager contents of keys, money clip, and fake cell phone.

She smiled. "Looks like you've got a bit more cash if you'd like to go another round. How about your back pockets?"

I turned so she could pat them.

"Nothing on your ankles?"

I often carry a knife on my ankle, so it wasn't an idle question. This time I reluctantly agreed to leave all the weaponry to Winnie. I hitched my pant legs up to show off pasty shins and wrinkled black socks.

"Cool. Then I guess it's time for you to step through that door and meet your Destiny."

"Bet you've never used that line before."

She brought a hand to her mouth to cover a near snort. "Sorry. Couldn't help myself."

I yanked open the door. Inside was a larger room with more faux Roman furnishings. A four-poster made with Corinthian columns and a drooping silk canopy dominated the space. A pair of Venus di

Milo statues with Beverly Hills boob jobs flanked that, and gilded mirrors shimmered from the ceiling and the wall behind. The only light came from a chandelier with twinkling little bulbs.

Destiny lay on the bed with her hands clasped behind her head. She was naked and as glistening as polished river stone. "Climb aboard," she urged. "The train is about to leave the station."

I stepped across the threshold, and the door closed behind me. Everything hinged on what I was about to find out now. I went to where she lay, and reached down to touch the back of her neck. She didn't attempt to stop me, didn't even shift her position.

When I felt what I was looking for, I pulled my hand back and sat next to Destiny. As we anticipated, she—and presumably all the girls at the brothel—had a stimulator surgically implanted at the base of her brain, just where it joined the spine. I didn't begin to understand the science, but I knew from my last run-in with the Winemaker that the stimulator overrode all motor impulses, replacing them with commands received from a radio transmitter. Rather than restoring self-directed mobility as Winnie's version of the technology did, it turned the bearer into an electronic puppet.

"Listen," I said in a hushed tone. "I know you're not doing this willingly. I have something I believe will break their control. But if it works, I need you to stay calm and do what I say."

"Shy, aren't you?" she said, as if she hadn't heard a word I'd said. "Well, quit your grinnin' and drop your linen."

Realizing there wasn't any point in talking further, I reached into my pocket and took out Ray's electronic gizmo. I powered it on as he taught me and immediately saw a green LED indicating a transmission in the area. I pressed the number 9 on the keypad, and a red LED began blinking as well. That meant the transmission was being jammed, and it also meant that an alert had been sent to the companion device Winnie was carrying.

Game on.

If I expected an abrupt change in Destiny once the signal controlling her movements was interrupted, I was disappointed. Freed of electronic slavery, she merely lowered her arms and stared at her reflection in the ceiling mirror, her mouth gaping slightly.

Others had a more animated response. "Get the fuck off me, you fat pig!" I heard a woman scream from next door.

Then came the boom of a shotgun, followed by two more booms in quick succession. "It's her!" shouted a panicked male from the front of the building. "Watch out!"

I heard answering shots from a handgun, and then the door flew open. I figured the Winemaker's men would be monitoring the women by hidden video, but I didn't think they would identify the source of the jamming so quickly. The bartender with the slicked-back hair peered around the door frame and aimed a revolver in our direction. Squeezed the trigger.

The mirror behind us evaporated into a cloud of sparkling shards, and I pulled Destiny and half the covers from the bed to the floor. The bartender advanced into the room, firing indiscriminately as he came. He took the shoulder off one of the Venus di Milos and put another slug in the floor less than an inch from my outstretched foot as I struggled to drag Destiny and myself farther under the bed.

"Winnie," I shouted. "A little—"

Help was the word I wanted, but I never got it out. A shotgun convulsed very loudly and very close. The bartender made a gurgling nose like tenement plumbing and fell to the floor with a wet smack.

From under the bed, I saw a pair of running shoes approach, and then Winnie leaned down to find Destiny and me tangled in a wad of silk sheets. She unholstered one of the 9mm automatics and slid it across the floor.

"Quit fucking around," she snapped, "and get to work."

CHAPTER 14

Winnie

HIDING IN THE LINCOLN'S TRUNK in front of the brothel, Winnie decided she would give Riordan ten more minutes before she launched out. For one thing, it was hot as hell inside. For another, she was far from convinced that Ray's jamming device would work or that it would provide an effective diversion. Better to skip the gimmicks and go in guns blazing.

A muted chime from the gizmo in her pocket put an end to her contingency planning. She let go of the rope tied to the trunk lid and watched it hinge open. Riordan hadn't thought of a clever way to allow her to unlock the trunk from the inside, so he'd simply removed the latch. She'd been holding the trunk closed since climbing inside a few miles from the whorehouse, but she hadn't given it a thought. She never felt fatigue.

She grabbed the sawed-off pump action and clambered out. The heavy door to the brothel banged against the interior wall when she kicked it open. The only people in the front room were a bartender with garters on his arms, and a troglodyte in black jeans standing by the bar, shooting the breeze with him. The guy in the jeans looked like a bouncer, but it didn't matter; she'd already decided it was open season on any male in the place. If they weren't working for the Winemaker, they were raping women forced into sexual slavery. She leveled the sawed-off at him and blasted away.

The shot caught him square under the arm as he turned to look at her. He grabbed the lacerated flesh above his heart and crumpled to the floor, his head conking the polished brass foot rail as he landed. Winnie jacked out the expended shell and immediately aimed the shotgun at the bartender. Her first shot vaporized the liquor bottles on the wall as he ducked for cover. Her second splintered the polished oak countertop.

"It's her," he shouted from his hiding place. "Watch out!"

She couldn't tell if he was warning someone nearby or yelling into a cell phone or a radio. She had no time to ponder the issue because in the next moment the oily black barrel of a handgun poked around the bar to belch two slugs. She dove behind a wingback chair and chanced a look from the side. She saw the bartender pop up and scurry down a hallway, holding his finger to a Bluetooth earpiece.

She sprinted after him. He darted into a room on the left, and almost immediately there were more shots. She heard Riordan call her name as she ran headlong through the doorway. The bartender was emptying his revolver at a huddled mass beneath the canopy bed. Her shotgun boomed, and she decoupaged his brains onto the rear wall.

She strode past the ruined corpse, bending down to take in the scene under the bed. There, wrapped in silk sheets, his hand clutching the boob of a naked girl, was Riordan. She knew the clown would have found a way to take advantage of the situation. She unholstered one of the Glocks and slid it along the floor.

"Quit fucking around," she shouted over ringing in her ears, "and get to work."

While Riordan struggled to disentangle himself from the girl and the sheets, Winnie topped off the shotgun magazine with shells from her bandolier. When she next glanced up, he was standing beside her with a sheepish expression on his face. The girl, who looked Middle Eastern, was still on her hands and knees by his feet.

"What?" she demanded.

"Thank you."

"You better thank me. I'm not even going to ask how you ended up under the bed with Miss Kuwait instead of guarding the door with a big stick or something. What did you think they would do when they found you had jammed the signal?"

Riordan grimaced, started to say something, and then swallowed it.

"What?" Winnie demanded again.

"We're sticking with the plan?"

"Yes, damn it. You take this wing. I'll take the other. Meet at the—"

A woman's scream interrupted her. It was shrill and panicked, but as much as anything, it broadcast surprise.

"Outbuilding," finished Riordan.

"That's right." She waved in the direction of the scream, farther down the corridor. "Your meat."

Riordan nodded and stepped around her, scoping both sides of the hallway over the outstretched Glock before he slipped through the door.

Winnie followed him through, hurrying back to the front room, intending to lock the outer door to stop or slow reinforcements before continuing on to her wing.

Too late. A scarecrow with a cowboy hat and a Hulk Hogan mustache stood just across the threshold with a shotgun of his own. He pulled the trigger as she dove behind the bar, the same sanctuary her earlier quarry had sought. She landed amid broken glass and spilled booze from the blasted liquor bottles. Had some of the shot caught her legs? Winnie wiggled her toes to test her mobility. Everything still worked, but when she looked closely, she saw dime-size blood stains peppering her right calf. Then she realized the sawed-off had flown from her grasp to a spot in the open, outside the cover of the bar.

"I reckon I winged you," said the cowboy from across the room. "And you lost your gun. Throw out any other weapons you have, and we can end things without more shooting. I don't want to hurt you."

She almost laughed aloud. He was underestimating her like many of the Winemaker's employees had, but she knew that he was also worried about damaging her valuable circuitry. She calculated the odds. She was a terrible shot with a pistol, so it didn't take long. "Okay," she said in a cowed tone, and slid the remaining Glock from behind the bar. "I'm coming out."

She stood with her arms raised and faked a limp as she came around, standing just in front of the bouncer's body. "Don't shoot me. I'm done."

The cowboy grinned and shook his head. "You got nothing to worry about, Missy, as long as you do what I say." He came toward her. When he was less than three feet away, he paused. "You've got some kind of Taser doodad, I see. Can't have that. Drop to your knees with your hands behind your head."

She nodded and put all her weight on her left leg while she made a show of slowly lowering her injured right leg to the ground. But then, instead of tucking her left knee underneath her, she slapped both palms to the floor and pivoted into a ferocious outside sweep kick. It was the perfect brute-force attack for someone who didn't have fine motor skills, and she had practiced it hundreds of times. She caught the cowboy with her right shin just below the knee. He yelped in pain as he toppled.

She was on him in an instant, pulling the handheld Taser from her bandolier and jamming it in his chest. She gave him the full five-second dose then reengaged the trigger for a second jolt. He twitched and bucked—and lay still at last. She scooped up his shotgun and stood to aim at his chest.

"Wait," said a voice she recognized as Riordan's, but it was too late. She splattered the cowboy's internal organs across the floor in a bloody swath.

"Jesus!" shrieked a new voice, a woman's.

She turned to find Riordan holding a blonde in leopard-skin hot pants by the hair. She was bent over with her face in her hands, racked with sobs. The gauzy blouse she was wearing had been torn, and there were bright-red scratch marks across her stomach.

Riordan looked at Winnie and shook his head. He said something, but the renewed ringing in her ears drowned him out.

"I can't hear you," she shouted.

"I said, was that really necessary?"

Without answering, she leaned down to retrieve the Taser and hurried back to the bar to pick up her sawed-off and the Glock. Then, after checking the corridor to the other wing of the building, she said, "What about 'Meet me at the outbuilding' don't you understand? We can't congregate here. They are bound to send reinforcements—they probably have the whole place wired for video."

"They do have it wired, but they don't have reinforcements. There's only one guy left, and he's a civilian. He's the tech weenie who controls the women."

"How do you know that?"

Riordan yanked on the blonde woman's hair, pulling her upright. "Meet Starlet. She told me. She's the madam or the greeter or something. I guess she's not very popular with the other women. When they got free, the more aggressive of them just about took her apart. It was her we heard screaming."

Winnie came up. "Maybe you shouldn't have stopped them. She's a traitor to her sex."

Riordan cleared his throat. "Let's stay focused on the Winemaker. No wars between the sexes."

"All right. So where is this tech guy?"

Riordan prodded the blonde in the back. "He's in the cabana," she said.

"The outbuilding to us," put in Riordan.

"And he's got no guns or weapons of any sort?"

"I don't think so. Oz is a skinny little nerd, and the place is filled with computers, video monitors, and other electronics. Nothing—nothing lethal."

Winnie laughed without mirth. "Oz? You're kidding."

"His real name is Ojas, but they call him Oz. You know, 'cuz he's the guy behind the curtain."

"Yeah. Well, if Oz called for help from outside—and he must have by now—how long will it take to get here?"

The blonde's eyes flashed through her tears, but she said nothing.

"Answer her, Starlet," said Riordan, tugging hard at her hair.

"All right, all right. There's two other guys in security. They're not on until evening, so it's hard to know where they are or if they're even reachable."

"Pretend they were sitting at home by their phones."

"They both live in Reno, so if he called them right away, about twenty minutes."

Winnie looked over at Riordan. "Assume we have twenty."

"Twenty it is. Let's get her parked and then we see Oz." He pulled Starlet back by the hair and maneuvered her into a three-point turn down the corridor on the left. "Follow me," he called over his shoulder.

He led them to a room a few doors from the one Winnie had chased the bartender into. It was a kind of lounge, and it was filled with six of the most beautiful women she had ever seen. It was also occupied by three naked men, arranged on the floor like so many tuna at a fish auction. All the men were white, flabby, and middle-aged. And all were restrained with classic S&M gear, including ball gags, wristcuffs, and spreader bars. One woman, a tall African American in harem pants and a vest, was idly switching the ass of the fattest man with a cane.

"Jasmine," Riordan said to the black woman. "I'm going to return Starlet to your tender mercies. But, please, no more rough stuff. If all goes according to plan, we'll be back shortly and we can figure out our next steps. If we don't come back, or someone else shows up in our place, use your judgment."

He shoved Starlet toward Jasmine, who caught her, shook her like a towel that she was about to fold, and passed her to an Asian. "Tie her up, Mei-Lien," she commanded.

Winnie stepped forward to hand Jasmine the cowboy's shotgun. "Here," she said, "this may come in handy."

Jasmine accepted the gun and immediately poked the muzzle of it against the ass of the man she had been tormenting. He grunted and tried to flop away. "Thank you," said Jasmine. "It just may at that."

Winnie pivoted and hurried out of the room, Riordan trailing after her. She knew from Google Maps that there was a door to the outside at the end of the corridor.

"Hey," called Riordan. "You're bleeding. You okay?"

"Nothing to worry about now."

"If you say so."

"Yes, I do."

They came to the steel door at the end of the hall, and she punched the push bar to exit. A large swimming pool yawned before them—a large *empty* swimming pool. Leaves and other debris peppered the bottom, and in spots the plaster flaked like patches of psoriasis.

Starlet's so-called cabana stood beyond the pool. Made of stucco and red tile like the main building, it was drab and shedlike with double French doors and no windows. A strange multimasted antenna sprouted from one side of the roof, and a bubble-shaped skylight protruded from the other. When they circumnavigated the pool to reach the building, they found a blanket tacked up on the inside covering the glass of the French doors.

Riordan chuckled. "There's the curtain." He jiggled the door handle. Locked.

"Stand back," said Winnie.

"Come on. Let's kick it in."

"Stand back."

He grabbed her arm and pulled her to one side. "At least stay out of his line of fire in case he does have a gun."

She shook off his grip and pointed the shotgun at the upper half of the French doors. She nuked all the glass above the door handle along with most of the frame. The blanket hung in tatters.

"You've got ten seconds to come out of there, Oz," she shouted.

"I'm coming, you freak," someone answered.

Furniture shifted, glass crunched, and a hand reached through the dangling strips of the blanket to unlock and twist the interior door handle. A short Indian man with thick black hair and long sideburns stepped out. He looked smug and churlish, and wore pointy leather shoes that Winnie disliked instantly. One hand was balled in his front pocket. The other, adorned with silver rings of intricate design, was flipping her off.

"Fuck you, cunt."

Beside her, Riordan made a noise in his throat that was more threatening than any words. "I'd tone it down if I were you, bucko."

"Fuck you, too, clown. I know all about you both. Talk about the perfect pair of losers."

"Shut up about us," snapped Winnie. "Where is the Winemaker?"

"I won't shut up. I've seen the design for your hardware. Except for the stimulator, it's inferior to everything we have now. What were you and your poor dead husband doing for all those years?"

Winnie took a menacing step forward. She knew she shouldn't let the little bastard get under her skin, but the mention of her husband and their company set her blood boiling. "Where the *fuck* is the Winemaker?"

Oz took a corresponding step back but didn't stop running his mouth. "And I've seen your crappy programming. There are security holes a mile wide. Did you know that it doesn't stop anyone from overriding your motor signals? From controlling your body externally?" He pulled his hand from his pocket and with it came a console of some sort. "Enjoy," he said, as he depressed a button.

Winnie stood stock-still for a moment, terrified at the thought of losing control, of being made to harm herself and Riordan, as Oz no doubt intended. But nothing happened. In a flash she knew why. Ray's RF shielding not only prevented her signals from being detected, it also stopped others from getting in.

She leaped at Oz with a roar, grabbing two fistfuls of his shirt. "Where is the Winemaker?" she screamed into his startled face.

He said nothing but made the mistake of grabbing at her throat. She spun him around in a wide arc, flinging him into the air as if he were an Olympic hammer as she repeated, almost manically now, *"Where is the Winemaker?"*

His body flew in a flat arc across the pool deck, over the edge, and into the deep end, where he landed head first.

Riordan dodged past her to stare at the wreckage. After a moment, he said, "We'll take our answer off the air."

CHAPTER 15

Riordan

"WHAT THE FUCK'S that supposed to mean?" asked Winnie.

I tugged at her jacket, pulling her back from the edge of the pool. "For someone who was so keen on torturing the Winemaker's men for answers, you hung up on Oz there pretty quickly without waiting for any. That's what it means."

"Do you understand what just happened? He was going to remote-control me into killing us both. If I hadn't been wearing Ray's magic underwear, he would have succeeded."

"Yep," I said, nodding my head. "I got that. Good thing I insisted you go back to your hotel room this morning to put it on even though you said no one would, quote, 'monitor my fucking signals at the fucking whorehouse,' unquote."

"Yeah, yeah."

"And what do we say when someone makes a helpful suggestion that ends up saving our life as well as his own?"

"We say even a broken clock is—"

"Exactly. And you're welcome. Now, if I may make *another* suggestion, why don't you starting searching the cabana for clues to the Winemaker's location."

"While you do what?"

"I'm going to update the girls, make sure they aren't flailing the hide off Starlet and the johns, and generally try to batten down the hatches in case Oz did call for help."

She narrowed her eyes at me, no doubt pondering the idea of me spending more unsupervised time with the women. "Maybe we should trade assignments."

"I don't think so. You're better with computers and whatnot. And I'm not entirely sure you won't join the girls in the flailing."

Winnie grunted. "Okay, but lock the front gate first thing. And don't let Starlet go. She's one person I *do* intend to question."

"Yes, boss." I wanted to broach the topic of her wounded leg again but was pretty certain she'd shut me down.

"Go," she urged.

I bit off the question and jogged around the pool to the door of the main building. I found the girls much as I'd left them, except that Starlet had joined the line of hog-tied bodies on the floor. She tried to say something through her gag when she saw me.

Jasmine, who was still brandishing Winnie's shotgun, put a slippered foot to the back of Starlet's head and forced it to the ground. "Hush up, bitch," she said.

"Oz," I announced, "has been dealt with."

"I hope 'dealt with' means torn from limb to limb. The peckerwood had his way with all of us multiple times while he was testing out the programming."

"And testing and retesting," put in one of the other girls.

I licked my lips. I couldn't help but feel I was being judged by my sex. "Yeah, well, I think you'd approve. Winnie helped him into a head-first dive into the deep end of the pool."

"The deep end of the *empty* pool," said Jasmine.

"That would be the one."

"Then you're damn right I approve. I figured that girl for a hellcat when I saw her."

"You figured right. Listen, I'm going out to secure the front gate. Hold the fort here for a while longer and then we can decide what to do about...all of this." I gestured to the men and Starlet on the floor.

"I've got some good ideas."

"That's what I'm afraid of." I started to leave but turned back. "Say, do you have the keys to any of the vehicles these gentlemen were driving?"

"Sure, we got their keys, their wallets, their cell phones, their condom packets, and their fake Rolexes."

"Can I borrow a set?"

A redhead in a black satin bustier reached into a wooden bowl on a sideboard and pulled out a key fob. She glanced down at the make. "How about a BMW—an SUV by the looks of it."

"Perfect."

She tossed it over to me. I snagged it midflight and hurried out of the lounge, down the corridor to the front room, where I had to dodge broken glass, congealing blood, and glistening bits of viscera on my way to the front door. Outside, I clicked the unlock button on the fob, which I realized for the first time was on a ring with a rental-car tag. A gleaming X5 chirped and flashed its parking lights in response.

I backed it away from the building and then barreled across the lot, angling for the entrance. As I approached, I saw the gate—essentially a segment of the barbed-wire-topped chain-link fence bolted to wheels—had already been rolled across the opening. Probably the guard had closed it before leaving for his showdown with Winnie. On the other side of the gate, crouched behind the open door of a pickup that was angled across the roadway, was a male figure dressed in jeans and a plaid shirt. The crown of his baseball hat peaked just over the roof line.

I swung to a stop about ten yards away, leaving the passenger side of the BMW to him. I eased open the door and crept over to the rear tire to peer around the back, holding my Glock just out of sight.

"We're closed," I yelled. "Get lost."

The man in the plaid shirt said nothing but hunkered down farther behind the truck. I saw the gleaming barrel of a handgun flash through the door window as he moved.

So much for the idea that he might be a customer. "Give it up," I said. "You're too late."

A three-count went by. "You're lying."

"I'll spell it out for you. The guard, the bouncer, the bartender, and Oz are all dead. The women are free. Starlet and the customers are tied up."

"Maybe you're alone. Maybe you're the only one left standing and you're trying to bluff me."

I cursed under my breath. I was trying to decide what I could say to convince him—or if it was just simpler to start shooting—when Winnie's electrified voice jumped out of the guard shack. Apparently, she had found an intercom system in the cabana.

"Listen, shithead," she barked. "There are plenty of us left. Come ahead. The crime-scene cleaners will be wet-vacing your pancreas off the asphalt by nightfall."

The man in the plaid shirt remained silent for another moment, then he ducked into the truck cab and started the motor. He K-turned away from the fence and zoomed up the road to the freeway.

I returned to the BMW and moved it forward, parking it behind the gate as I had originally intended. I wanted it there as an additional barrier in case the Winemaker's men tried to crash through.

"Hey," said Winnie's disembodied voice from the guardhouse.

"Yes, ma'am."

"Get the hell back here. I found something I want to show you."

I opened the half door to the guardhouse and stepped inside. I could see Winnie on a monitor attached to the wall. A red light on a video camera glowed just below it, leading me to think she could see me, too. "What about the other guy? Starlet said there were two guys, remember?"

"If they didn't come together, I doubt the other's going to show by himself. He may be gathering even more reinforcements. There's an alarm system and video cameras all the way up to the freeway, so we'll have some warning, but I don't want to hang around here any longer than necessary. So, like I said—"

"Yeah, yeah. Get the hell back there. All right. I'm going to put a note out to dissuade any legitimate customers and I'll be right with you."

"Legitimate my ass," she said, and then she was gone.

I hunted around for some paper and a pen. On a sheet I tore from a clipboard I wrote, "Closed due to herpes outbreak. Come back next week," and scotch-taped it to the fence.

I jogged across the parking lot, continued through the main building—ignoring requests from several of the girls—and out the rear door to the cabana. I found Winnie staring at one of the computers at the back of the room. I heard a male voice issue from a speaker and thought she was watching a video until I got a clear look at the screen. It showed a darkened office or cubbyhole with rough plaster walls. Beyond a short section of desk, hunched in an electric wheel-chair like a curled-up daddy longlegs, was a man I recognized with a start. He had shaved his head, he looked older and wizened, but he had the same gangly limbs, the same flat nose, and the same thin-lipped, grim-looking mouth. Winnie had taken it upon herself to Skype the Winemaker.

"... prevent venereal diseases and provide comfort to soldiers," he was saying in his high-pitched voice.

"It's forced prostitution," snapped Winnie.

"Here, in the Land of the Free?" said the Winemaker. "Perhaps. But in Yemen or Nigeria where we are fighting Islamic terrorists? No one will object to using the enemy's women in this way. We will use their propaganda against them." He paused. "Who walked in behind you?"

"Never mind. Just know that Oz is dead and the Bridle Bit is shut down. You're not going to win."

The Winemaker's smile was like a crack in an ice cube. "Ted said something very much like that to me once."

Winnie lurched forward to yell at the screen. "You're not allowed to call him that."

I reached down for the mouse and clicked every Skype button I could find until the video call was terminated. I put a steadying hand on Winnie's shoulder, but she slapped it away.

She stared up at me defiantly.

I waited a long moment then asked as calmly as I could, "What was he telling you when I came in? His justification for the Bridle Bit?"

"Yeah. It's like I said. He and Donovan plan to use the technology for military applications. One of their warped ideas is comfort stations for soldiers."

"Like the Japanese in World War II?"

"Exactly. He was particularly expansive about the idea of turning the jihadist reward of seventy-two virgins on its ear. Instead of the terrorists getting seventy-two virgins, his men get a thousand Islamic women."

"I see. This may be a sensitive question, but may I ask why you were talking to him in the first place?"

She turned back to the computer and began banging on the keyboard. "To find his location."

"How?"

"I figured that Oz had to talk to the Winemaker some way, and Skype is as good as any. When I saw that Skype was installed on this computer, I went through the contacts list—"

"And you found him listed. But what did you hope to accomplish by calling him?"

"Hold on. He wasn't in the listings, exactly. I found a cryptic entry that I thought could be his. I called it to trace the IP address. When you make a call on Skype, you establish a connection between your computer and the receiver. And while that connection was open, it's possible to use a system utility to get the address."

I'm not much of a computer person, but even I knew IP addresses were unique identifiers for computers and other devices on the Internet. And I also knew that once you had an address, you could associate it with a physical location. "So you know where he is."

"I know where his computer is, anyway. Healdsburg, California."

CHAPTER 16

Riordan

"Guess we're heading back to California," I said.

Healdsburg is a town in Northern California's wine-producing region. It's more rural than Napa and Sonoma, the principal cities involved in the area's wine industry, so it didn't surprise me that the Winemaker might pick it as a place to lie low.

Winnie rubbed the back of her neck and nodded. I'd noticed she often found excuses to touch her head and neck. "Yeah, I guess we are. But we need more than just the town. I think it's time to talk to your friend Starlet."

"She's not my friend."

"You let somebody who's not your friend handle your junk?"

"Very funny. I should never have mentioned that part of brothel protocol. You want me to fetch her?"

"That's the idea. I need to keep an eye on the security cameras."

I shrugged and went to retrieve Starlet. I had Jasmine remove the spreader bar from her ankles but kept the handcuffs and ball gag in place. As I herded Starlet back through the rear door of the main building, a scraping sound came from the pool. Winnie hadn't exactly stayed glued to the computer monitor. She was dragging Oz by the ankles along the bottom. Starlet and I watched as she painted the plaster with a streak of blood from a wound on his forehead.

"He was still breathing," said Winnie, when she saw us.

"Was?"

"Yes, was." She leaned down to retrieve the device he had pointed at her and then rifled his front and rear pockets for a cell phone and wallet. "Brain dead, probably," she amended, "but still breathing."

Starlet made a strangled noise.

"Now you know what you're dealing with," I said to her in an undertone. "Don't expect me to control her. She's going to ask you some questions and you damn well better answer."

I got a twitchy nod and a gurgle in response. Starlet seemed to have grasped the point.

We met Winnie at the cabana, where she resumed her place in the chair by the computer. I stood Starlet up in front of her and undid the ball gag. She whimpered a little when it came off but said nothing.

"You know who I am?" began Winnie.

"You're the one they've been trying to capture," said Starlet.

"And?"

"And you're like the—the other girls, but you move on your own. They were going to get the implants from the back of your neck and said you might be coming here. They also said..."

"Yes?"

"They also said that the Winemaker hated you for what you and your husband did to him."

Winnie smirked. "Did they say anything about my friend here?"

"I don't think so. Who *is* he?"

"Riordan. They might have referred to him as a detective or a private investigator."

"Oz did say something about a detective once. Said he was a bozo who was going to be killed."

"Please," I said. "No need to sugarcoat it." Both women ignored me.

"Did they say we might be working together?" pressed Winnie.

"No."

"Or where they thought we were?"

"No."

Winnie leaned back in her chair and regarded Starlet for a moment. "How did you get involved with them?"

Starlet looked down and then away. "I was managing another brothel—a regular brothel—when they approached me. They offered me a lot of money. At first, I didn't understand what was different about the women, but it didn't take long to figure out that something was odd. I started asking questions—and finally they told me. They said they would kill me if I went to the police. I was just as much a prisoner here as the girls."

"By 'girls' you mean slaves, don't you? And I'll bet you were."

"No, it's true," Starlet insisted without looking up. "I didn't have a choice."

Winnie rolled her chair forward. "Here's the big question. I want you to think very carefully before you answer—think about what happened to Oz, to the bartender, to all the men who worked here. Where is the Winemaker?"

Starlet's breath caught. "I—I don't know."

Winnie leaped out of her chair and took hold of Starlet's throat with both hands. The suddenness of it surprised me, to say nothing of what it did to Starlet. She yelped and toppled into me.

"Did they tell you how strong I am?" asked Winnie.

Starlet managed a truncated nod.

"But I can't feel anything. I get no feedback. I might start squeezing your throat to encourage you to answer my question and, without even meaning to, strangle you or break your neck. Don't take that risk. Tell me—where is the Winemaker?"

Starlet's body trembled like a thunder sheet in a radio play. Liquid spread from her crotch to darken the fabric of her tights. "I really don't know," she sobbed.

"Winnie," I said softly over the head of the terrified woman. "She's not lying."

"Don't take her side."

"I'm not taking her side. I'm taking yours. Ask her something else. She wants to be helpful."

Winnie released Starlet's throat, shoving her back into me. "All right, bitch. Did the Winemaker come here?"

Starlet rode over sobs and deep hyperventilating breaths to answer. "He never came here."

"How did you communicate with him?"

"I've never met him or talked to him. No one spoke to him but Oz."

"How exactly?"

The question seemed to surprise her. "I don't know. I assumed the phone."

"Did anyone else ever visit?" I asked. "Any of the Winemaker's other employees?"

"Two guys came through about a week ago. They spent time with Oz. He told me they were after her."

"What'd they look like?"

"One had red hair. The other was Hispanic. Looked like he worked out."

I raised my eyebrows and nodded at Winnie. "Did they say anything about where they'd come from?"

"No..."

I tugged on the short length of chain between her handcuffs. "Think harder."

"I hardly spoke to them. I set each of them up with a girl—"

"Bitch," Winnie said sharply.

"And—and I talked to them a little at the bar before they left. They didn't say anything about where they came from... Well, one little thing."

"Let's have it."

"They left after the drink, but the redhead came back into the building with a bunch of garbage for me to throw away. He said the other guy was a pig and he was tired of having it in the car."

"So?"

"So there were fast-food wrappers from a place I'd never seen before. Nation something. I asked the guy about it and he said it was a chain in California."

I chuckled.

"What?" said Winnie.

"Nation's Giant Hamburgers. And it's not a chain in California. It's a chain in *Northern California*. I bet there are not more than two dozen of them. I'm sure we can find out if there's one near, ah, the place we're concerned about."

"Big fucking clue," said Winnie, settling back in the chair. Her eyes wandered over to the computer screen and she quickly grabbed the mouse to resize a window. "Somebody just pulled up in front in a cab."

"That's got to be a customer."

"Yeah. The guy's getting out to read your note." A beat went by, and she smiled for the first time in what seemed like a very long time. "Jesus, what did you write? He looks like he's been slapped."

"I'll tell you later. I'm going to take Starlet back to chill with our other detainees. Then I think we need to figure out our next steps."

"Fine. I'll do a Google search on your burger place."

I escorted Starlet back to the lounge, where Jasmine got her resituated next to the johns. Apparently, Starlet wasn't the only one with bladder-control issues, as there was now a dark stain shaped like India on the carpet under one of them. I suggested that Jasmine get the girls packed up and ready to go.

"There's not much packing to do," she said, "but we may have a problem with Destiny."

I looked around the room and realized for the first time that she wasn't there. "Why? What's the matter?"

"For one thing, I don't think she speaks English."

"But I heard her."

Jasmine blew air through her lips. "They can make you say whatever canned phrases they want. Like those fucking dolls with the pull strings. Maybe the bigger problem is her emotional state. She's almost catatonic. Apparently, they kidnapped her from some Middle Eastern country. She was a burqa-wearing virgin. No experience at all with men, and certainly none with the shit they made us do here."

I thought back to what the Winemaker had said on the Skype call.

"Oh."

"'Oh' doesn't even begin to cover it. I don't know why I'm telling you this. We'll take care of her. My impression is you have other fish to fry."

I ran my hand through my hair. "Yeah, we do. Look, let's meet in the front room in ten minutes. With the brothel's cars and the ones these guys came in, we should have enough to transport everyone."

"Yep. And I'm certain Starlet will be happy to open the safe to provide a little traveling cash."

I laughed. "No doubt."

When I got back to the cabana, I found Winnie yanking cables and cords from the back of one of the computers. "I'm taking this with us," she said. "In case there's any more information on the disk."

"Did you look up Nation's Giant Hamburgers?"

She nodded as she extracted an oversize laptop from the tangle of wires. "You were right. There's one in Healdsburg. I guess it's confirmation of a sort, but it doesn't tell us anything new."

"I've got another question for you."

She straightened and looked at me with a quizzical expression. "What? You want to know if I date older men?"

"Hardly. The question is did you really finish off Oz in the pool?"

She curled her upper lip at me. "That bother you?"

"It seemed a little extreme—even for you."

She walked by me, patting my shoulder as she passed. "Relax. He was already dead. I wanted his cell phone and stuff, and it didn't seem like a bad idea to make Starlet think I was administering the coup de grâce before we questioned her."

"Very—" I started to say, but a scream from the main building interrupted.

Winnie chucked the laptop, retrieved her sawed-off from a table by the door, and sprinted out. I pulled the Glock from the small of my back and followed. We rushed through the rear entrance, hugging the left side of the corridor until we came to the lounge. Outside stood the redhead who had given me the keys to the BMW. She was staring into the room with her hands held to her face in a silent-movie pantomime of shock.

The redhead backed away from the doorway, and Jasmine emerged, holding Destiny in a bear hug. She was wild-eyed and pale—and had blood on both of her hands.

Jasmine looked over Destiny's head to meet my gaze. "She killed all the johns," she said. "Starlet, too. Cut their throats with a bar knife."

"Sweet Jesus." They were culpable, but did they deserve death? Did Destiny even understand what had been done to her and who was responsible? I turned my head away. "Clean her up and let's get the fuck out of here," I snarled. "I've had a bellyful of this place."

I cajoled, prodded, and otherwise force-marched all the women into three of the vehicles for which we had keys. I backed the BMW away from the front gate, pulled it wide open, and waved them through in caravan.

Jasmine drove the last car in line. She paused to roll down the window as she pulled up. "I just wanted to say thank you."

"You should really be thanking Winnie," I said. "But you're welcome. Where will you go?"

"I'm not going to tell you. If you're going up against the people who did this—who thought up this technology and enslaved us—I don't want you to know anything more about us. Far away from here is all you need to know."

I kicked a pebble across the blacktop. "I understand. You should get those things off your necks as soon as you can. You're vulnerable as long as you have them."

She nodded and pressed the button to roll up the window. I heard her say, "We'll cut them out with a nail file if we have to," and she was gone.

I walked back to the Lincoln, which was still parked in front of the brothel. Winnie was waiting for me in the passenger seat. "Ready?" I asked.

She looked at me with an opaque expression. She'd been strangely subdued since I'd blown my top. "Almost," she said quietly. "I realized I left the computer in the cabana. Would you mind going back for it?"

"Why ever not?" I said snidely, and trod the short flight of steps to the entrance. I strode through the building, averting my eyes as I passed the lounge, nabbed the computer, and then made my way back.

As I came through the bar area, I nearly tripped on the broken neck of a wine bottle. I looked past the bar to the wall behind and spotted a shelf with a display of more of the same sort of bottles, a few of which had escaped Winnie's shotgun volleys. I crunched over to take one from the shelf. It was a pinot noir from a winery called Marionette Vineyards. It was no place I'd ever heard of, but somehow I knew the label would read BOTTLED IN HEALDSBURG, CA.

CHAPTER 17

Winnie

WINNIE DROVE BACK with Riordan to their hotel in Reno to pick up their luggage. They decided that they needed to put more mileage between themselves and the Bridle Bit before dark, but Riordan insisted on stopping at a drugstore to pick up bandages and disinfectant for her leg. By the time he finished swathing her calf with Neosporin, gauze, and tape in the parking lot of a Walgreens, she looked like she was ready for burial in an Egyptian sarcophagus.

"You know the first line of the Hippocratic oath?" she asked, as he knelt on the asphalt by the passenger door of the Lincoln.

"Something about collecting the co-pay?"

"No, something about not doing any harm. Are you sure you didn't cut off the circulation?"

"If your foot turns blue, we'll know." He stood and looked down at her. "Seriously, this should help with infection and bleeding, but it looks like you took some buckshot. We should see a doctor and have them removed."

"That goes back to the do no harm thing. If you get hit by some buckshot, it's better to let them come to the surface as the wound heals rather than trying to dig them out. And there's no way I'm going to a hospital with a gunshot wound. Those have to be reported. Even if we didn't draw the attention of the Winemaker's men, we'd certainly have the Sparks or Reno cops breathing down our necks."

Riordan sighed. "You always have a comeback, don't you? If you won't see a doctor, you're still going to have another consultation with me. We need to do a better job of cleaning the wounds than I can do in a frigging parking lot."

He tromped to the other side of the car and, after flinging the medical supplies in the back, dropped into the driver's seat to start the motor. He paused then, his hand poised over the gear selector, and turned to look at her.

"Waiting for a pat on the head?" Winnie asked. "Okay, thank you. I appreciate it."

Riordan harrumphed and drove off.

They crossed into California and covered another sixty miles or so along Highway 20 until they came to the tiny Gold Country town of Nevada City. It was nearly eight p.m. They were both tired and hungry and ready to stop for the night. Making good on that decision was another matter altogether. It was "high season" in Nevada City, and the town's few hotels and motels were full of bratty kids and their parents looking to fish, hike, or pan for gold. It was only after the clerk of another motel directed them to a dump called the Prospector Inn that they were able to find rooms.

They weren't even rooms, exactly. They were cottages set around a tract of land that the hotel brochure referred to as a park. The only place Winnie could think of where weeds, dead pine trees, and skids of bare red earth would qualify as a park was Chernobyl.

The cottages themselves were just as bad. Filthy, ramshackle, and decorated with furnishings that looked like they'd been purchased at a yard sale—she'd seen ice-fishing shacks that were more livable. After unloading the luggage, they sat down at the scratched dinette table in her cottage to feast on the half-vegetarian, half-pepperoni pizza they'd picked up in town. A chandelier with missing globes dangled above them.

Whether it was the depressing surroundings, the crappy food, or the tragic ending to their assault on the brothel, conversation was at a minimum. Winnie found herself wondering whether she should even go on—or whether she should continue to drag Riordan with her. She knew that he wasn't comfortable with her aggressive tactics and that the death of Starlet and the johns at Destiny's hand had upset him.

"Maybe we should split up," she said abruptly. "We've found where the Winemaker's holing up. That's the most important thing. There's no need for you to come with me to Healdsburg. Maybe you should—"

"Cut and run?" Riordan chugged the last of his beer and set the bottle aside. "Look, I know you are a death-dealing bitch on wheels, but there's no way you—or anyone else—is going to take the Winemaker down by herself."

"The odds don't improve much with two of us."

"Yes, they do—they aren't good odds, but they're certainly better odds. You've saved my bacon several times now, and whether you admit it or not, I've helped you through my association with Ray, with my clever—"

"Cockamamy"

"—stratagems, and the simple and rather startling fact that, at times, I'm more prudent than you."

"Prudent like when you nearly choked yourself to death on the bench press?"

"I said *at times.*"

She smiled in spite of herself. "Okay, I'm not going to say you complete me, but we've made an okay team. Still, it's really not your fight. If you leave now, and do a good job of keeping your head down, I doubt the Winemaker would bother to chase you. It's me—and my hardware—he's after."

Riordan took another Bud from the six-pack. He twisted off the cap and held it up by his ear to snap it across the room. It whizzed through the bathroom door where it clattered into the sink. "Two points," he said. "But I digress. That's bullshit. It's always been my fight, as you said yourself when you came to the Springs. The Winemaker has killed everyone who crossed him. He won't exempt me no matter how far I run. And that's just looking at it from his side. From my side, there's no way I'm calling it quits now. Not after seeing what he did to the women at the brothel—and what he caused them to do to others—and not after..."

Winnie waited a moment, then prompted, "And not after what?"

Riordan took a hurried swallow of beer and bought more time by wiping his mouth with the back of his hand. "Not after all I've invested in you."

"Invested in me? What am I? Some kind of mutual fund?"

Riordan flashed a grin. "What you are—exactly—is a longer discussion. But there are two things about you that I've been trying to figure out how to tell you since we stopped at the Pizza Hut."

"Namely?"

"One is you've got dried blood in your hair—on the left side, just above your ear. I don't think it's yours."

"All right. A little icky, perhaps, but pretty low on the ickiness scale when you consider all we've been through today. What's the other?"

"You've also got dried blood on your butt. It's yours. You were also shot in the ass."

Winnie understood why Riordan had mentioned Pizza Hut. She'd gone to the bathroom there, and he had expected her to see the blood on her underwear when she pulled down her pants. She also might have seen the blood on her hair in the restroom mirror. She hadn't noticed either because the toilet was so dirty that she'd been more concerned about hovering over it to avoid contact, and the light over the mirror was busted.

Then it dawned on her that he must have spotted the blood much earlier—certainly by the time they stopped at the Walgreens. *That* was why he was so keen on getting her to see a doctor, and *that* was why he'd lingered before driving off. Without someone else's help, he knew he would have to treat the wound. And he didn't want to be the one to tell her.

She looked over at him and felt her face go flushed.

"Now you know how I felt about dropping trou at the Bridle Bit," he said.

"I'll patch it up. I don't need your help."

"The hell you don't. You'd have to use a mirror and you don't have the motor skills or the patience. Go into the bedroom and close the door. Ditch your pants and underwear, and lie on the bed on your stomach. Holler when you're ready. Unless you have an embarrassing tattoo, I won't see anything that exciting."

"My ass is pretty damn exciting."

"With the blood and the buckshot, I'm sure I can hold myself in check."

"I'm not finished with dinner."

"You already ate your measly two slices and there aren't any mushrooms or peppers left to scavenge from the others. Go."

Winnie stood and kicked the chair back. She strode into the bedroom and slammed the door shut. She pulled off her shoes and socks, and then slipped out of her track pants. Riordan was right. There was a small hole on the left side two inches or so below the waist that was crusted with dried blood. She walked over to the bed and considered it. The bed was swaybacked and lumpy. The mustard-colored spread was dusted with a white powder she hoped had nothing to do with fleas or bedbugs. She peeled it back to reveal graying sheets with several obvious mends. She sighed, hooked her thumbs in the waistband of her panties, and shimmied out of them. Holding them to the light, she examined the small Rorschach of blood, then kicked them under the bed.

She put a knee to the mattress then thought better of it. Instead, she went to the luggage she left by the dresser, found her purse, and extracted a makeup compact. "Okay," she called out, when she was at last positioned diagonally atop the bed, feeling as vulnerable as a shucked oyster.

Riordan entered the room carrying a large bag of stuff from the drugstore, trying his damnedest to look serious but not pulling it off. Propped on her elbows, Winnie watched as his eyes zeroed in on her backside. She expected a leer or a grin. He surprised her by grimacing.

"That looks worse than your calf," he said.

Her butt was the one thing she hadn't inspected before calling him into the room. She flipped open the compact and used its mirror to look now. He was right. There was a mottled ring of bruising and discoloration. The wound did look a tiny bit worse than the one on her calf.

"But I'd totally hit it otherwise," Riordan assured her. "Talk about two creamy scoops of vanilla ass cheeks."

"Shut the fuck up," Winnie snapped.

"Should I have said rock hard instead of creamy? I could definitely get behind rock hard."

"I don't want you to get behind any goddamned thing. Just hurry up with the doctoring."

Riordan laughed. "I'll be right with you. I need to wash up."

When he returned from the bathroom, he spread a hand towel beside her with a variety of first-aid supplies arrayed across the top: gauze, cotton balls that smelled like they'd been doused with alcohol, tape, a tube of Neosporin, and a pair of tweezers. She was pleased that at least the hotel's towels looked clean, but she wasn't so pleased about the tweezers.

"We already talked about this," she said. "You're not going on a fishing expedition for buckshot."

He knelt on the bed beside her and began rubbing around the wound with a damp washcloth. "We're not talking fishing here," he said. "I can see one right near the surface. No doubt it bounced off your rock-hard gluteus maximus."

"Right." She held the mirror over her shoulder to monitor what he was doing. "You don't need to be so dainty about it."

"You really can't feel anything?"

"No, I really can't. But don't get any ideas about doing a reacharound. I'm watching."

"In your rearview mirror."

"Oh, please."

He scrubbed more vigorously with the washcloth, but he surprised her with the careful, almost fastidious way he approached the task. She wouldn't have thought it in his repertoire. When he was finished, Riordan picked up the tweezers and an alcohol-sodden cotton ball and thoroughly scrubbed the tips.

"I did this in the bathroom already," he said, "but just to be sure."

She nodded. "I'm glad you're disinfecting them, but you only get one go. No digging around in there."

"Yes, boss." He reached down to pinch the sides of the wound then brought the tweezers in for the kill. Now even she could see the shot in the mirror, and he didn't have any trouble plucking it out. He dabbed at an ooze of blood with a dry cotton ball and applied a generous layer of Neosporin. He finished with a laminate of fresh cotton, gauze, and tape, making a surprisingly neat job of it.

"That's the only way I'll ever get to pinch your ass," he said.

"You got that right. Are you done?"

"Almost. I want to change the bandage on your calf."

"Do I have to be naked from the waist down for that?"

"No, feel free to get up and pull your pants on."

"Bastard."

He made quick work of it, but rather than leaving the room to let her dress as she wanted, he returned to the bathroom and brought out a bath towel. "Wrap that around your waist and strip down to your bra. I'm going to wash your hair."

"The hell you are. I'm perfectly capable of washing my own hair."

"I know, but this will be nicer. Like a massage."

She used to have Ted wash her hair. It *was* like a massage—the only sort of massage she could ever feel. She shook her head. "It's a nice thought," she said, her voice softening. "But it'd be too awkward. We can't use the sink and I'd have to get down on all fours to use the bathtub faucet."

"No, you don't. I got one of those sink-rinser hoses at the drugstore. I already attached it to the faucet."

"Jesus. You've been planning this since before we left Reno. You knew about my butt before we left Reno, too, didn't you?"

He dipped his head, embarrassed. "I didn't know how to tell you. When you wouldn't agree to see a doctor, I thought for sure you'd—"

"Yeah, yeah, figure it out on my own. Okay, if you're man enough to play ladies' hairdresser, I'm woman enough to let you do it. Wash my hair."

Riordan grabbed one of the stick-back chairs from the dinette table while she wrapped the towel around her waist and stripped down to her bulky sports bra. *At least,* she thought, *it wasn't some skimpy black-lace number.*

He got her situated in the chair near the sink, draped another towel around her neck, and leaned her back over the basin.

"How's the water temperature?" he asked.

"Oh, God, it's wonderful." For the first time in months, Winnie let herself relax. She closed her eyes. She thought back to the times Ted would wash her hair while they stood in the shower of their designer bathroom. She was so far away from that now, but Riordan's touch felt as good or better, massaging her scalp through the shampoo, kneading the muscles in her neck.

A sudden constriction of emotion—loss and loneliness—tightened her throat. Moisture welled in her eyes. "Stay with me tonight," she heard herself whisper.

CHAPTER 18

Winnie

RIORDAN INSISTED ON GOING BACK to his cabin to shower. Winnie did the best she could with a washcloth while she perched on the edge of the scaly bathtub. When he returned, she was waiting on the sofa with the lights down, nervous and harboring second thoughts.

She ditched them quickly. They locked lips and fell prone on the sofa, rocking its wobbly legs one way and then the other while they made out like a couple of hormone-soaked teenagers. To say Riordan was enthusiastic was putting it mildly, but he was also surprisingly gentle and considerate. He had some trick of kissing and lightly tugging her earlobes that she found especially pleasurable.

Yet for all his enthusiasm, he seemed reluctant to take the obvious next step. Finally, she forced the issue by reaching for his belt buckle.

"Wait," he said. "What's in it for you?"

She was too embarrassed to explain the complexities of her sexual response—there were actually circumstances under which she could come—so once again Winnie took shelter behind a cutting remark. "What makes you think *any* of the women you sleep with achieve orgasm?"

Riordan sat up, his face slack with hurt. "Look," he said. "I was only trying to be respectful of—of your situation."

"I don't need pity."

He made an exasperated sound. "And I don't need to hug a cactus. Maybe this wasn't such a good idea."

He shifted away and started to get off the couch.

She knew she'd bungled it. All he really wanted was some reassurance that he wasn't being selfish. "Wait," she said, and pulled him back so forcefully they knocked heads. "I'm sorry. You're a wonderful kisser, and I'm sure you're a wonderful lover, too. I'm happy to continue as we were, but you've got a boner like a railroad spike. Since I was the one who asked you to spend the night, I thought I should follow through on the implied commitment."

Riordan looked down at his lap and demurely crossed his arms over it. "I played college ball, but I was never a very good base runner. Let's stick with first tonight."

"Are you sure? You've been taking a pretty good lead toward second."

"Just patting you down for other injuries."

"Very considerate, I'm sure." Winnie grabbed him by the back of his neck to pull him closer.

They continued for well over an hour, and although she could have gone on all night, it was late and *she* had begun to feel a little selfish. The "terms of engagement" were clearly taking a toll on Riordan. When they finally managed to peel themselves apart, she felt flushed, content, and more upbeat than she had in months. Riordan, on the other hand, looked jittery and pale.

"Well," he said, "I guess I'll go back to my cottage."

She reached over to touch his face. "No, I asked you to stay the night with me."

"But—"

"Don't say it. I won't feel you next to me, but I'll know you're there."

He nodded. "That would be nice."

Fearing bedbugs or worse, she refused to sleep on the bed. They took spare blankets and pillows from the hallway closet, and spread them out on the living-room floor. She pulled off the dress she'd put on for him and slipped under the covers in her bra and panties. Riordan ducked into the bathroom before joining her and came out a few minutes later wearing only his boxers and a sheepish expression.

"Feel better?" she asked.

"Officially, I don't know what you're talking about. But unofficially, yes."

He turned off the light from the globeless chandelier and crawled in beside her to spoon.

She reached back to pat his hip. "Next time we won't leave you to handle things on your own," she said, but it was wasted breath. He was already snoring softly in her ear.

•

She woke with a start and a vague impression that a slamming door was to blame. She couldn't tell if the sound was real or dreamed. Judging from the pale light filtering through the front window, it was close to dawn. She disentangled herself from Riordan and stood up.

She felt exposed. The tattered lace curtains in the window drooped like Spanish moss, providing spotty coverage at best. She crossed her arms over her chest and crept to the side to look out.

There, idling in the hotel lot across the weedy park, was an ambulance.

Exhaust billowed beneath it, and as she watched, it rolled toward the exit. Ambulances weren't exactly harbingers of health and good fortune, so its appearance was troubling enough. What was more troubling was the pair of figures jogging away from the place it had stopped.

Both wore baggy gray sweats. Both jogged in a stumbling, herky-jerky gate, as if they were injured or had leg braces. They couldn't have been dressed more differently than the last time she saw them, but she recognized them immediately: Jasmine and Destiny from the brothel. They jogged together until they reached midfield. Jasmine veered left, and Destiny came straight at the cottage.

She knew what it meant, and she knew it wasn't good. She dove back to where Riordan lay, shaking him roughly.

"Wake up," she hissed. "We're in trouble."

Riordan mumbled something and tried to push her away. She slipped past his defenses to slap his face and then yanked off the covers.

"Come on," she yelled. "Get up."

He was too slow. She took hold of his arm and uprooted him from the floor.

"What's going on?" he demanded, awake enough now to be angry.

"We need to get away from the door."

She drove him toward the bedroom, but Destiny was close behind. Winnie heard sharp footsteps on the tread boards of the stairs then deeper ones on the long planks of the porch. A booted foot came smashing through the sash window, rattling it in its frame and spraying glass across the floor. The last thing she saw before slamming the bedroom door shut was Destiny thrusting her head through the window, heedless of the sharp edges. Her eyes had the look of a disbelieving and completely horrified spectator.

Winnie punched the flimsy button lock on the door. "Try to block it. I'll see if we can get out through the bathroom."

"Was that Destiny?"

"Yes. She's on a suicide run. Come on."

Riordan didn't need any more convincing. He denuded the bed and dragged the mattress against the door.

She ducked into the bathroom. Last night, she'd hardly glanced at the window above the toilet, but now she saw it was hopeless. It was too small for either of them to fit through, and it was firmly painted shut besides.

When she returned, Riordan had the mattress and the box springs against the door, and was shoving the dresser behind them. He looked over at her, and she shook her head: *no go*.

"Come on, then," he said. "The bathtub."

It was his turn to manhandle her. He bulldozed her back into the bathroom and slammed the door shut. He shoved her face down into the tub and dove on top of her. He'd no sooner reached to take her outstretched hands when a crumping explosion shook the cottage to its foundation. Toiletries fell from the sink, and plaster rained from the ceiling.

With her cheek mashed into the chain of the drain plug, she whispered, "Is that it?"

"I don't know," he whispered back. "It seemed too—"

The bathroom door blew open with a tremendous roar. Winnie and Riordan were slammed against the tub as the floor, walls, and ceiling convulsed around them.

CHAPTER 19

Riordan

I PRIED MYSELF OFF WINNIE and peered over the tub. The air was choked with dust; the light from the shattered window wavered in swirling eddies. Through the canting door frame, I could see the items I stacked as a barricade blasted across the bedroom like so much doll-house furniture. There was no sign of Destiny—no sign, at least, of the dark-haired beauty I had selected from the Bridle Bit lineup less than twenty-four hours earlier. There was only an ominous finger of blood creeping from beneath the ruined bedroom door.

Winnie shifted under me, her butt rubbing against my crotch in a manner I would have found arousing under different circumstances. Plaster clung to her skin like a coating of powdered sugar. She coughed then spat into the drain. "Motherfucker," she said with a kind of wonder.

"Are you okay?" I asked.

"As far as I know."

I nodded and reached for the bar over the soap dish to lever myself up. I stepped out and then offered a hand to Winnie. "You've got to get back into the RF shield. They're using the signal from your transceiver to track us again."

Winnie clambered out beside me. "But how did they know to send Jasmine to the other cottage?"

"Jasmine? Jesus. I didn't realize."

Winnie shook her head. "Sorry. I forgot you didn't see them. But the question stands. How did they know to target your cottage?"

"Ray's decoy transmitter. I left it running there."

She stared hard into my face, and then her gaze softened. "I'm not sure whether that was smart, brave, or foolhardy."

On impulse, I leaned over to kiss her full on the mouth. "Only half smart. I forgot to make you put on the shield last night, so they targeted both signals. Now hustle. They have to be coming. It's better if they think you and your transceiver are dead."

Winnie's purse and bag had flown from the place she had parked them to the far corner of the room. While Winnie searched through the jumble for the transceiver, shield, and shoulder holster, I found the duffel bag we confiscated from the Winemaker's men. As I rummaged inside for the sawed-off and my Luger, it dawned on me how lucky we'd been. Lucky that Winnie had insisted we sleep at the front of the cottage where she heard Destiny coming. Lucky that she had left the transceiver in her purse in the bedroom, where it would be relatively protected from the explosion. Lucky that Ray had made the device more shock resistant. The harsh truth was, even though she didn't sustain any physical injuries, Winnie could just as easily be lying paralyzed at the bottom of the tub.

I wasn't the only one pursuing this train of thought. "I'm never taking this fucking thing off again," said Winnie, as she struggled to pull the shield over her head. She'd already strapped on the holster and transceiver. "We really dodged a bullet. I really dodged a bullet."

"Don't think about it."

"Too late for that. I suppose I'm the bait this time."

"It is your turn. But unlike me at the brothel, you can be armed." I passed over the sawed-off.

"Yeah. How about if I lie under the mattress with just a leg sticking out?"

"That works. Let's see if we can arrange it like a lean-to. Put you facing the door, far enough back so the rest of you can't be seen by someone without getting on all fours. You'll still have an excellent shot at their feet."

"Good."

We dragged the mattress back to the bed frame and leaned the long edge against the rail closest to the door. We left about a foot of space between the elevated edge and the carpet, just enough for Winnie to squeeze under. She crawled in place, leaving out half a leg as bait.

I took up a position with the Luger on the side of the door nearest the bathroom. The door had been blown off its hinges and was leaning well into the room, resting on the toppled dresser. I thought about moving the dresser to make it easier for someone to enter and to disguise the fact that the entrance had been barricaded, but I decided that was pushing it. The way it stood, it would be clear that Winnie had anticipated the attack and tried to block the door, but it would hopefully suggest she'd been caught building the barricade when the bomb when off.

"Okay," I whispered. "I'm set. Don't shoot or reveal yourself unless you hear me call."

"Don't screw up."

"Quiet."

I had told Winnie that the Winemaker's men must be coming, but as I crouched by the doorway in my boxers, it occurred to me that the first person to enter the room might be a cop, a paramedic, or even someone from the hotel. All the more reason for Winnie to wait for my signal. I hoped our conversation the night before about prudence had sunk in.

No sirens preceded the steps I heard on the porch mere seconds later. That eliminated the police or other first responders. No one called out, "Are you okay?" That eliminated hotel staff or guests. The next thing I heard was the sound of someone crunching over glass in the front room, no groans or involuntary expressions of shock or horror at finding Destiny's body. That seemed to eliminate just about anyone else with a shred of decency.

The top of the unhinged door swept down, then drew back across the overturned dresser with a scraping noise. It landed with a thud on something just the other side of the doorway. Destiny. The intruder was using the door as a bridge across the gore of her mangled corpse.

A heavy tread reverberated off the door, and then a pair of booted feet landed atop the dresser. I was surprised to find the feet went with a man dressed as a paramedic, and for the briefest moment, I doubted my assessment of the situation. Then I saw the gun in his right hand and recognized him as the beefier of the two ersatz utility employees from Palm Springs. More puzzling was the power drill he held in his left hand and the clear plastic shield he wore over his face. It looked like the rig a dental hygienist would wear while cleaning teeth.

All confusion faded when I realized that the power drill wasn't that at all. It was a battery-operated surgical saw. He was there to harvest the stimulator from the back of Winnie's neck and had worn the shield to protect against blood splatter.

So much for prudence. It was bad enough they'd sent Destiny and Jasmine on involuntary suicide missions. Now they'd come to slice up Winnie like so much chuck roast—and they were going to pay.

The man in the paramedic uniform spotted Winnie. He grinned to himself beneath the shield just before my left hook collided with his kidney. He gave a strangled yelp and pitched forward, landing in a sprawl in front of the dresser. I was on him in an instant. I ditched my gun and took two handfuls his hair, bouncing his head up and down on the carpet like a basketball. Blood from his nose collected in the shield and flew in the air like sea spray.

By the time Winnie pulled me off him, he was long dead or unconscious. "Stop it," she hissed. "He's done. We need to find his partner."

I was so angry I couldn't form words. I grunted my agreement and hurried to gather my clothes from the bathroom where I'd left them the night before. I threw them on and then collected my gun and the surgical saw from the floor.

Winnie had taken a post at the front window of the cottage, peeking out from the side. I stepped across the door that covered Destiny's body, simultaneously horrified that I was desecrating her remains in this fashion and thankful that I didn't have to look at them. But there was no ignoring the detached arm lying underneath the dinette table.

At the window, I could see sunlight filtering through the pine trees on the eastern edge of the property. It couldn't have been later than six. "Anything?"

"There's nothing stirring in the office. I've seen a few pale faces in the windows of cottages, but no one's come out. The ambulance they pulled up in is gone or out of sight."

"Ambulance?"

"Yeah. Another thing I didn't have time to tell you. I guess it goes with the paramedic uniform. Camouflage if the cops show up."

"You're right. But they can't have gone far. Probably the driver is the redhead from Palm Springs. He must be waiting for this one to come back with the goods."

"Probably."

I took hold of her arm, forgetting again that she couldn't feel my touch. "Look, I'm sorry for what happened. You were right about dealing with them in the Springs. They must have posted bail the next day."

"If it wasn't them, it would have been another team."

"But they wouldn't have been on our ass so quickly. And they might not have recaptured Destiny and Jasmine. Get everything packed up and ready." I glanced down at her bare legs and grinned. "And put on some pants. I'll deal with our redheaded friend."

"Don't be silly. We—"

"No, Winnie. I'm going to handle this. It's the right thing tactically, and it's the right thing for me."

"Be careful."

"You, too."

I slipped out of the cottage door. From the vantage point of the porch, I could see that a few brave souls had gathered in front of the other cottage. They stood in a huddle with their backs to me, pointing at smoke boiling from the roof. Jasmine's bomb had evidently ruptured a gas line. I hurried down the steps and dodged to the back of the building, cutting through a stand of scrawny pines to the main road that ran by the hotel.

I found an ambulance parked on the shoulder of the road, the red lights on its roof sweeping through the branches above me. The window of the passenger door was down, but I could see only a bit of the dashboard and nothing at all of the driver.

My original plan was to sneak up on him and take him alive for questioning. Questioning I intended to motivate with the surgical saw—at least the threat of it. Now that I was here, I could see too many things that could go wrong. The most likely being that he would simply drive away before I could overpower him. I threw down the saw and double-checked the safety on the Luger. It was rush him with guns blazing or nothing.

I sprinted out from the trees, bending low to draw less attention in the side mirror should he be looking that way. When I reached the ambulance, I planted a foot on the running board and hoisted myself over the edge of the open window, shoving the Luger into the cab to threaten or shoot the driver.

Only he wasn't there.

I found out exactly where he was when a slug thudded into the side panel of the ambulance just to the left of my hip. I had no place to go but forward. I pushed off the running board, flopping and dolphin-kicking all the way into the cab. It would have been comic if it wasn't so terrifying. More bullets hammered the side panel, vaporizing the glass of the sliding door and destroying the side mirror. I slithered across the bench seat to see if the keys had been left in the steering column. No such luck.

I reached for the driver's door handle and popped it open. Another shot whinged off the center post as I dropped to the asphalt. How the redhead had gotten behind me, I didn't know. He might have grown tired of waiting and gone to check on his partner, or been assigned to check the other cottage. He might even have stepped out to take a piss. But now he was somewhere in the stand of pines taking pot-shots at me while I hid behind the ambulance. His ambulance. The realization that he was shooting up his own getaway vehicle gave me the idea.

"Hey, asshole," I shouted. "You got run-flats on this thing?" I pointed the Luger at the left rear tire and pulled the trigger. The sidewall exploded with a bang that seemed louder than the pistol. I gave the left front the same treatment. The ambulance lurched, resting on the bare metal of the wheels. "How you going to get home now?"

I risked a look around the front bumper and saw him in full flight back to the hotel. My guess was that he intended to steal another car from the parking lot, but he hadn't reckoned on Winnie. She stepped out from behind a tree with the sawed-off, shot him where no man wants to be shot. He went down in a heap, clutching at what was left of his genitals.

I watched as she kicked him onto his back and put her foot down on the wound. He writhed under her as she barked a question. He shook his head no, but Winnie ground in her heel and shouted, "Tell me!"

He blubbered something. She asked another question and received a response. She dropped to her knees. I thought she was getting closer to hear, but I was wrong.

She took his head in both hands and snapped his neck.

CHAPTER 20

Riordan

IN SPITE OF MY PRONOUNCEMENT that she was right about dealing with the pair of them in Palm Springs, I was shocked. The anger that caused me to savage the one in the cottage was a puny thing compared to the white-hot fury that drove Winnie. This was total war to her, pure and simple.

I ran up to where she knelt by the body, watching as she patted the dead man's pockets. "Nothing doing," she said, when she came up empty.

"Okay."

"'Okay?' That all you've got to contribute? Get the Lincoln. I'll get the shit from the cottage and meet you by the ambulance."

"Sure," I said, happy to be doing anything but standing over her and the dead guy. "Got it."

I broke into a trot, dodging between scrawny pine trees until I came to the clearing in front of the cottages. Across the way was the hotel office and, in a parking spot next to the entrance, the Lincoln. The only problem was the green and white Nevada County Sheriff's car lurching to a stop behind it.

The driver's door flew open and out gushed three hundred pounds of khaki-clad, wispy-haired deputy. He wore a tactical vest with the word SHERIFF stenciled across the front, but it was at least two sizes too small for him. With his fat belly bulging out beneath it, it looked more like an armor-plated bib. As I came up to him, I saw that he was not only dressed for a SWAT-team response, he was packing heat for one, too. He held a powerful FN Five-seven pistol in a combat grip. I just had time to shove my own Luger into the small of my back before he caught sight of it.

"Officer," I said. "Thank God you're here."

His face was flushed and he was already sweating. My guess was suicide bombings were a far cry from his usual duties of wrangling drunk drivers and juvenile delinquents.

"What's the situation?" he asked in a Joe Friday voice.

"All I know is I woke up to the sound of an explosion. Then, a split second later, I heard another one, not quite as loud as the first. I was afraid to go outside, but then I just had to take a look. The cottage next to mine is on fire, I guess from the first explosion. I don't know about the second one."

He gestured over my shoulder with the gun, still holding it in a two-handed grip. "So that cottage with the smoke coming out of it— that's the one on fire?"

I had to bite the inside of my mouth to keep a straight face. "Yes, that's the one on fire. From the explosion. I was staying in the one next to it."

"Did you see the occupants?"

"Yeah, I did. Good-looking middle-aged guy with a heavy build. Looked like he worked out."

Apparently this description of my self-image didn't ring any bells with him because all he said was "Right."

"What are you going to do?"

I expected him to say, "Wait for backup," and then I would find some excuse to ask him to move his car. Unfortunately, he seemed to take the question as a challenge.

"Go into the cottage to look for survivors, of course."

"Shouldn't you—"

"You wait here for the sheriff. Give him your story when he arrives."

"But—"

"And stay back," he called over his shoulder, as he rumbled past me, the ring of fat beneath his tactical vest bouncing like a rubber doughnut.

I watched him galumph toward the burning cottage with a kind of obsessive fascination and then forced myself back to the problem of the stuck Lincoln. There was no escape from the front. The tires were jammed tightly against a concrete parking block a sidewalk's width away from the slab-sided hotel office. At the rear, the passenger door of the cruiser lurked no more than a yard from the Lincoln's bumper.

A siren wailed in the distance, followed by a much nearer squawk from the cruiser radio. "Unit 131, check in," it commanded.

Hearing the radio made me curious. I ducked my head through the still-open door and, wonder of wonders, spotted a ring of keys dangling from the ignition. The prudent thing would have been to pull the cruiser out of the way and then vamoose in the Lincoln. But the driveway was narrow and I worried about the time it would take to get the sheriff's car completely clear and the Lincoln pointed in the right direction.

I dove into the cruiser and cranked the starter. The engine caught immediately. I shoved it into reverse and backed down the drive, the transmission whining like a living thing.

As I crawfished out onto the road, the radio squawked once more. "Unit 131, report. We're two minutes from the Prospector Inn. What is your situation?"

I risked a glance back at the fat deputy. As near as I could tell, his situation was disbelief. He stood with the rubbernecking guests in front of the burning cottage with his mouth hanging open while a little girl next to him pointed gleefully at the fleeing cruiser.

I slammed it into drive and zoomed around the wide corner to the back of the complex. Winnie skulked by the ambulance with the duffel bag and her suitcase. She caught sight of the sheriff's car, took a guilty step back, and tried to hide the sawed-off she was still carrying by her side. When I screeched to a stop just in front of her—and she recognized me through the front window—she cursed and hurried forward with the duffel bag.

I popped the rear-door locks and jumped out.

"What about 'go get the Lincoln' didn't you understand?" she nearly screamed into my face.

"Believe me, I would have brought it if I could. More cops coming, less than two minutes out."

"Tremendous."

I yanked the back door open and she flung the duffel bag into the caged rear seat. She hustled back to get the remaining bag while I dove back behind the wheel. She joined me in the passenger seat, and we were away.

"I vote for Highway 20 heading west," I said. "It's only a few miles to Yuba City. We can ditch the cruiser and rent a new car there."

"No. Highway 20, heading *east*. The way we came. Three miles out of town, we exit on Coyote Ranch Road."

"What's on Coyote Ranch Road?"

"A heliport."

"A heliport? Are we going to get away in a helicopter?"

"No. The reason those two assholes were on us so fast is that the Winemaker flew them in. A helicopter is waiting to take them back."

I risked a glance over at her. She looked as grim as I'd ever seen her. "You got that from the guy you shot in the crotch?"

"Yeah. He gave me the name of the place. I used my cell phone to check it out on Google Maps and it's legit. It's a private heliport for a ranch."

I didn't say anything for a moment. "Seems like the risk-reward ratio is a little skewed. It's a big risk to double back. They might not be there when we arrive, and even if they are, a helicopter doesn't exactly qualify as a priority target."

"What if the Winemaker is sitting there waiting for them to report? What if he's sitting there and we let him fly back unmolested? We'll never have this clear a shot at him again."

"*If* he's there."

"Yes, *if* he's there. But I know some of them are there because I found a radio in the ambulance. They keep calling to check on our buddies from Palm Springs."

I thought about it. From what I knew of the Winemaker, it wasn't beyond the pale for him to try to be in on the kill, no matter how bad his disabilities. "Okay," I said. "I'm in."

I steered us along roads that paralleled Highway 20, staying off the highway proper until we were almost out of town. After that, it was a two-minute ride to the turnoff for Coyote Ranch Road. As we bumped over the cattle guard that fronted the gravel track, the cruiser's radio came to life once more.

"All units, all units, be advised Unit 131 vehicle stolen. I repeat, Unit 131 vehicle stolen. Suspect is a white male in his early fifties. He is armed with an assault rifle. Approach with caution."

Winnie clutched at the dash as the car jolted over a washboard section of the road. "Armed with an assault rifle? Where'd they get that idea?"

I gestured with my thumb. "I guess you missed the little beauty behind us."

Winnie glanced back at the strangely shaped weapon hanging in the gun rack behind us. It looked more like an overgrown staple gun than an assault rifle, and it was the cousin to the pistol the deputy had been carrying. Like the pistol, it was made by FN Herstal in Belgium and fired a nasty little 5.7x28mm cartridge with a polymer tip that had been designed to penetrate armor. For all the wallop the bullet packed, it was smaller and lighter than conventional 9mm ammo, making it possible to cram an astounding fifty rounds in the rifle's clear-plastic magazine.

"Stop!" barked Winnie.

I stood on the brake and the cruiser skidded to a halt just before the road began the climb to a flat-toped hill. "What the hell?"

"I'll drive. You're a better shot than I am. If we've got that thing in our arsenal, I'd rather have you hanging out the window taking potshots than me."

I nodded as I shoved the gearshift into park. We raced past each other at the back of the car, and Winnie got the cruiser rolling again before I had even pulled my door closed. As she tore up the hill, I snatched the P90 assault rifle from the rack, cleared the safety, and set the selector to automatic. Then I mashed down the electric-window button.

When I thought about it later, I realized that a cop car was just about the worst vehicle we could have chosen to approach the helipad. They were expecting the ambulance, but they might have at least waited to see who was driving if an unmarked car approached. There wasn't any question about a Nevada County Sheriff's Department cruiser.

We caught a little air as we came over the crest of the hill. About a hundred yards to left was a slab of concrete painted with two concentric circles. A helicopter with its rotors spinning was perched in the center.

Winnie didn't waste any more time with the road. She bounded over the shoulder, angling directly for the helipad. The ground was rough pasture, bumpy and covered with thick grass, but that was the least of our problems. The helicopter was already airborne and too high above us for me to shoot out the window by the time we reached the concrete.

I tumbled out and pointed the P90 at the belly of the ascending beast. Pulled the trigger. The 5.7x28mm ammo had less recoil than 9mm rounds, but it was louder and produced a brighter muzzle flash. I felt the ejected shell casings bounce off my thigh as they streamed down from a chute behind the grip. The first few rounds missed the helicopter entirely, but as the pilot dipped the nose to bull forward, I saw an angry little hole appear in the aluminum skin near the tail.

I stitched a line all the way to the front of the craft and then crossed the T at the place I imagined the pilot must be sitting. Abruptly, I ran out of ammo and the P90 bolt locked open. At first, I thought it had all been for naught. The helicopter beat serenely forward, no flames or even oil trailing in its wake. Then the craft rolled, flipping on its side like an overloaded wheelbarrow. It dropped straight down.

The rotor hit first, churning up dirt and debris like a giant weed wacker and causing the main shaft to wobble. The entire craft shook in response. Then the blades shattered, sending fragments scything through the grass. The fuselage pancaked into the earth, twitching and wrenching across the pasture as the amputated rotor continued to spin. By the time the motor finally died, the helicopter lay in three steaming pieces. I didn't see how anyone could have survived.

Winnie had watched the crash from behind the driver's door of the cruiser. Now she shouted for me to get back in, and we bounced over the pasture to the wreck. She leaped out.

"Are you sure this is a good idea?" I called to her back. "What if the fuel catches fire?"

She waved me off, hurrying toward the cockpit as she worked the pump action on her sawed-off. If the Winemaker was in that wreck and alive, she was going to make damned sure the second condition was temporary.

I ran after her, drawing the Luger as well. Winnie leaped onto the nose by the cockpit door. The door itself had sprung off and was lying several feet to the side. The remains of two men in paramedic uniforms were strapped in the front seats. There was very little blood, but heads, torsos, and limbs were twisted and mangled in ways that I didn't think possible. The seats behind them had ended up in a separate section of the wreck, but they were empty. The Winemaker hadn't made the trip.

"Fuck," said Winnie. "Double fuck." She stared down at the mangled flesh. "Check their pulses."

"You're kidding me."

"Do it."

I clambered onto the nose and stepped gingerly into the wreck. The first whiff of aviation fuel came to me, and I thought how ironic it would be if we were to die from an explosion at this point. I touched the throat of the guy strapped in the chair to the right—the uppermost chair now since the helicopter was lying on its side—and felt for a pulse. There wasn't any. Seeing how two of his shattered ribs protruded from his chest, that wasn't very surprising.

I squatted down to check the pilot. At first he seemed to be in better shape, but as I turned his head to get better access to his throat, I found a bloody red laceration under his chin. It wasn't a neat round hole—P90 slugs tumble as they fly—but it was clear to me he'd been hit by one of the last shots I'd fired into the cockpit. He'd died instantly and had sent the helicopter gyrating into the ground when he lost control.

"They're both goners," I assured Winnie. "Now can we get the hell out of here?"

She didn't answer. Instead, she slid off the helicopter and trooped over to the detached door. Grumbling under my breath, I hoisted myself up to follow. By the time I reached her, she had flipped the door over and was reading the print on the outward-facing side: MARIONETTE VINEYARDS, HEALDSBURG, CA.

"Bastards," she said.

We got back on Highway 20 and drove to Yuba City as I'd originally suggested—but not before Winnie stowed the helicopter door in the cruiser's trunk. In the bustling metropolis of Yuba City, we found a freight forwarder to ship it to Marionette Vineyards. Winnie took a Sharpie and scrawled on it in big black letters before she let the shipping guy nail the lid of the crate in place.

YOU'RE NEXT! she wrote.

CHAPTER 21

The Winemaker

I WAS IN MY OFFICE in the ambulation lab when Sergy—one of my "projects"—brought in a heavy wooden crate. I couldn't have been more proud. The crate was the size and weight of a grand piano, yet he manhandled it as if it were a stage prop.

He's as strong as a bear—much stronger than Winnie. And like Winnie, he is nearly impervious to pain. He is lacking only her agility, and that will come.

The contents of the crate are proof of that. Inside was the door to one of our helicopters, a juvenile threat scrolled across it. It represented proof that my latest attempt to ensnare Winnie and Riordan had failed, and for the tiniest moment after Sergy had pulled it out, I was angry. I was angry at the taunt, the loss of men and material, and the additional delay. But then I realized what the door really meant. It meant that Winnie had determined my location—how could she help but do so with the name of the winery writ large?—and now she was coming to me rather than running. She was delivering herself and her technology into my hands.

I will be ready to receive her.

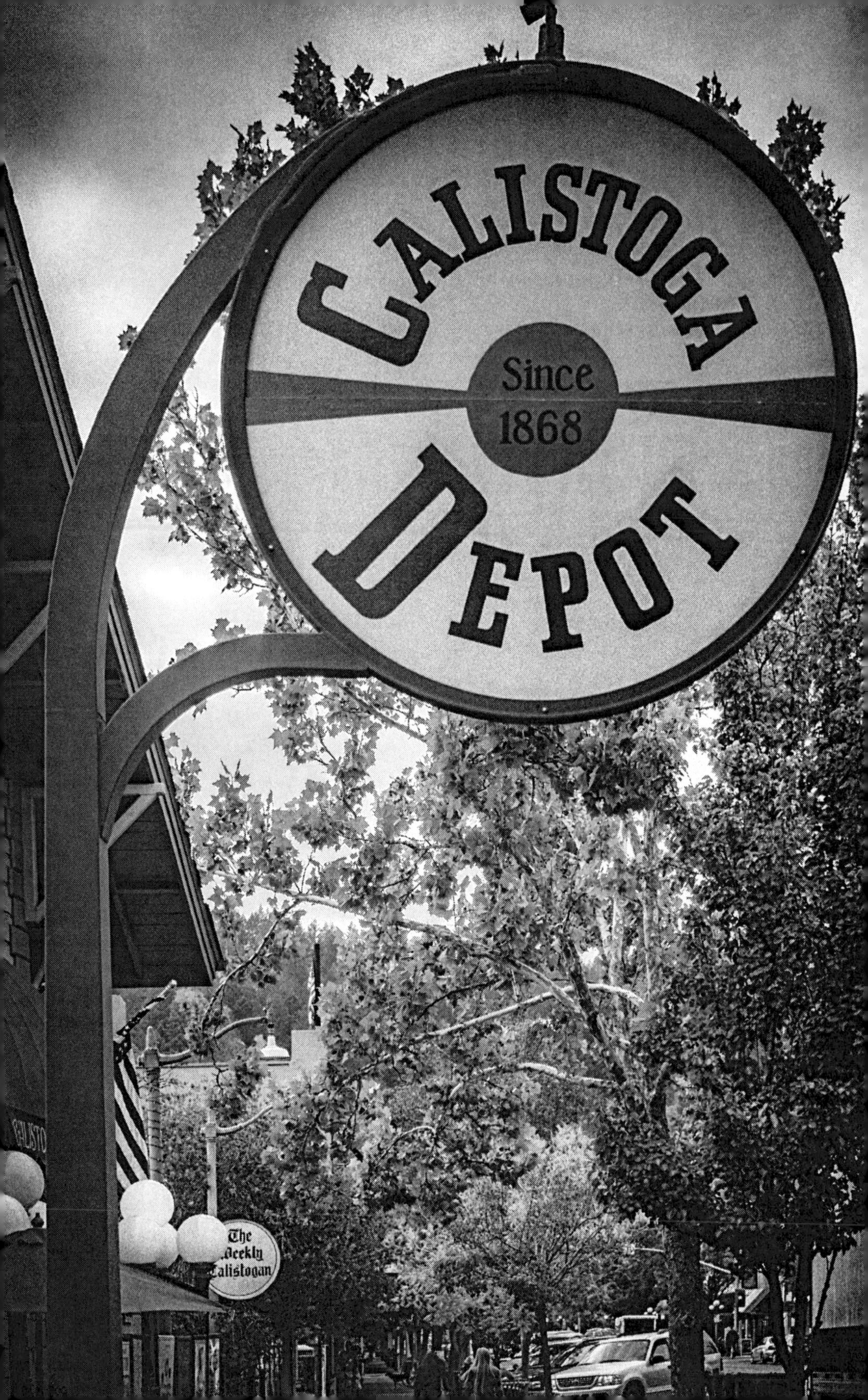
CALISTOGA
Since
1868
DEPOT
The
Weekly
Calistogan

CHAPTER 22

Winnie

WINNIE WATCHED FROM A PERCH on the couch as Riordan paced across the hardwood floor. He had brooded all the way from Yuba City to the wine-country town of Calistoga, where they had checked into the last available room of a touristy bed and breakfast. She had wanted to head right into Healdsburg, another twenty-five miles down the road—and another valley over—but Riordan had ignored her protests as he veered off the highway into the parking lot of the B&B.

Now he stood over her, stabbing the air with an index finger. "Do you know what I was dreading until you flipped over the helicopter door?"

"How could I forget?" she sneered. "You couldn't stop talking about it. The wreck catching fire."

"Yes, I was worried about that. Anyone would be. Even you must have given it some thought. But apparently this other concern never even crossed your mind."

"Which was what?"

"That the helicopter didn't belong to the Winemaker's men. That we might rush the helipad, machine gun blazing, only to shoot down a helicopter full of innocent people."

She frowned at him. "Are you saying I made it up? How would I even know about the helipad if the Winemaker's man hadn't told me?"

"I'm not saying you made it up. Obviously, you didn't. Obviously, it turned out...for the best. I'm just saying there could have been another helicopter on the pad when we arrived."

"Whose?"

"How about one from the ranch? It was their property after all."

She jumped up, forcing Riordan to take a step back. "We've already had this conversation. Another version of it, anyway. Yes, there was a possibility that the Winemaker's helicopter had flown off and another one had taken its place, but that possibility was tiny. If we're going to win, we're going to have to take risks. We're going to have to be aggressive, go after their jugular. Bottom line—we're going to have to operate outside your comfort zone."

He looked her in the eye for a long moment then something in his face shifted to signal acquiescence. He let his arms fall to his side. "All right," Riordan said. "But did you have to mail him the fucking door with a death threat scrawled across it? Wouldn't it have been better to let him wonder what happened than to know for sure that we killed his men and were coming after him?"

The anger Winnie felt when she hadn't found the Winemaker in the helicopter flared once more. She brought a finger up to point at Riordan, as he had pointed at her. Then she understood. There was a place past his comfort zone—maybe well past it—where they had to operate. But that place—that zone of compromise—was also well before the red line where rage began affecting her judgment. They had to be aggressive but not foolhardy. She relaxed her hand and gently reached it around his neck. "Yes, it would have been," she said.

"Would have been what?"

"It would have been better to leave him wondering than to send a warning that we were coming."

Riordan covered his surprise by leaning over to kiss her forehead. "Then you also agree it's better to stay *here* than in Healdsburg, where we risk being spotted by the Winemaker's men?"

"I'm not completely sold on that one." Without warning, Winnie dove forward, pushing Riordan back onto the posh sleigh bed, where she landed with her knees on either side of his hips. "But as long as we're here, we'd better take advantage of it."

•

An hour later, Winnie stood under the shower, enjoying the sensation of warm water flooding over her scalp. Riordan had already stepped out of the stall and was busy toweling himself off in the spacious bathroom. He had picked the B&B at random, attracted by its proximity to the highway and its prominent vacancy sign, but she had to admit that it was much better than the hotel in Nevada City. The sex was much better, too: more give and take and, judging from Riordan's reaction, a more satisfying conclusion. The one thing that puzzled her was where he managed to find a condom when all his luggage had been destroyed in the suicide bombings. It could only have been the convenience store at the station where they'd stopped for gas. Apparently, he had been brooding on more than just the helicopter during the drive.

After Riordan stepped out of the bathroom, Winnie cut the water and took her turn with one of the B&B's fluffy towels. She hurried into her clothes and the RF shield and the holster she used to carry the transceiver. The less time out of them the better, especially now that they were so close to the Winemaker.

Riordan was waiting for her in the main room, clean and glowing from the shower but relegated to the same outfit he'd worn to her cottage in Nevada City the night before. He had also strapped on a holster, but his held the Luger. After shrugging on a windbreaker to cover the rig, he said, "Let's walk into town. We can grab some dinner; maybe find some locals to ask about Marionette Vineyards."

"Sounds nice." She pinched her nose between two fingers. "And maybe we can also buy you some new clothes."

He held out his arms, staring down at his slacks. "That bad?"

"Not really. A little rumpled and dusty is all."

"Plaster dust from the explosion. Okay. We'll add a new wardrobe to the shopping list. You can help me pick it out. That's what women like to do, right?"

"Some women."

He grunted and held open the door.

It was early evening, and the main drag of downtown Calistoga was clogged with tourists shuffling from spas to antique stores to bars and eateries, all of which were housed in quaint Victorian buildings dating from the late 1800s or early 1900s. As they made their way down a covered wooden sidewalk, Riordan took Winnie by the elbow and steered her into a wine shop. The interior was painted to look like an underground wine cellar or cave, the metal racks along the sides displaying a daunting menagerie of wines for sale. There seemed to be bottles of every variety, vintage, and style, many with laminated sheets dangling nearby to explain just how exalted they were.

The proprietress, who was wearing a red quilted vest, was a middle-aged blonde with rather large teeth. As they entered, she came out from behind the register, beaming at them like they were family. "May I help you?"

"I hope so," said Riordan. "We had a bottle of wine at a restaurant the other night. We really enjoyed it, but we forgot to write down the name. We were wondering if you could help us identify it."

"I can try," said the woman. "What sort of wine was it?"

"A pinot noir."

The blonde nodded, still smiling. "Anything else? Done in a Burgundy style or more fruit forward?"

Riordan turned to Winnie, a panicky look in his face. She almost laughed aloud. She knew what he was doing, of course. He was trying to ask about Marionette Vineyards without being completely obvious, but he barely knew red from white, much less a Burgundy from an American-style pinot noir.

Winnie couldn't drink because alcohol interfered with the function of the stimulator. She knew the industry, though. For good or ill, it was the common thread that bound her to both the Winemaker and her late husband.

She put a hand on Riordan's forearm and gave a gentle squeeze. "I think more fruit forward. I remember from the label that it came from the Alexander Valley."

"Okay, that helps, but there are still a lot of producers there. You said you read the label. Do you remember what it looked like?"

"I remember," said Riordan. "There was a painting of a wooden puppet. The kind that dangles from strings."

The wine-shop owner pushed her lips together and exhaled through her nose. "I see," she said. "It sounds like Marionette Vineyards."

"Yes, that does sound right. Do you have any in stock?"

"No, I'm afraid that we don't carry Marionette."

"But why? Alexander Valley's just a few miles from here, isn't it? I would have thought you'd favor local producers."

"We do in general. But they are relatively new, and there are so many wineries that, well, we just can't stock everyone."

Winnie thought she saw an opening to play the good cop. She leaned toward the blonde with her hand cupped over her mouth as if she didn't want Riordan to hear what she said next. "To tell you the truth, Ralph here is the one who liked the wine. I didn't much care for it. It seemed pretty generic and drab to me. I wouldn't have even known it was a pinot if I hadn't seen it on the bottle."

The owner clasped her hands in front of her and dipped her head. "Yes, I could see how you might say that. It's not their best varietal."

"What is?"

"Oh, the cabernet. They are known for their cab."

Winnie nodded. It was the Winemaker's specialty. It fit his brute-force, take-no-prisoners style. Something subtle like a pinot would be beyond him. "Why not just carry the cab?"

"I did try," said the blonde, "but—" She stopped, clearly worried about saying something that could come back to haunt her. "Are you from California?"

"Oh, no. We live in Omaha." Winnie smiled and touched the woman's arm. "We work in the same office, but no one knows we're a couple. We're here on a naughty little getaway."

The blonde laughed. "Your secret's safe with me."

Winnie hoped that sharing a confidence would loosen the women's tongue. Despite her hesitation, it was clear that she wanted to talk about what evidently was a charged subject. "You were saying about Marionette?"

"Oh, yes. The thing is, they sent a salesman around to the store. That in itself is unusual. We can only buy through distributors. I listened to his pitch anyway, and when said I'd be placing an order for just the cabernet, he was very rude."

"Rude how?" asked Riordan.

"It was juvenile. Just vague warnings about discouraging other wineries and distributors from selling to us. I told him if that was the way he was going to do business, I wouldn't order anything at all."

"Of course. You mentioned they were new. Could that be the problem? Maybe they don't understand the way the industry works."

The owner looked down while she combed her fingers through her pageboy cut. "Yes, they are new," she said, and then looked up. "They bought an existing winery about a year ago and promptly dropped another ten million to improve the production facilities, dig wine caves, and plant more acreage, including more pinot noir. When it all grows to maturity, I'm told they'll be one of the largest producers in the valley. You should see the property now. Well, you can't because they did away with tours—but it looks more like a prison than a winery."

"I'll bet that ruffled a few feathers. A newcomer throwing around all that money trying to buy his way to the top."

"That's exactly what people said." She shook her head, as if to distance herself from the sentiment. "I shouldn't be running on like this. You came in to learn about a bottle of wine and instead you got a soap opera."

"We don't mind," said Winnie. "The truth is we have an ulterior motive."

Riordan and the shop owner both looked at her with concern. "You do?" said the owner.

"Yes, my Ralph here is the best orthodontist in Omaha—and I'm the best dental assistant—but when he retires, he wants to move to California and start his own winery."

The owner smiled. "Well, take it from me, it's not nearly as romantic as it seems. It's a tough business, and it's getting tougher all the time with competition from new wine-producing regions like New Zealand and South America. I'd stick with straightening teeth if I were you."

"Maybe I better," said Riordan. "But what about the owner of Marionette? What's he like? Is he a retired orthodontist?"

"I doubt it. The truth is no one knows very much about him. He has no prior history in the region, no prior history from anywhere as far as anyone can tell. He rarely leaves his property, and when he does, he's completely surrounded by his entourage. You see, he's disabled. He has a number of people to help him get about, including one giant fellow who lifts him in and out of his car and his wheelchair. Things like that."

Winnie made eye contact with Riordan. "How creepy," she said.

"Yes, it is a little bit. Let's switch to a happier subject. Would you like to sample the absolutely yummy zin I've got open?"

They nodded their agreement, and in the end Riordan purchased two bottles of the expensive zinfandel. *He is such an easy touch*, thought Winnie.

Outside, he hefted the bag containing the wine. "I'm worried this will be too fruit forward."

She reached over to ruffle his hair. "I thought you'd be more worried about being Ralph, the orthodontist from Omaha."

"I admit that stung a bit. But being your boyfriend on a naughty getaway instead of your father on a walk around the neighborhood made up for it."

CHAPTER 23

Winnie

AT A LITTLE AFTER TWO IN THE MORNING, Winnie walked with Riordan along the side of Highway 128 in a semirural area of Healdsburg. There were no lights on the road; the only illumination came from a quarter moon dipping below the hills to their left. They'd parked their car in the lot of a sad, isolated elementary school comprised entirely of prefab buildings and were hiking east a mile or so back to Marionette Vineyards for a reconnaissance.

They were dressed for the job. Winnie was in her standard uniform of dark tracksuit with the RF shield and one of the body-armor vests they had taken off the Winemaker's men in Palm Springs. She also had a pair of the captured night-vision goggles.

Riordan was wearing the black pullover and jeans she'd picked out for him in Calistoga, coupled with a pair of matching black Chuck Taylors and ankle socks. Even the underwear she'd selected for him was black.

He'd been fine with everything but the socks. Standing at the checkout counter at the sporting-goods store, he'd said, "When I wore Chuck Taylors in grade school—when Converse USA still made the shoes instead of sweatshops in China, and when basketball players in the NBA endorsed them instead of hipsters in coffee shops—no man would be caught dead wearing ankle socks. Those were for girls who played tennis. And the only people who wore black socks with athletic shoes were old men with pasty white legs."

"Well," said Winnie, "the fifties weren't exactly the decade of fashion."

"This was the sixties and you know—"

"The part about old men holds, though."

"Thank you for that," he'd said, after he'd absorbed the comment.

In addition to the clothes from Calistoga, Riordan wore the second body-armor vest and carried the other pair of night-vision goggles. The P90 assault rifle hung from a strap on his shoulder. Winnie was armed with her sawed-off, and both of them had their faces blacked.

On the drive past Marionette, they'd seen that the western border of the winery was delineated by a row of widely spaced trees. As the trees—and the towering chain-link fence in front of them—came into view, Riordan gestured to the left, toward a vineyard in the neighboring property. She nodded her understanding. They jumped an irrigation canal that ran beside the road and threaded between strands of a barbed-wire fence. They jogged down a vineyard row, the stumpy, contorted vines on the trellises projecting threatening-looking shadows at their feet. Twice Winnie stumbled on the uneven ground, and twice Riordan stopped her from sprawling facedown in the mustard grass that grew between the vines. Without feedback from her feet and legs, it was hard enough to walk on level ground in the daylight, much less run a veritable obstacle course at night.

At the end of the row, they zigged right along a tractor path to within a hundred yards of Marionette and then zagged up another row in another patch of vines. Winnie was breathing hard now and she felt the heat of her body rising through the turtleneck of the RF shield. The warm night, the uphill slope of the terrain, and the extra insulation afforded by the body armor were conspiring to make the jaunt more of a workout than she'd planned. She wondered how the old man in the black socks was handling it.

When they reached the end of the second row, they squatted by the end post of the trellis to peer down a second tractor path at the fence and trees guarding Marionette. At this distance, Winnie noticed details she had missed before. The fence looked new, most likely installed after the Winemaker bought the property. It was over ten feet high and was topped with a coil of concertina wire. The trees she recognized as olive.

Riordan brought his mouth to her ear. In a panting whisper, he said, "Let's sneak forward to a row closer to the property line and then duck back into the vines."

She gave him a thumbs-up and watched as he scuttled past the end post and down the tractor path. She followed a moment later, running in a crouch to the row he had selected.

By the time she rounded the corner, he had already thrown himself on the grass. He rolled onto his stomach and swiveled around to peer beneath the vines. She flopped at his side, and they both struggled to position the bulky night-vision goggles over their eyes.

At first, the eerie green tableau projected through the goggles failed to add much to what Winnie had already observed. But gradually, as she accustomed herself to the absence of color cues and the flattened depth of field, she was able to pick out details she'd missed before. Well inside the fence line, a row of stainless-steel tanks gleamed faintly under an open-walled shed. Farther back, a three-story warehouse with a roller door partially open abutted the hillside. Between the tanks and the warehouse, a portal trimmed in stone seemed to lead directly into the hill—the newly dug caves the Calistoga wine-shop owner had mentioned.

But there were details closer to the fence that she'd missed entirely. Riordan reached over to grab her arm, forgetting again that she couldn't feel his touch. She noticed the movement anyway, and when he pointed emphatically to the far left, she saw what had captured his attention. A man in a zippered one-piece suit walked along a well-worn path just in front of the olive trees. Strapped low on his back was a metal box that looked like it housed electronic equipment. Protruding from the box was a girderlike strut that extended to a point just above his head. Atop the strut was a spherical object with cameras and other devices embedded across its surface. It reminded Winnie of the cameras Google put on top of the cars they sent to photograph streets for their maps, and she suspected it had a similar function. Certainly it was taking pictures—most likely video rather than still—and it was probably listening and detecting motion as well. It was a portable electronic watchdog, no doubt beaming all the information it captured back to a central control room.

The obvious question was why the Winemaker needed an electronic watchdog when he had a human to do the watching. Winnie was pretty sure she knew the answer. The first clue was the stilted, choppy gate of the watchman. He walked like a robot. Further clues could be gleaned from his failure to "watch" anything but the middle

distance in front of him and the absence of any extraneous gesture or motion, like scratching an itch or running a hand through
his hair. He was another electronic slave, like the women in the
Nevada brothel. Winnie didn't doubt that this was another effort to
militarize the technology. It wasn't hard to imagine a combat post
patrolled by captured enemy insurgents equipped in this fashion.
There would be any number of advantages, not the least of which
was psychological. Who would want to fire on former brothers
in arms?

Winnie got Riordan's attention and pointed to the back of her
neck. Then she pointed toward the watchman. Riordan nodded, the
goggles amplifying the motion in a cartoonish way.

They watched as the guard passed behind one of the olive trees
and emerged in the clearing in front of them. He stopped, and they
hugged the ground in response. The guard did a slow pirouette, turning
so that his back faced them. A light on the spherical object winked,
and Winnie could only guess what sort of instrument or sensor had
been aimed their way.

Seconds leeched by. The light winked once more, and then at last
the guard turned to face the path and began walking along the olive
trees in his stilted gate. She propped herself up on her elbows, and
Riordan followed suit. He held his hands out in a "what was that?"
gesture. She shook her head.

The loamy smell of the soil wafted up to her. The ground was soft
and damp, and Winnie was sure that if she had sensation in her limbs
she would feel a clammy wetness soaking into the fabric that covered
her elbows and knees. She decided there were diminishing returns to
staying any longer. They'd gotten a feel for the layout of the property
and learned that it was patrolled by zombie/machine hybrids, but

what else was to be gained? This was—as Riordan had emphasized in the car—only a reconnaissance.

The appearance of another guard on the path seemed to underscore the point. He walked in the same robotic gait and carried the same pack of instruments, but he was taller and older than the first one. She and Riordan hugged the ground once more, but the new guard didn't stop to aim an instrument in their direction.

As soon as the guard passed, Riordan made an emphatic gesture with his thumb, pointing back the way they had come. Winnie nodded just as emphatically.

But they had dallied too long. A tongue of fire flashed from beyond the fence and she heard the muffled farting noise of suppressed rounds. Dirt kicked up inches from her face. Winnie leaped back and led Riordan in a hunched, scrambling run to the end of the row and down the tractor path. More rounds chased after them. She weaved as she ran, having learned from her very first encounter with the Winemaker's men—when her husband had been murdered in an ambush—that going in a straight line was an invitation for a bullet in the back.

A tractor parked on the side of the path offered temporary sanctuary. She dove behind the oversize rear wheels and then heard a sequence of heart-slamming sounds. A bullet ricocheted off the metal of the tractor, thudded into a softer target, and a body dropped to the ground.

"Fuck," groaned Riordan.

She slithered around the tire to grab his arm and hauled him to cover behind the wheel, more shots whizzing overhead as she worked. Riordan groaned again and brought up his free hand.

"Where are you hit?" she demanded, louder than she meant to.

"Vest," he wheezed, struggling for breath. "Okay."

Anyone else would have run their hands over his body, checking for blood. Instead, she yanked off the night-vision goggles, shoved her face inches from his chest, and scanned for a wound. She found it, after a manner: a ragged hole torn in his pullover just below his right pectoral. She poked a finger into the hole and saw that the lighter-colored fabric covering his body armor had been shredded as well, but the plate beneath it was only pockmarked. The round hadn't penetrated.

She felt herself tearing up. "You're one lucky bastard," she croaked.

"Lucky? I'm in agony," he said, returning to his sarcastic self. "I think I cracked a rib."

"Can you move?"

"Yeah. But in case you didn't notice, there's more than just the guy behind the fence. I saw three or four muzzle flashes from the vineyard on *our* side. They sent a whole squad of Donovan's ex-Navy SEALs after us. The first shots were only meant to flush us out."

"I hope you got a good plan."

"There's no way out but the way we came. But as soon as we pick a vineyard row, they're going to triangulate on it and the place it dumps out. We've got to start down one and then crawl under the vines to another."

"We should crawl to one *closer* to them, then. They won't expect it."

"Good. You go first. I'll lay down a suppressing fire."

"You go first. I don't want you to get stranded."

"No. You can't do dick with that sawed-off."

She realized it was the right thing tactically, but she hated to abandon him. She pulled the goggles back on and crept forward to the front tires while he struggled to crouch by the back ones.

Without warning, he popped up and began raking the vineyard with slugs from the assault rifle. "Go!" he shouted.

She covered the distance to the grapes in two hungry strides. She combat-crawled a short length down the row she landed in then rolled under the vines to lie in the one to her left.

Riordan nearly dove on top of her a moment later.

"Christ, that hurt," he hissed next to her ear. "Keep the party going. Let's get over four or five more."

They rolled, crawled, and slithered their way across another five rows, ending only a few rows from where they had been stationed by the fence. Sporadic shooting continued, and Winnie thought she could hear men talking in hushed tones not so very far away. She helped Riordan to his feet, and they hurried down the row to the next tractor path, making sure to keep their heads well below the tops of the vines.

Riordan peered around the trellis post, looking east toward Marionette and then west toward their car. He twitched visibly at something in the western view. He stepped back and held up a single finger, pointed in the direction that made him twitch, and then held his hands out a few feet apart.

She nodded. *One bad guy very close.*

He made a gun with his hand, pantomimed a shooting motion, and then pointed over the tractor path to the next section of the vineyard.

Winnie nodded again.

Riordan took a knee by the end post, laid the P90 gingerly against the wood, and leveled it on a line about three feet above the ground. Just as she was thinking the bad guy must be squatting, too, the P90 coughed, and Riordan lurched forward out of his crouch.

She grabbed him by the collar as he rose and hauled him across the tractor path to the relative safety of the next plot of vines. She saw a man dressed in camo sprawled facedown on the ground as she passed.

More suppressed gunfire erupted to the west and north, but it was far enough away that she was certain the Winemaker's men were aiming at shadows. They hurried down the row until they came to the barbed-wire fence that protected the property from the road. There was only one problem. A white van was parked fifty yards down facing them. Another man dressed in camo leaned over it with an assault rifle laid out on the hood.

They stepped back into the vines to huddle.

"We can get under the wire and across the road without him seeing us," said Riordan.

"No way. We'll be sitting ducks if he *does* see us, and you aren't exactly moving at top speed."

"I'll pick him off, then."

"With that grease gun at night at that range? Even if you hit him, you'll alert the rest of them."

"All right, then," he said. "What's your suggestion?"

"You stay here and keep him covered."

"While you go where?"

"Back under the vines to a row nearer to him. Then I'll crawl under the wire and finish him off quietly."

He stared down at his feet while he rocked from one to the other like a little boy who didn't want to go to school. It was hard for either of them to let the other take risks now. "Okay," he said finally. "But be careful."

A smart remark formed on her lips, but she bit it off. She pulled off the night-vision goggles and held them out to him. "Hold these for me. I don't need them for this."

Riordan took the goggles without comment and reached around to the small of his back to produce one of the captured Tasers. "But you might find a use for this."

"Why in the world did you decide to bring that?"

He grinned. "I tried to bring the Luger, but these new pants are too loose and it kept slipping. This is lighter and bulky enough to stay in place."

"You're lucky you didn't electrify your ass."

"I love you, too. Now get going."

She pocketed the Taser and dropped to the ground. She combat-crawled beneath the first trellis and kept going until she was even with the center of the van. She could just see the left foot of the gunman sticking out from the front tire. All that remained was the barbed-wire fence and the irrigation ditch.

The barbed wire was relatively easy. The lowest strand was several inches above her highest points—her ass and her head. She cleared it without catching either part on the wire. The ditch was another matter. It was too wide to crawl over without putting some part of her body in it, and while it wasn't full of water, there was a dark puddle of indeterminate depth at the bottom. Her main worry was slipping and making a splash. The sawed-off, which she'd been holding by the barrel as she crawled, was also going to complicate any maneuver that required two free hands. Winnie considered standing upright, or partially upright, to leap across but decided there was too much chance of attracting the gunman's attention.

In the end, she edged into the canal like she was merging onto a highway, crossing at a much shallower angle than she would have if she crawled directly across. Winnie moved slowly to avoid making splashes, and the shallow approach allowed her to keep the hand holding the sawed-off clear of the water. The strategy did mean she was thoroughly soaked with mud and water by the time she slithered across to the other side. Yet another time lack of sensation proved an advantage.

Once out of the canal, Winnie realigned herself to intercept the gunman and snaked under the van to a point inches away from his feet. Above her, she heard him clear his throat. He said, "Base is still clear," into some sort of radio. Then, "Roger that. Base out."

Winnie laid the sawed-off to one side and pulled the Taser from her pocket. She knew the weapon was more effective if aimed at the torso or the thigh, but it would be folly to clamber out from under the van to get a better shot. The lower leg was the best she could hope for. She cleared the safety and aimed the targeting laser at a meaty portion of his calf. Then she yanked the trigger.

The probes jumped out from the Taser and embedded themselves mere inches apart. That was also less than ideal. The weapon worked better with a larger distance for the current to flow.

These ruminations were lost on the gunman, who made horrible growling noises and did a back flip onto the shoulder of the road, writhing in the dirt as he clutched at his calf. His rifle bounced off his chest and then clattered to the ground. Winnie pumped the trigger once more to insure the full discharge and then scrambled on top of him. She soon found that he was down but not out. He slammed the heel of his hand into her chest, knocking her back. He thrust up with his hips, attempting to buck her off. Then he twisted to reach his rifle.

It was a mistake. Winnie rained a vicious blow down on the side of his head, smashing his ear with her palm. His eardrum ruptured and he howled in reaction, instinctively cradling his head with his arms. She reached across him for the rifle and mashed the upper receiver into his throat. He was fighting back, trying to push the rifle away, when Riordan came charging up.

He dropped by her side and added his strength to hers. The gunman gurgled and kicked, but finally went limp. By unspoken agreement, they held the rifle in place for another long minute until they were absolutely certain he was dead.

Winnie looked over to Riordan. He'd taken off his night-vision goggles, and his face was drawn and concerned. He started to say something, stopped himself, and settled on "Was that your idea of getting rid of him quietly?"

She knew he meant to say something more serious, but she was glad of the lighter tone. "The only noise I heard was you wheezing on the way over." Winnie retrieved the sawed-off and stood.

Riordan stood with her. "Well, you're welcome."

"I had it under control. What next? Hike or take the van."

"The van, no question—if they left the keys."

The keys, it turned out, weren't in the van, but Riordan found them in the gunman's pocket. They climbed in and made the short run to the grade school with the lights off. They passed no one on the road, and they didn't see or hear anything more of the Winemaker's men in the vineyard.

At the school, Riordan parked beside their rented SUV and clicked the keyless opener. He was out of the van and on his way to the driver's door when he checked up and detoured to the rear of the van.

"We might as well see if they left us any other goodies."

"Sure," she said. "They've been generous so far."

Riordan yanked open the cargo doors. There, lying side by side, as unblinking and stiff as tin soldiers, were two Hispanic men outfitted with bulky packs of electronic instruments.

CHAPTER 24

Riordan

"THOSE," I said, "aren't exactly the goodies I had in mind."

"They don't even belong in the goodie category," sneered Winnie. "Let's get the hell out of here. It looks like they are frozen in place, but that doesn't mean the electronics on their backs aren't transmitting. Some guy in a control room could be watching us right now."

"No, the other backpacks had little blinking lights all over them. These must be shut down. Hold on a second. I want to try something."

I leaned back into the van. I had noticed a toggle switch on the dashboard covered with a red protective cover, like some sort of missile launcher. Maybe it was the power switch for the backpacks, but I had an idea it did something else. I flipped up the cover and pushed the toggle down to what I hoped was the off position.

"Notice anything different?" I called out the door.

"Yeah. They're groaning and squirming around. One guy just pissed himself. You switched off the signal controlling them, didn't you?"

I hurried back to the rear. From what I could tell, there was more groaning than squirming. Their muscles had to be in knots from being held rigid for so long. "Help me undo the straps on the backpacks."

"Do we need another conversation about mission?" asked Winnie, but nonetheless she reached to unbuckle the straps on the nearest guy. "Freeing them is fine and dandy, but it doesn't do anything about the Winemaker."

"Don't jump to conclusions. This isn't entirely altruistic." I fumbled open the buckles at my guy's chest and hips, and then stood back, gripping the place I had been hit by the ricochet. Every movement felt like an ice pick in the ribs. "Go, man," I said. "Get away while you can."

All he did was hug himself.

"Maybe they don't speak English."

Vamos," I shouted, pulling him by his arms. I was pretty sure that meant "let's go" rather than "get up," but that was the best I could do. Eventually, he tottered to his feet to join his friend—who Winnie had decanted with a more ruthless efficiency than I had.

"You better not be taking them with us," she warned.

"I'm not, but I am taking one of the packs." I worked the clicker on our SUV and yanked open the rear door. By the time I turned around, Winnie had already snatched up one of the packs, and now she flung it into the back and slammed the door shut.

"Okay, you got your pack. What *are* we going to do about them?"

I stepped in front of the guy Winnie had been wrangling. He was the one with bladder-control issues, but he seemed a lot steadier on his feet now. I took his hand and slapped the van keys into it. *"Adios, amigo,"* I said, and then pointed to the van and made a steering motion like I was driving. He looked at me like I'd told him to grow wings and fly.

Winnie elbowed me out of the way and slapped him none too gently on the cheek. She barked, *"Escúchame,"* and proceeded to unreel about three paragraphs of rapid-fire Spanish. He started nodding about halfway through, and when she broke off, he wobbled over to the driver's door to hoist himself behind the wheel.

I offered him a hand up while Winnie gave the other guy the bum's rush into the passenger seat.

We watched as they backed out of the parking lot, getting all the way into the middle of the road before they found the D on the gearshift. Then they lurched forward and boiled down the highway.

A minute later, we gained the road ourselves, charting a circuitous route home to elude pursuers and avoid another Marionette drive-by. We were still running without lights, but I risked a glance over in Winnie's direction. "I didn't know you could speak Spanish."

"Well, I can. It's pretty much a requirement if you hang around wineries. All the workers are from south of the border. Speaking of surprises, what's with the backpack? Seems like a big old Trojan horse to me. What do you think you're going to do with it—except allow the Winemaker to spy on us?"

"It's not what *I'm* going to do with it. It's what Ray is going to do with it. It's time to call for Q."

Winnie stared through the windshield into the darkness. "I don't mind having him come up and join us—as long as he understands the risks. But I don't see what you expect him to do with the backpack."

"Take it apart. Understand how they work and how to defeat them. We'll never be able to sneak onto the property if we can't avoid detection by those zombie guards and the instruments they carry around."

"Who said anything about sneaking onto the property? When the time comes, I'm going to make damn sure they know I'm there."

"The operative phrase being 'when the time comes.' There are only two of us. We have to have the element of surprise."

"Maybe. But I don't like taking that thing back home. Even if it's not lit up like the others, it could still have some sort of geolocation tracker on it."

"If you believe that, then why did you help me load it into the SUV?"

She reached over to give my arm a squeeze. "Because, lover boy, I didn't want to have the argument in the parking lot. I wanted to get the hell out of Dodge. Let's ditch it. Now. Before we turn back toward Calistoga."

"But—"

She squeezed my shoulder again. "Please."

I found a wash along the highway next to a sign that read NO DUMPING. There was already a camper shell, a box spring, and a refrigerator lying amid a field of other flotsam and jetsam. We pulled to a stop by the guardrail, and I stepped over. Winnie handed me the backpack and I stuffed it through the door of the camper shell, nestling it among a sea of Bud and PBR empties.

Back behind the wheel of the SUV, I wagged an index finger at Winnie. "To be continued," I said.

Winnie grinned, wrapped a hand around my finger, and gently pushed it down. "I hate sequels."

•

Ray arrived two days later at about five in the afternoon. We had moved from the B&B to a cheaper motel at the other end of town. He wheeled into the parking lot in his 1987 Dodge Aries—the Chrysler K-car he'd bought the year he retired from McDonnell Douglas—pulling a cigar-shaped trailer he'd made to haul around his model-airplane junk.

I saw him through the window of our room and stepped out into the breezeway that fronted the parking lot. "What'd you bring that for?" I asked, after he had hoisted himself out of the car.

Squinting at me, he brought a hand up to block the afternoon sun. "Did you expect me to walk?"

"I don't mean the funky car. I mean the funkier trailer."

"I've got my reasons." He paused. "Nice to see you, too."

"Sorry," I said, and stepped out to shake his hand, gripping his bony elbow at the same time. It *was* good to see him. "Thank you for coming. It means a lot to me—to us."

He gave me a lopsided grin, pulling me closer to ask in a stage whisper, "You doing her yet?"

I laughed and pushed him away. "You don't need to whisper. She's at the gym."

"Swell, but you didn't answer the question."

"Let's just say we have only one room."

"Ha! I knew it."

I spent the next hour filling him in on everything that had happened since we left Palm Springs. He merely grunted when I told him how his electronic countermeasures had helped at the brothel and Nevada City. It was the helicopter that drew the biggest reaction.

"You're telling me you shot down a fucking helicopter?"

"Yeah." We were sipping watery coffee from the decrepit motel coffee maker. He was on the couch and I was balancing on two legs of the scratched desk chair. I brought the legs down with a bang. "We thought the Winemaker might be on it."

"But he wasn't."

It wasn't really a question, but I answered anyway. "No, he wasn't."

Ray took a sip of coffee, frowning as he swallowed. "It's really not going to end until you kill him or he kills you."

"I tried to make that clear on the phone, Ray. You don't have to do this. You can turn around and drive right back—and I won't think any less of you."

"I heard what you said on the phone. I just didn't realize you meant it." He shook his head. "I'm staying. As far as I can tell, you'd both be dead if it wasn't for me."

I laughed, eager to cut the tension. "That's almost certainly true. Thank you, Ray."

"Now tell me about this instrument pack."

I explained about the zombie guards patrolling the Winemaker's property and the packs they wore—and how they seemed to have detected Winnie and me in the dead of night from at least a hundred yards away.

He nodded. "Could be radar, could be infrared, could be a lot of things."

I was describing the disagreement Winnie and I had about keeping one when she stepped through the door in a black Lycra half suit, fresh from her workout at the gym.

Her face was flushed, and her muscles pumped, but that only made her more attractive—like some kind of female superhero come to life. Ray stood awkwardly, staring at her with obvious carnal interest almost exactly as he had the first time they met.

A huge smile spread over Winnie's face, and she hurried over to wrap him in a hug. "It's good to see you, Ray. Thank you for coming."

He was as flushed as she was by the time she released him. "Now that's the sort of greeting I expected."

"Your expectation has more to do with the greeter than the greeting," I said.

It was close to dinnertime, so we ordered Chinese delivery to limit the chances of being spotted by the Winemaker's men. Sitting cross-legged around the motel coffee table, we feasted on kung pao chicken while Ray entertained us with a story about a prank he played on old Mrs. Grenshaw from our trailer park. But by the time we got down to the fortune cookies, I steered the conversation back to the disputed instrument pack.

"Winnie's right," pronounced Ray, once he understood the crux of the disagreement. "It almost certainly has some kind of geolocation device, and that device will almost certainly have a separate power supply from the main instruments. Think about it—they need to know where these guards are at all times, and they need to deal with the possibility of an intruder killing the guard and disabling the pack. They would need a way to determine where the downed guard is, so they would know where the breach took place. It would have been foolhardy to bring the pack back here without removing the geolocation tracker first. They would have been on you in hours."

Winnie held out her hand, palm up. "I rest my case."

"But he's right, too," said Ray.

"Come on," said Winnie. "Now you're just trying to split the baby. We can't both be right."

"Yet you are. You're right because you shouldn't have taken it without removing the tracker. He's right because you need to get your hands on one to understand what makes it tick. They've got a nearly perfect defense system—an unlimited supply of expendable zombie guards, patrolling the ground with sophisticated detection electronics. You'll never get through if you can't subvert or disable them."

"You know what I'm going to say next," I said.

"Yes, I do," said Winnie. "And I don't like it."

"We have to go back to the one we ditched. Have Ray defang it and bring it back here."

"That's what I thought."

CHAPTER 25

Riordan

WE SET OUT AT ABOUT ELEVEN the next morning, Ray cheerful and keen in the front seat with me, Winnie grousing in back. Although I didn't remember the exact location of the no-dumping zone, I knew it was on a stretch of Alexander Valley Road five or six miles from the Healdsburg city center. We found it at the apex of a broad curve in the road across from a forested tract of land. Traffic on the road was light but constant, so it was unlikely we would be able to retrieve the pack from the camper shell completely unobserved by passersby. More to the point, a baby-blue Pacific Gas and Electric van was parked by a power pole fifty yards down on the same side of the road. A guy in a yellow hard hat stood by the pole with a pile of insulated wire spooled at his feet.

"Right there," said Winnie. "That's one of them. He's watching to see if we come back."

I powered around the curve until we were well out of sight of the

PG&E guy and pulled over. I turned back to Winnie. "Why would they think we were coming back?"

"Good question. Anyone with an ounce of sense would know better."

"He could be one of them," admitted Ray. "Remember the bogus power-company people in the Springs?"

"Yeah, but he might be Joe Working Stiff who could give a rat's ass if we rummage around in the garbage dump. We have to find some way to find out without tipping our hand."

"I'll do it," said Ray.

"How?"

"I walk along the road like I'm a vagrant looking for cans and such. I'll wander down into the dump site and nose around in the camper shell. If he reacts, I'll just play dumb and let him roust me out of there. If he doesn't, I'll take the pack and go."

"Okay, that could work. But we can't let you risk it without backup. If he really is one of them, he might not buy your story."

"Let's just shoot him and be done with it," snapped Winnie.

"Now who's forgetting the conversations about mission parameters? No civilian casualties."

She let out an impatient sigh. "We'll double back on foot through the wooded area and take a position in the trees on the other side of the road. If Ray gets into trouble, we'll be with him in an instant."

"Better."

It turned out that Ray needed very little help to make a convincing dumpster diver. We gave him the black plastic garbage bag we had used to collect trash on the drive from Nevada City and found him a long stick for poking and prodding. He already had the shabby clothes, the long gray beard, and a general air of malnourishment.

"Go slow," I told him, "and make it look good. We need time to get into position."

He nodded and trotted across the road, where he almost immediately stooped to pick up a can from the shoulder.

"He's found his calling," said Winnie.

"A little eerie, isn't it? You ready?"

"Yeah, let's roll."

We jogged into the stand of oak and eucalyptus trees, the uneven ground carpeted with leaf litter, curling eucalyptus bark, and acorns. Winnie carried her sawed-off by her leg. I had my Luger in a shoulder holster strapped under my windbreaker. The slap, slap, slap of it against my side as I ran did nothing to ease the pain in my ribs.

We came up behind a wide-trunked oak at a spot halfway between the PG&E guy and the garbage dump. If he moved to interfere with Ray, he would have to cross directly in front of us.

From our vantage point, he certainly seemed legit. His van looked right, he was dressed right, he had all the right tools on his belt, and there was definitely something going on at the top of the power pole. One end of the cable coiled at his feet ran to an insulator on a cross-piece above. The only problem was that he didn't appear to be doing anything. He stood by his pole, dividing his attention between the wire at his feet and the view down the road in either direction.

When Ray came shuffling around the curve, the PG&E guy didn't pay him any particular attention. When Ray gingerly negotiated the guardrail and the drop to the wash, the man still didn't react. Same when Ray traded his stick for a rusted golf club taken from a ripped bag. But when Ray started poking the club in the camper shell, the PG&E guy turned to face the dump, bringing his hand to a leather pouch on his belt. And as Ray reached into the camper to pull out the pack, the man produced an automatic and broke into a sprint.

Winnie and I launched out from behind the tree. "You grab him and I'll finish him," she shouted.

It was a good plan, but it wasn't going to be as easy as that. Just as we reached the asphalt, a Frito-Lay truck came barreling around the curve, heading toward Healdsburg. We skidded to a stop inches from the yellow line. The truck rumbled past, buffeting us in its slipstream and momentarily blinding me with dust. It delayed us for a three-count—but it also shielded us from the view of the phony PG&E guy. Now we used that to our advantage.

I did a steeplechase number over the guardrail, managing to land upright at a point equidistant from Ray and the Winemaker's man. I let my forward momentum carry me into a diving tackle just as he leveled the automatic on Ray's crouching form. We crash-landed into the baked earth, jolting the hard hat from his head and—despite the cushion of his ample gut—punishing my injured ribs.

I doubled up in pain, losing my hold around his torso. He kicked at my shoulders and head with his work boots, rolling and squirming out of range as he did. I tried to snag his ankle, but managed to grab only a handful of the fabric of his work pants. He was trying to kick free when Winnie's feet flashed by. He yelled, "Get off me, bitch." Then came the sound of vertebrae popping, and his leg went slack.

I trundled to my feet, gripping my injured ribs with one hand while I explored a bump over my right eye with the other. Winnie already had the PG&E guy by the collar and was dragging him back toward the power pole. "Get the pack," she said. "I'll hide the body in the van."

"Right."

Ray watched me approach with a look of sick fascination. He was sitting by the camper shell surrounded by beer cans with the instrument pack pulled halfway out the camper door. "Jesus," he said. "This really is for keeps."

"I keep telling you that."

"Yeah, you do. Help me get the instruments out of the pack. We need to find the tracker module."

We yanked the electronics out of the nylon harness. I'd never seen the goods in the daylight until now. It was clear that most of the smarts were in the ball-like turret that protruded over the wearer's head. Ray pointed out a central spine that ran from the turret down the girderlike pole into the boxy base. "That's the communication bus for all the sensors and instruments," said Ray. "These modules on either side are the batteries. And, unless I'm mistaken, this doodad right here is the GPS tracker."

He pulled out a module the size of a matchbox from the communication bus at the base of the pack. A USB connector protruded from it. Ray read the writing stamped along the side. "Yep," he said. "This is a commercial model with its own power source." He tossed the tracker back into the camper among the empties where it landed with a tinny clatter. "Consider it defanged."

I started to thank him, but a scream cut me off. Winnie was yelling my name at the top of her lungs.

I twisted back to find her being dragged along the ground, clutched at the ankle by something the villagers outside Frankenstein Castle would have chased with pitchforks and torches. He was wearing a PG&E uniform like the other guy, but on him it was laughably small, coming up inches short in the legs and arms. He was seven feet tall if he was a foot, and he had to weigh over three hundred pounds. He moved with robotic jerkiness, but I didn't feel—like I did with the guards the night before—that someone else was calling the shots. He seemed to be driving solo.

I jacked out the Luger and fired two rounds into his chest. It didn't affect him in the slightest. He had to be wearing body armor but, as I knew from personal experience, the pain and shock of being hit while wearing armor was debilitating. I aimed for his thigh. The first shot went wide, but the second bit into his quadriceps inches above his knee.

This time I saw blood blossom from the wound, but if it slowed him in the least, I failed to discern it. If anything, he dragged Winnie faster, snapping her leg like a rope to whiplash her into the ground.

And there was more bad news. The toggle action of my Luger had jammed open. I reached to clear it with sweaty fingers, but I was too panicked and jittery to do the job properly.

"In the head," Winnie yelled, "in the head."

I stooped to pick up the golf club Ray had been using and ran toward the giant, holding the club above me like a samurai sword. The giant dropped Winnie's leg and went into a defensive crouch, but he moved like a sumo wrestler in Jell-O. I dodged past his outstretched arms and brought the club down on his hard hat. He lurched backward, tripping on the coil of wire by the power pole.

The hard hat popped off as he hit the ground, and I skipped forward to tee off on his noggin like I intended to drive it three hundred yards. I connected at a spot behind his left ear, sending a jolt of pain to my ribs and detaching the club head, which went gyrating off into the weeds. The giant slumped facedown into the dirt, dead or unconscious—I wasn't sure which.

Winnie struggled to her feet. We linked arms and jogged toward

Ray, who was already hefting the instrument pack. We dodged across the highway, slipping back into the trees for the hike to the car. But just a few steps into the woods, Winnie paused to look back at the downed giant.

"He's one of me," she said, and hurried on.

MOUNT
ST. HELENA
TRAIL

NORTH PEAK

4.2 MI

CHAPTER 26

Riordan

RAY UNWRAPPED his third Little Debbie Banana Pudding Roll and dispatched it in one bite. It was a little after seven in the evening, and we were parked on a twisty section of Highway 29 in his Dodge Aries just a few miles north of Calistoga. We'd gone there to wait for sunset and the closing of Robert Louis Stevenson State Park, home to Mount Saint Helena, the tallest peak between the Napa and Alexander valleys.

"Really?" I said. "How many LDBPRs are you going to eat?"

"*Mumph,*" said Ray, his mouth still full of rubbery sponge cake and ersatz banana cream.

"A person of your advanced years should pay more attention to your diet."

Ray threw the wrapper over his shoulder, where it fluttered onto the backseat. "You're one to talk."

"Yeah, but Ray, *banana*? Little Debbie makes a fine line of snack cakes. Stick to her chocolate Devil Squares or her Cosmic Brownies. There's no need to get involved with banana."

Ray waved me off, wagging his chin at a white pickup coming around the corner. "The park ranger. That's our cue."

"Have I mentioned this is crazy?"

"You're one to talk," he repeated, and drove off.

A hiker going to the top of Mount Saint Helena, I knew from Ray, would start at a trailhead near the park entrance. He would pick his way a mile or so through the pine forest ringing the mountain until he came to a dirt fire road. He would turn left onto the road and follow it another four miles until he reached the summit—and a thicket of communication towers.

Ray had a different idea. We passed the park entrance, which wasn't much more than a wide spot in the highway, and continued to a gate made of galvanized pipe guarding the fire road. I jumped out with a set of bolt cutters, and after bit of fumbling, managed to dispatch the padlock securing it. Ray rattled through, funky home-built trailer and all. I shoved the squeaky gate closed, snapping on a new padlock once I latched the gate in place. We didn't expect anyone to come tootling along at this time of night, but if they did, we hoped they'd assume they'd brought the wrong key.

I piled back into the Aires, and we began the ascent up the mountain. The road was steep and rutted with switchbacks every few hundred yards. Ray drove without lights and steered a wavering course that hewed a little too close to the edge for my taste. I brought my hand up twice to make what seemed a needed course correction, and twice I restrained myself out of respect for Ray. He kept the car on track nonetheless. The third time I didn't have a choice. We nearly drove right off the edge. I squawked and yanked the wheel over. Then I pulled on the headlights.

"I think we can risk a little illumination," I said. "You know, to help keep you on the straight and narrow."

"Sure," he sniffed.

We made the rest of the ascent without incident, passing not one but two blocky white buildings with attendant communication towers before we reached the summit and the biggest tower of all. Beside it was another blocky white building, and beside the building was a football field's worth of smooth black asphalt, presumably for parking service vehicles. There weren't any service vehicles now, though, so Ray bumped off the rutted fire road to the blacktop, pulling the Aires to the rear of the pad.

We got out of the car and walked forward to the overlook. There, stretched below us, was the Alexander Valley, dark except for the winking lights of Healdsburg, the odd blip from a farmhouse or winery building and the slow stream of headlights from cars trolling along Highway 128. And, just in front of the highway, less than ten miles southwest as the crow flies, was the cluster of lights that marked Marionette Vineyards.

"Nice view," I said.

"Yes, it is," said Ray. "Why don't you stay here and enjoy it while I get set up."

"You don't need any help?"

"No. It's all stuff I don't trust anyone else to do."

"Thanks, Ray."

"You know what I mean."

I nodded and watched him trudge off toward the car. A minute later, the headlights snapped on, and he pulled open the trailer door and began rummaging inside.

I returned to the overlook. On the drive from Reno, after we had figured out the Winemaker's location, I had made a crack to Winnie about targeting him with a drone strike. Ray's idea wasn't a drone strike, exactly. It was more of a drone reconnaissance. He planned to do a fly-over of Marionette with one of his model airplanes.

He had pitched the idea that afternoon at a meeting in our motel room.

"But, Ray," I said, "we already did a reconnaissance."

"You call getting chased away from the property by machine guns doing a reconnaissance? You haven't seen a tenth of the place. You have no idea what other defenses they have and, more to the point, what vulnerabilities there may be. The only practical way to get that is by air."

"Then let's use the satellite function of Google Maps. We won't even have to leave our room."

"I already looked. The satellite photos on Google Maps were taken two years ago, before the Winemaker bought the property. They won't show any of the changes he's made."

"Oh."

I looked over at Winnie. She was sprawled on the couch, working on her hand exercises with an improbable level of concentration. There was no help coming from her. "How about a real plane, then?" I said. "Why don't we rent a plane and fly over?"

Ray shook his head. "Why don't you drive up to the front gate in your rental car? Because they'll get the plate number and track you down. They'll do the same with the N-number on the tail of the plane. The whole point of a drone is it's safe and untraceable."

"I think this is just an excuse to play with your models. You must have installed the cameras in Palm Springs right after we invited you. You planned this from the beginning."

That got him going. "You asked me up here to help," he said, punctuating his words with a stab of his index finger. "*This* is how I'm helping."

"I asked you here to reverse engineer the instrument packs on the guards. We risked life and limb to get one. Seems like you should take a little time to look at it."

"I will. Once we have the full picture of their defenses."

I glanced over again at Winnie. She stood, tossing her hand exerciser onto the couch. "I'm going to the gym. Let me know when you boys determine the *grande stratégie*."

I battled on for another few minutes, but this wasn't an argument I was going to win. I remained convinced that the exercise was a complete waste of time, but I conceded it was at least a relatively safe and anonymous one.

A sputtering metallic cough brought me back to the here and now. Then a piercing whine I recognized as a model airplane engine. I turned to find Ray lining up his prized Fokker triplane in the light thrown from the Aires's headlights. The plane was painted bright crimson like Red Baron Manfred von Richthofen's fighter from WWI. Trimmed with black Iron Cross decals on the tail and fuselage, it had a wing-span of more than six feet and it had won awards for best custom-built model at many radio-control conventions. I was surprised Ray had picked this of all his planes to use.

I jogged over to where he stood by the door of the car. He held a remote control with a long antenna and was busy testing the elevator, ailerons, and rudder of the triplane. Lying on the hood beside him was a tablet computer that seemed to be receiving a video feed from the craft.

"Why the Red Baron?" I shouted at him over the whine of the motor.

"It needs the shortest amount of space to take off and land."

Ray had at least relied on Google satellite maps for one thing: finding the best launch point for the reconnaissance. Mount Saint Helena was perfectly positioned, but he didn't trust the scale of the satellite photos and was concerned about the condition of the blacktop. As it turned out, the pad seemed plenty big enough—and was relatively smooth and unweathered, too.

"All right," said Ray, "we're ready to go. Hold the tablet, will you? I'll need that to navigate once we get off the mountain."

I picked up the tablet and held it up like a book for him to read. The bulk of the screen had the video feed from the plane, but there was also a small box in the upper-right corner showing a map of the area. The map had a flashing red dot at the summit of the mountain. The geolocation of the plane, I assumed.

Ray pushed the slider that controlled the throttle, and the motor screamed. The aircraft shot forward, and then Ray pulled the elevator back and it jerked into the air like a hooked trout. It seemed the triplane needed very little runway at that.

The plane sailed over the edge of the mountain, Ray executing a full barrel roll as it disappeared from view. Just the video feed of the maneuver was enough to make me nauseous.

"Show off," I said.

"That's so you don't start doubting my piloting skills."

"Only on the ground, Ray, only on the ground."

The volume and pitch of the motor decreased as the plane flew away from us, and soon I could hear nothing at all. The flashing red dot on the map steered a true-enough course west by southwest, but the video seemed very jerky, as if the plane was being buffeted or shaken.

I pointed at the screen of the tablet. "What's going on?"

"That's normal. There are thermals rising from the mountain and the foothills, and a triplane is particularly sensitive to those. It'll smooth out once we're farther into the valley."

As Ray predicted, the motion gradually dampened. Five minutes after takeoff, if you told me I was watching footage from the Goodyear Blimp, I would have believed you.

"I'm steering clear of the winery on the way out," said Ray, a few minutes later. "We'll turn at Highway 128, drop down to about three hundred feet and then come right up their gullet. That way, we'll get good video from the entrance to the eastern property line. We can make multiple passes if we see anything interesting."

The highway came into view just a minute later. Ray banked the plane to fly on a line above it, dropping from what must have been several thousand feet until I could clearly identify the models of the cars below us and even make out the arms of farmers resting elbows in the open windows of their pickups. The dual driveways leading into the Marionette property appeared, and Ray banked right to fly over the vineyard between them. We crossed a section of road that connected the drives in a U and then flew over the office and the old tasting room of the winery. In the halos of floodlights, I picked out the aluminum shed and the entrance to the wine caves I'd seen when Winnie and I had sneaked onto the adjacent vineyard. The fence and the guards patrolling the perimeter were visible, too, marching lockstep with more than military precision. From the air, they were like mechanical people in a gigantic clockworks.

Ray reached over to tap a control on the tablet computer, and the display flashed into night-vision mode. More details became visible, including oak barrels stacked in shadows beneath a tree and even a dog barking at the plane.

The dog was not the only thing to take note of the plane. As Ray circled to make another pass at the office and outbuildings, the guards closest to it stopped marching. They made no obvious move to threaten or even observe the aircraft, but I couldn't help feeling they were capturing and relying information about it to the Winemaker's men.

I pointed out their attitude to Ray. "Maybe it's time to cut and run," I said. "You've already gotten more than I ever expected."

"That's because you expected so little. We'll make another pass here, and then I want to cover the full perimeter of the property. There's got to be a chink in their armor."

Ray swung over the highway once more and then lined up for another run past the twin drives. That was when the chink was found—and, unfortunately, it belonged to us. As we came over the office buildings once more, the door to the wine cave swung open and out charged a group of four men. All of them wearing night-vision goggles, and all of them armed with rifles or shotguns.

"Ray," I warned, but he had already seen them.

He shoved the stick over, goosing the throttle and pulling back on the elevator to climb as we turned. The view on the screen shifted from the ground to the foothills, and then farther east to the mountain on which we were standing.

We never saw what hit us. One moment the sky was clear, the next there were bits of wood and fabric obscuring it, and then the picture went dark. The plane had been shot down like an overgrown mallard.

Ray made a noise like he'd been kicked in the stomach. I looked over to find him slack jawed, moisture already welling at the corners of both eyes. In the eerie light projected from the tablet computer, I saw a tear detach itself and run down his cheek.

"Ray, I'm sorry, man. I know that plane was important to you."

I realized the loss of the plane was the first time he truly understood the stakes of the game. Yes, he had expressed shock about the downing of the helicopter, and, yes, watching Winnie dispatch the fake PG&E lineman had disturbed him, but this, *this* was personal. Building model airplanes was what had kept him going after he retired and his wife left him. And this particular plane was the one he prized most, the one he had invested with the most sense of self.

Given all that, it's not surprising what he did next.

He shoved the controller over to me and marched around to the far side of the trailer. He yanked open the door, and I heard a rattling of contents. Piece by piece, he extracted the parts of a plane that I had never seen before. It was huge for a model and made of metal. And it did not have a propeller.

I walked around the car to get a better look. I recognized it as a military plane. I was vaguely aware that it was not entirely modern, that it looked like something that might have been flown by the U.S. during the Vietnam War. Knowing Ray's association with McDonnell Douglas and the F-4 Phantom II, I had an obvious guess.

"Is that what I think it is?"

He ignored me and reached back into the trailer to haul out a heavy tank on wheels. He wheeled it over to the plane, attached a hose to the side and began working a pump to transfer whatever was inside the tank to the plane. An oily, varnishlike smell wafted over me.

"It's not an actual jet, is it? I mean, you can't make a model airplane with a jet engine, can you?"

Still ignoring me, he took hold of a metal bar attached to the nose of the plane and pulled it around to the front of the Aires where he'd parked the Fokker triplane. He detached the rod and tossed it to one side.

"Gimme that," he said, pulling the radio controller back from my hand.

He turned a dial on the controller to select a new frequency and put the control surfaces on the plane—elevator, rudder, and ailerons—through their paces like he had with the triplane. Then he took hold of my shirtsleeve and hauled me about ten feet to the side.

"You might want to put your fingers in your ears," he said.

There was no way to do that without putting the tablet computer down, but he wasn't giving me time for that. With a look on his face that was as grim as I'd ever seen, he pressed and held a red button on the side of the controller.

At first, I thought the buildup had been for nothing. All I heard was a faint whirring noise. Then something else caught inside the plane, something larger, louder, and more primeval. A screaming, snarling whine rent the night air, rising in pitch as the motor gained speed. Exhaust washed over the Aires, melting and then charring the paint on the bumper. Ray pressed the throttle slider forward and the jet roared down the blacktop, seeming to separate wheels from ground just as the plane gobbled up the last bit of runway. The jet held a flat trajectory out over the summit and then sagged from view. My stomach dropped, and I felt certain Ray had lost another plane.

A loud bang seemed to confirm the impression. But an instant later, the plane rocketed back into view, and I understood the bang hadn't signaled the plane's destruction but rather the tapping of some other source of power. The jet disappeared into the night, the tiny glint from its aluminum fuselage lost quickly among the lights of Healdsburg.

I glanced at the tablet computer. The terrain in the video feed was streaming by like a fast-forwarded version of the picture from the Fokker.

"Christ, Ray," I said. "What the hell is that?"

"An F-4 Phantom II, of course."

This was a literal interpretation of my query, but it didn't really get at the questions I had. "How many minutes of fuel do we have?" I tried instead.

"Ten minutes."

"But it'll take that long just to fly there."

"No, we'll be there in one." Ray pointed at the video feed. "In fact, we're already there."

Highway 128 glowered below. Ray dropped into a power bank toward the winery so steep and fast that my stomach did the dipsy-doodle again as I watched. He was on the property and over the main buildings in an instant. Clustered around the wreckage of the tri-plane like a pack of dogs worrying fallen prey were the men who had shot it down. Ray dove straight toward them. Two dove flat on the ground. Another pair veered off in opposite directions. Ray chased a shorter, fatter man with a shotgun until he tripped and did a face plant.

"Bastards," he snarled. He pulled out of the dive and began a wide looping turn—apparently intending to make another pass.

"You got your revenge," I said, mustering the calmest tone I had. "Let's finish the job we came to do."

"One more pass."

"Ray, does your ten minutes of fuel include the sort of aerobatics you're doing now—or are you already eating into your reserve? Come on, bring this one home safe."

He took a deep breath and let it out slowly. "All right." Holding the rudder over, he transitioned into a corkscrew climb that left him several hundred feet higher, heading east by northeast directly on a line back to our mountain. He feathered the throttle back, gaining us a few extra seconds to observe the remainder of the property.

More vineyards passed below us then the ground rose to broken foothills. A moment later, we passed the fence delineating the back of the property. Guards patrolled it, too, and it looked every bit as formidable as the other sections.

Now that we had seen everything, I decided I'd been right about the whole enterprise. We hadn't learned a single new thing—with the possible exception that the instrument pack carried by the guards was capable of detecting aerial as well as terrestrial threats.

I was fighting the urge to crow "I told you so" when I saw something on the screen that put the lie to my whole train of thought.

Well past the Marionette fence, in a notch in the hills near a dirt road built to service high-tension power lines, loomed a large steel door sheathed in concrete.

"The back door to the wine caves," said Ray, "or I'm Baron von Richthofen."

CHAPTER 27

Winnie

DAY SPAS, yoga studios, Pilates emporiums, and pink-trimmed, female-only health clubs were legion in the area, but the only gym that met Winnie's requirements was Jimmy's, a Spartan, no-frills establishment in Healdsburg founded by a former champion bodybuilder. It was housed in a wedge-shaped building that had undoubtedly started life as a warehouse or a factory. She pulled into a parking spot on the side, well away from the other cars, and reached under the passenger seat to pull out a zippered pouch.

Inside the pouch was a clutch of disposable syringes and several glass ampules of metenolone enanthate, one of the safer anabolic steroids for females. Winnie used it as part of a twelve-week training cycle—a cycle she'd been following ever since the Winemaker's men had come after her. She knew it wasn't the best thing for her long-term health, but "long-term" was relative in her world. She needed every edge she could get in the coming showdown.

She broke off the stem of the ampule and then dipped the needle of the syringe in to draw out 50mg of the steroid. She had been told to use a filter needle to avoid pulling in glass fragments, but she never bothered. She pulled up her shirt to expose her stomach and jammed the needle home. When she had injected the full 50mg, she wadded up the ampule, the syringe, and the packaging in a napkin from a fast-food restaurant. She dropped the whole mess in a trash can by the front of the gym, where she imagined it settling in with discarded steroid paraphernalia from other bodybuilders.

The guy at the front desk was a good-looking kid with curly black hair who was twenty or, at most, twenty-two years old. When she explained that she wasn't a member and just wanted to use the gym for the day, he used her presumed ignorance as an excuse to flirt while talking up the gym facilities. He finished with "And we also offer a variety of spa services, including massage."

Winnie looked around skeptically at the scuffed white walls, concrete floor, and acoustic-tile ceiling. "And exactly where do you do the massages?"

He grinned. "We can find a place."

"I'll bet you can." She pointed at the refrigerator full of sports drinks to the right of the desk. "Just give me a day pass—and bottle of Muscle Milk."

"Eight ounces or sixteen?"

"Sixteen."

The kid went over to the refrigerator to retrieve the Muscle Milk and returned to the desk register to ring up the sale for the drink and the day pass. "That'll be $24.95 total."

Winnie passed over a twenty and a five, and the kid slid back a nickel. "Hey," he said, "haven't I seen you around town? At one of the wineries maybe?"

Winnie snatched the drink from his hand and pushed the nickel back across the counter. "Maybe. Do you know my son, Percival? I think he goes to your high school."

She didn't wait for a response but turned to go up the metal staircase running along the back wall. The second floor was where they kept all the serious workout equipment.

Winnie started with the heavy bag, working on her kicks. She did front kicks, roundhouse kicks, and side kicks, singly and in combinations. Then she lowered the bag and worked on the outside sweep kick that she had used at the Bridle Bit. When she was finished, she moved on to punches. Winnie focused on hitting accurately with power. She knew she was never going to overwhelm with speed.

Flinging sweat with each punch, Winnie tapped into a growing frustration. She cared for Riordan and she valued his assistance, but she never should have let him send for Ray. *Whack.* The effort to retrieve the guard's instrument pack had been a dangerous waste of time, and the business with the model airplanes was plain silly. *Whack-whack.*

It was time to move against the Winemaker. Each day of delay only heightened the chance of discovery. *Whack.* The run-in with the giant had thrown her for a loop. Winnie was shocked to discover that he was like her: paralyzed and mobile only with the benefit of the stimulator technology. *Whack-whack.* Yes, the Winemaker hated her and wanted revenge. Yes, he sought her version of the technology to improve his own. But until now, she assumed he was interested only in controlling others through preprogrammed scripts. She punished the bag with a last uppercut, sending it jittering and twisting on its chains.

She wiped down with a towel and chugged half the Muscle Milk. Old-time medicine balls were next. She started by throwing one up against the wall and then moved through a series of exercises that worked her arms, core, and legs. She liked the medicine ball because it helped with balance and gave her a workout that mimicked the physical challenges she'd face in close combat.

As she drilled, Winnie continued to ponder the Winemaker's motives. Was he trying to create an army of soldiers like her? Fighters who felt no pain and advanced even when wounded? If that was the goal, the giant might well represent the peak of his achievement: balky, slow, and clumsy. Although her own reactions were not as fast as a normal person's, she could run circles around him. He'd only captured her by the PG&E van because he'd flung open the rear door at the precise moment she came up behind it.

Still, he was incredibly strong. Winnie imagined him as an opponent as she moved through her routine, pivoting with the ball left and then right as if she were locked in a titanic struggle. If he survived the blow to his head and she chanced to run into him again, Winnie would not underestimate him.

But there were worse things to consider. Like she did, the giant moved under his own direction. It was a relatively benign application of the technology. What was truly terrifying was the possibility of the Winemaker controlling others through *his thoughts* rather than a script. Winnie would destroy herself before she let him use her technology to make that more practicable. She pivoted a final time and hurled the ball down to punctuate the point.

She drank the rest of the chalky Muscle Milk and then moved on to pure strength training. This involved the sort of exercises Riordan did in his driveway in Palm Springs, but unlike Riordan, she knew what she was doing. He followed some sort of Charles Atlas regimen from the 1960s—with shots of bourbon thrown in. She'd read the latest studies and did what they suggested to maximize her results. She used free weights instead of machines whenever possible and went for a relatively small number of reps—six to eight—with as much weight as she could handle for each exercise. She typically did three sets of reps, with no more than two exercises per body part.

Although she spent over an hour on the heavy bag and the medicine ball, it was the strength training that took the lion's share of her time. She was about to begin one of the last exercises in her routine—wrist drills with kettlebells—when she checked the time on the old grade-school-style clock on the wall. It was already eight p.m.

The wrist drills would take at least another forty minutes, the drive to the motel would consume another thirty, and she'd promised Riordan she'd be home by nine. She decided it was time to pack it in.

She toweled off a final time and hurried down the staircase to the first level. A middle-aged Hispanic woman had taken the kid's place behind the desk. Winnie said good night to the woman and was going toward the door when she caught sight of the merchandise in the pro shop. It was mostly T-shirts, leotards, and other workout attire, but nestled among the clothing was a limited selection of equipment—including kettlebells. Invented by the Russians for strength and endurance training, kettlebells were like little cannonballs with handles. They were quite versatile, and if Winnie bought a pair to finish her wrist exercises at the motel, she was certain she could use them later for other training—assuming there was a later.

She paid the Hispanic woman for a pair of ten pounders and shouldered her way out the front door, one kettlebell dangling from each hand. The sun was dipping below the hills to the west, and the parking lot was almost completely deserted. She walked around the side of the building to her car, the faint breeze against her cheek pleasant after all the hours in the stuffy gym. As she put the kettlebells down to fish out her car keys, a pickup truck pulled into the lot, cruised past her, and turned into a spot several places down. She didn't catch sight of the driver, but two German shepherds sat alertly in the back, ears perked forward. Both wore bright red service vests.

Although they weren't growling, something about the dogs put Winnie on alert. She let her keys fall back into her pocket and leaned down to pick up one of the kettlebells. She watched as the driver of the pickup got out and lumbered onto the sidewalk. He was blond and huge. He turned to whistle to the dogs, and both of them bounded out of the pickup to join him.

He felt Winnie's eyes on him and glanced up. She had never seen him before, but she knew instinctively that he was like the giant at the PG&E truck. He was another of the Winemaker's pale imitations of herself. A simpering grin crept onto his heavy features. He recognized her, too.

He looked like the other man, but not like him. Winnie didn't see a family resemblance so much as a type or a shared development process. Given their towering height, protruding jaws, and oversize hands and feet, she wondered if both men suffered from a growth disease of some sort. But compared to the giant at the PG&E truck, this man seemed even slower and more clumsy. She guessed he had received the stimulator implant more recently than the other and was coming to the gym for physical therapy. His use of the service dogs fit with that interpretation as well.

She soon learned that the dogs were intended for more than service. The man clapped his hands together awkwardly and shouted, *"Fass!"*

She didn't recognize the word, but the dogs clearly did. They scrambled around the pickup, snarling as they charged. Winnie turned to place her left foot on the SUV's tire. She took a big step up onto the hood with her right. She felt a tremor and heavy resistance as she tried to pull her trailing foot onto the hood to join the other. The lead dog, a muscular black animal with almost preternaturally white fangs, had clamped its jaws around her ankle.

She pivoted, leaning down to sweep the kettlebell in a scything motion. It caught the animal in the side of the head just below the ear. The dog went slack, and she nearly toppled as it detached itself from her ankle and dropped to the ground, dead or mortally wounded. She overcompensated for the forward pitch and fell back on the hood, banging the kettlebell on the sheet metal with a clang.

The second dog—a black and brown brute—leaped and snapped at her, launching onto the hood with each jump and then sliding back down. Winnie scrambled to her feet and stood towering above the snarling animal. The loss of its partner seemed only to have enraged it further. Its eyes were wild and foam frothed at the corners of its mouth.

Winnie held the kettlebell high over her head, waiting for an opening. It came when the dog leaped up once more, nipping at her feet. She launched the kettlebell straight down at its back. The animal howled and sloughed off the car. It whined as it pinwheeled miserably along the ground, pawing at the asphalt while it dragged its dead hind legs after.

"You cunt," yelled the blond giant. He had tottered off the sidewalk and was bending to retrieve the kettlebell she had set down when he arrived.

Winnie knew nothing good would come from this development. It was now or never. She flew from the hood, lifting her legs to land butt first on his shoulder. The impact flattened him to the ground, but she had not hit squarely, and she ricocheted off his massive scapula to fall in a jumble by the dead dog. She felt nothing from the impact but a jostling and a mild disorientation, as if she were someone watching a video from a POV camera.

She rolled to the side and levered herself upright. The blond monster was struggling to push himself up. She took a deliberate step forward and executed one of the roundhouse kicks she had practiced so assiduously in the gym. Her right shin caught him square in the forehead. He groaned and slumped back, down but not out.

She was lining up another kick when a voice called behind her. "Stop! What are you doing?"

Winnie wheeled to find the woman from the front desk peering around the corner of the building. Probably there was a security camera. Probably she'd seen the commotion from a monitor inside.

"Anatoly," shouted the woman. "Are you okay? What happened to your dogs?"

"He sicced them on me," said Winnie. "That's what happened." She knew there was little hope of convincing the woman, but she wanted to engage her long enough to slow the inevitable call to the cops.

"Anatoly would never do that. He's a gentle—"

"Giant?" Winnie laughed harshly. She snatched up the kettlebells and hurried to unlock the SUV door. "Check the tape, lady," she said, before piling in.

She reversed out of the parking space and snapped the transmission into drive. The last thing she saw before accelerating out of the lot was the woman running out to kneel by the blond man's side.

She took a long, circuitous route home, both to avoid the police and to insure that none of the Winemaker's men were following her. When she arrived at 9:20, she found Ray and Riordan huddled over a laptop, staring at video shot from the air. They looked up at her, clearly eager to impart some news.

She didn't give them the chance. "That's it," she said. "We're done fucking around. D-day is tomorrow."

CHAPTER 28

The Winemaker

I HAVE TO SMILE every time I see an article in the press breathlessly announcing a so-called breakthrough in stimulator research. Headlines such as PARALYZED MAN MOVES COMPUTER CURSOR WITH THOUGHTS ALONE, NEW IMPLANT HELPS PARALYZED PATIENTS REGAIN PARTIAL USE OF THEIR LEGS, and MIND-CONTROLLED CYBORG LEG MAKES THE WORLD CUP'S FIRST KICK are legion. And laughable. It's like reading about the Wright brothers while ensconced in the first-class compartment of a 787 Dreamliner.

As it happens, we are nearly ready to exploit one of the significant breakthroughs we have made. Donovan tells me he's located the number two man in the leading Islamist terrorist organization. His name is Abu Asim al-Qasim, and he serves as the organization's spokesperson. He is a preeminent scholar of the Qur'an and Islamic law while—perhaps paradoxically—possessing unrivaled mastery of modern PR and social media. He blogs, he tweets, he makes YouTube videos, and he gives interviews to Al Jazeera and the Western press—in both English and Arabic. He is also thought to be the producer of the group's beheading videos.

Our plan is to capture him and surgically implant a neurostimulator at the base of his brain. This will enable us to control his body as we have the bodies of the guards and the comfort women, but unlike with them, we will not be limited to simple scripts that we have painstakingly programmed in advance. A specially trained individual—a specially trained and equipped *puppet master* (for, in truth, there is no better name for him)—will directly control al-Qasim with his thoughts.

We will set him up in a broadcast studio with the puppet master off camera. The first few videos we release, the first few Skype interviews al-Qasim gives, will be nearly indistinguishable from the others. He will vomit forth all the usual propaganda, condemning the West, Jews, Christians, and modern morality; but careful observers will begin to notice small inconsistencies, small deviations from the path of Allah and the organization's goals.

Over time, these inconsistencies will become more obvious, more blatant. Perhaps al-Qasim will be seen wearing a crucifix or a Star of David, enjoying a drink of alcohol, or listening to Western music. Perhaps he will talk of accommodating the enemy or encourage misguided acts.

Later, he will become a complete apostate, an utter traitor. There is no limit to the depraved, sacrilegious, and disloyal acts the puppet will be seen committing. (Sex with Jewish men? Wiping his ass with a page from the Qur'an?) He will change from the guiding voice of the organization to a source of shame, confusion, and anger.

And then, after removing the stimulator, we will reunite him with his fellow zealots…

CHAPTER 29

Riordan

"D-DAY," as Winnie had phrased it, wasn't the next day. Nor was it the day after. It was a little more than three days later, and it seemed like Ray and I had spent nearly as much time convincing her that we *weren't* ready as we did working to get that way.

Eventually, we agreed on a plan—or, more accurately, Ray and I agreed on a plan—assigned roles, and determined a zero hour: two a.m. on the fourth day. I didn't think we had a chance in hell, and I was pretty sure Ray felt the same. Winnie didn't brook any discussion. Lying in bed the night she returned from the gym, I mentioned how difficult it would be to get past the Winemaker's fence. Without a word, she slid from beneath the covers to curl up in a far corner of the room. We didn't kiss, touch, have sex, or share any sort of affection from that point on.

When zero hour arrived, I was alone once more—this time at the controls of a backhoe on the shoulder of Highway 128. I'd stopped in front of the vineyard to the east of Marionette and was shining the work lights at a sign posted at the edge of the grapes. It read KNOW WHAT'S BELOW. CALL BEFORE YOU DIG.

I'd done exactly what the sign suggested. That's how I knew the power lines that supplied Marionette and all the other buildings on this side of the highway were buried four feet down.

Backhoes and I had a complicated relationship. I'd been caught up in several cases involving them, but I'd never had occasion to operate one. It was for that reason that we elected to rent rather than steal the yellow behemoth beneath me. I needed practice with the thing, and I didn't figure to get it if I hot-wired one at a construction yard the night before.

Now, just as I had practiced earlier in the day, I drove into the vineyard—past the place the power lines were buried—dropped the front loader to the ground, and lowered the stabilizers on either side of the rear wheels. The idea, I'd read, was to take some of the weight off the wheels, but not all of it. You wanted a broader, stabler base from which to dig and not push the whole rig off the ground. Next, I swiveled the driver's seat to face the highway and took hold of the pair of levers that controlled the boom and the bucket. This was the fun part.

I extended the boom past the power lines, curled the bucket inward, and took my first swipe. I came in too shallow, barely scratching the ground with the teeth of the bucket. It was the same mistake I'd made earlier in the day. I wound up for another go, this time overcompensating with too big a bite. The motor of the backhoe growled with the strain, the tractor rocked against the stabilizers, but the soil was loose and sandy, and the bucket bit through the earth to come back full. I swung it over to the side and flipped it open to release the load.

My next pass came in too shallow once again, but the one after came in at just the right angle: 40 degrees. I fell into a rhythm, the engine rising and falling as I scooped out more and more dirt from the trench in front of me. At last, I felt the bucket snag on something at the bottom of the hole. I pushed the boom out for a deeper bite and then scooped beneath something. When I was sure I had got hold of it, I pulled the boom toward me a few nervous inches and stopped. Then I stood in the cab, leaning out over the boom to take a closer look.

Laced across the teeth of the bucket was a gray plastic sheathing about the thickness of a man's wrist. Inside the sheathing, Ray had told me, would be two or three high-voltage power lines.

"And exactly why won't I be electrocuted?" I had asked.

"The metal of the tractor and the ground under it will be energized once the bucket comes in contact with the bare wire. As long as you stay in the cab, you should be okay. But you're a dead man if you panic and bail out."

"Can't you do any better than 'should be okay'?"

"No, I can't. Get free of the wires as quickly as you can. The current will flow from the tractor through the tires to the ground—"

"But I thought rubber was an insulator."

"Only to an extent. The current's got to go somewhere, and that place is the ground. The spot where the tires touch is going to heat up, and eventually they will melt. If you don't break contact quickly, they'll blow and it will be even harder to get free."

"Swell."

I took a last glance at the power line, imagining the kijillions of volts coursing through it. I shook my head to clear the image and dropped back into the cab. If I was going to do this, I wanted to do it quickly. I reversed the seat, raised the front loader, and brought the stabilizers up. Then I put the tractor into gear—and floored it. The motor snarled and the back tires spun. The backhoe found traction, but the resistance from the straining cable held progress to a crawl. Just when it seemed the tractor would stall or even slide back, the cable snapped. The night behind me crackled and exploded. Sparks danced at the edge of my peripheral vision. I felt the hair on my arms stand on end, and the tractor seemed to hum beneath me. The smell of ozone and burning rubber filled the air.

I plowed into the vineyard, knocking down trellises as I went. I was so frightened of the cataclysm behind me that I didn't stop until I had crashed and bounced across three rows of grapes. Finally, I slammed on the brakes and turned to look at the ditch behind me. There were no sparks, no arcing current, just a faint trace of smoke floating in the moonlight. Across the way, nearly a mile from where I was stopped, the buildings on the Winemaker's property stood huddled in the dark.

As I watched, lights snapped on around the property. There were not as many as there had been before, and they were not as bright. As we had learned from our reconnaissance, the Winemaker had a backup generator, which was now kicking in.

I took both feet off the dual brakes and steered a course out of the grapes to the nearest tractor path running north toward Mount Saint Helena. I thought of Ray and his assignment, and hoped that he was progressing as well as I was. A lot depended on him—a lot depended on all of us.

When I came to an intersecting path, I turned left toward the Winemaker's property and rumbled another quarter mile or so until I came to a second path going north. I zigged along it and then zagged a final time along a path that led straight to the tall fence guarding the property.

As I drove, I flipped the toggle switch that Ray had taped to the console. The switch controlled a box of electronics he had shoehorned behind my seat. And sprouting from that box were coaxial cables that ran up the side of the cab to two large antlerlike antennae secured to the roof. Jamming equipment. The idea was to prevent the instrument packs the zombie guards carried from transmitting information about my approach.

I hoped it worked because, as I came within one hundred yards of the fence, I could already see one of the guards stopping to monitor my approach. He pirouetted in place, turning so that the ball atop his pack was aimed in my direction. Colored lights winked at me and, as Ray determined when he reverse engineered the captured pack, video, infrared, and radar sensors worked to capture a wealth of information. The trick was in making sure it went no farther.

When I was fifty or so yards from the fence, I pulled to a stop and put the backhoe in park. Partly I was waiting to see if the jamming really worked, partly I was trying to screw up my courage. I had come to this section of the fence for a reason. As Ray and I had learned when we researched fence construction on the Internet, chain-link fences were strongest when the fence segments stretching between the supporting poles were long and continuous. Attempting, for example, to drive a backhoe through a segment that stretched across several poles would be nearly impossible because the tractor would have to pull down all the poles attached to the segment.

On the other hand, if you could identify a seam—a place where one segment of the fence ended and another began—the force of the backhoe would be spent in detaching the segment from its anchor pole rather than toppling it. After watching Ray's reconnaissance video, we decided that there had to be a seam right at this place.

The tractor path ran along the base of a hill. The Winemaker's fence ran relatively straight and level from the highway to this point but climbed thereafter. Since the shift in grade was so abrupt, we hoped that the crew building the fence had been forced to end one segment at the pole that stood at the end of the path and then to begin another to accommodate the steeper grade.

I could have climbed down from the tractor to check, but I was too nervous to bother, and I knew whatever I discovered wouldn't affect what I did next. Either I was going to get through this segment of the fence or I wasn't. I didn't have a plan B.

I buckled the lap belt—there wasn't a shoulder belt—and raised the loader to the same level as the hood, figuring it would be best to hit the fence as squarely as possible. I shoved the backhoe into gear and hit the gas. I was aiming at a point just to the left of my target pole, as far from the guard as possible. I braced my arms on the steering wheel and watched as the speedometer climbed. I was only a few feet from the fence when it reached twenty miles per hour, nearly the top speed of the beast.

The backhoe hit with a fearsome rattle, followed by rapid-fire popping and the snap, snap, snap of something bouncing off the Plexiglas of the cab. The bands holding the fence to the pole were zippering off. As I bulled past the fence line, a portion of the chain link became ensnared on the blade of the loader, stretching the fence tightly over the cab as the zipper opened wider and wider, eventually reaching the cross bar at the top where the concertina wire was strung. The bar grated as it sprung loose from the top of the pole then dropped with a clang on the boom behind me.

I jerked to a stop past the fence, ensnared in chain link. I had hoped to use the backhoe for the next part of my mission, but I doubted I could disentangle it without help, and I was no longer sure that Ray's jamming technology was working. At the very least, the antennae on the cab had taken a beating, possibly limiting their range. I slung the P90 assault rifle over my shoulder, grabbed the bulky pack Ray had prepared for me, and abandoned ship. I found the guard lying flat on the ground, knocked over by the collapsing fence. Rolling him over to check his condition, I realized he was one of the men we had liberated on our earlier reconnaissance. He blinked back at me in shared recognition. He was alive but still enslaved. I patted him on the shoulder and whispered, "Keep a good thought."

As I straightened, I saw another guard descending from the hillside. When he came within range, he began the familiar maneuver of training his instrument pack in my direction. It was time to boogie—well past time. Even if the jamming still functioned, someone must have heard the fence being breached.

I ran uphill toward the deep thrumming noise of a diesel motor. My destination was a fenced enclosure on a terraced section of the hill. It was well away from the cluster of buildings at the entrance and, as far as we could tell, sat above the roof of the wine cave that extended back into the hillside.

The pack I was lugging was heavy and it bounced against my shoulders with a metallic clang as I ran. At first, I tried to move stealthily, dodging from an oak covered in Spanish moss to stainless-steel aging tanks to a toppled stone wall. Stealth went out the window as I became winded and approached the dual halos of light thrown by the sodium-vapor lamps planted at the ends of the rectangular enclosure. With the clanging of the backpack and the area lit up like a stage, there was no sneaking up on the Winemaker's generator, and I was too tired to try.

I had drawn level with the enclosure and was moving to cross behind it when the first shot cracked. It came from down the hill and passed inches in front of my face. I dove for cover behind the back fence as two more shots rang out. One thudded into the corner of the front-facing fence. Another kicked up dust a foot or so from my torso as I bucked and clawed my way behind the back fence. Although I wore the captured body armor, the shots carried an extra risk now. The armor wouldn't do a damn thing for me if a bullet hit the backpack.

Behind the enclosure, I struggled to sit upright on the hard-packed earth and yanked off the pack and the assault rifle. A flood of shots from below provided an arrhythmic counterbeat to the thrumming of the diesel generator. I had to move quickly or I would soon be outflanked. With shaking hands, I unzipped the pack, reached inside to grasp a black plastic handle, and pulled out a two-gallon pressure cooker. Ray had taken a page from the terrorist handbook—as well as black powder harvested from about $150 worth of fireworks bought in nearby Petaluma, one of the few cities in the state that still allowed their sale—and had fashioned an improvised explosive device.

I set the pressure cooker on the ground and got to my feet to squat beside it. The harsh yellow light from the sodium-vapor lamps gave its aluminum skin an evil cast. I took hold of the handle, spun in a semicircle, and heaved the cooker over the eight-foot-high wooden fence. It hit something hard and metallic—the generator—bounced off the interior of the fence, and clattered onto the concrete pad.

I snatched up the pack and the assault rifle, and scrambled farther up the hillside. I needed to get away from the coming conflagration, but as soon as I left the cover of the rear fence, I would be visible from below. I ran a dozen yards and took another headlong dive into the earth. Just as I heard someone shout, "There! Above the generator!" I rolled and reached into my pocket to grasp the electronic gismo Ray had given me. I slid a switch on the back to arm it and then pressed a button on the front. That gave me five seconds.

I lurched onto my stomach and pressed my face to the ground. At first I was disappointed. There was an explosion, but it sounded puny and flat. The diesel generator, we knew from the reconnaissance video, was a high-capacity model made by Caterpillar. The generator itself sat atop a four-hundred-gallon fuel tank. Ray intended for the shrapnel in the pressure cooker—ball bearings, nails, and scrap metal—to rupture the tank, allowing the accelerant he'd packed into the bomb to ignite the diesel fuel and blow the whole thing to smithereens.

I don't know whether the high ignition point of the diesel slowed the accelerant or the shrapnel didn't penetrate the tank in many places, but the bigger explosion was long in coming. Yet when it arrived, it didn't disappoint. A shock wave rumbled through the ground beneath me. A pressure wave assaulted me from above. A cataclysmic roar tortured my eardrums—even through ear plugs—and an orange light flooded my vision even through squeezed eyelids. The conflagration sucked the oxygen from the atmosphere, burning the back of my hands, the back of my neck, and the tips of my ears. And as a kind of exclamation point, a tertiary explosion sent something massive gyrating over my head, where it embedded itself in the hillside not six feet away.

Even safe and secure in his custom-built cave twenty or thirty feet below ground, the Winemaker had to know that Winnie and her ragtag posse had come a-calling.

CHAPTER 30

Riordan

I WOULD HAVE LIKED nothing better than to rest on my laurels—or on my singed backside—but knocking out the Winemaker's power was only the first step in our plan. The first step in our "OCD, fucked-in-the-head plan," as Winnie had called it.

I snatched up the pack and the assault rifle, and rumbled down the hill to the toppled stone wall. Once there, I unzipped the pack to draw out a cell phone. One of a trio of throwaways we had purchased at the local Walmart, it was programmed with the numbers of the other two phones, which were carried by Winnie and Ray. I sent a text to both of them about the power being out. No doubt they already had a pretty good idea, but the thing about OCD, fucked-in-the-head plans was that they had to be executed in a certain order.

I opened the pack again and extracted a pair of the captured night-vision goggles. After the glare of the cell display, it took a minute or so for my eyes to adjust to the ghostly green of the goggles. It was worth the wait. The few men I could spot were running around like ants from a dug-up hill. Given the breach of the fence and the pyrotechnics at the generator, it must have seemed like they were defending against the Normandy invasion rather than one guy with a backhoe and a pressure cooker.

But even an ersatz Normandy invasion wouldn't be complete without an air assault, and that's what we had in mind for them next. I heard Ray's plane before I saw it. He wanted to build one especially for the mission, but there was no way Winnie was sitting still while he assembled it from scratch. Instead, I coerced him into using a store-bought model of a Piper Cub—with the equivalent of a Molotov cocktail jury-rigged to each wing. I watched as the barely airworthy craft wobbled by overhead, making toward the L-shaped complex of the winery office and tasting room. Fewer than a hundred yards from the tasting room, the whine of the motor rose and the Piper made a kamikaze dive straight into its pitched roof.

It hit with a brittle crunch, and twin fireballs blossomed three feet in the air. Ray had filled the Molotovs with carbon disulfide, white phosphorus, and sulfur rather than the traditional recipe of gasoline and motor oil. The alternative brew ignited upon exposure to air, avoiding the requirement to fly the plane with prelit wicks.

It seemed to burn every bit as well as gas and motor oil, though. Flames from the accelerant ran down the hip of the roof, igniting the shake tiles as it went. Soon the entire face was engulfed, and sparks from the fire were threatening the other wing of the complex and even some oak barrels stacked by the eaves.

The point of the fire-bombing wasn't to catch The Winemaker in the buildings. We had pretty good intelligence that he—and most of his men—were holed up in the wine cave. The point of it was to sow confusion and tie up a portion of his force in fighting the blaze while we took our assault underground. Ray was supposed to report the fire next. We figured the arrival of several wailing, hook-and-ladder trucks would add that much more distraction, particularly since The Winemaker would not want anyone in authority to get a good look at his zombie guards.

When the light from the fire grew too intense to watch through the goggles, I turned my attention to my flanks and the slope below. Men were still scurrying hither and yon, but what before had seemed like random movement resolved into an outright retreat. Somewhere, someone had called the ants back to the nest and a good half dozen men in military fatigues were charging pell-mell down the hill toward the entrance to the wine cave. No one was even pretending to care about the fire.

With a short burst from the assault rifle, I picked off one guard who crossed in front of me. He dropped his own rifle and did two Slinky-like somersaults down the hill before colliding with a tree. I squeezed off several more bursts at retreating men—as much to keep up the illusion of a full-scale assault as anything—but no one else went down.

When the only ones remaining were me and the zombie guards, I scrambled to my feet and ran in a crouch toward the cave. I heard the doors clang shut just as I set foot on the concrete pad in front. The entrance itself was set back in the hill like a gigantic mouse hole, surrounded by a retaining wall of river rock. The dual oak doors were great iron-bound things with rounded tops. In spite of how sturdy they appeared, a single metal door would have been stronger, if less attractive.

I dodged behind a vineyard sprayer parked a dozen yards from the entrance, still concerned about being observed or shot at from a bolt hole. Rummaging nervously through stacks of extra magazines for the P90 rifle, I eventually located the only other thing in the pack: a six-inch length of galvanized pipe filled with black powder. At first glance, even the bombs Boris Badenov hurled looked more sophisticated, but Ray had at least upgraded the hissing fuse with a twenty-second detonation timer. In theory, I was supposed to walk calmly up to the doors, affix the bomb, and throw the switch. In practice, I was shaking so badly I nearly dropped the thing on my toes. My experience with the pressure cooker had really spooked me, and the more I stared at the pipe bomb, the more frightened I got. I knew that if I didn't get rid of it soon I would vapor lock entirely.

I slid the detonation switch forward impulsively, committing myself to action. Jumping out from behind the sprayer, I assumed my league-leading form and bowled the pipe along the concrete toward the door. Things went swimmingly at first. The bomb rolled straight at the door, and it was clear I'd put enough oomph on it to cover the distance. Then I saw the channel drain directly in its path. The drain was meant to keep water out of the cave, and in my haste, I'd overlooked it entirely. When the pipe hit the metal grate covering the drain, it bounced several inches into the air and thudded into the oak doors.

I dove for cover so I heard, rather than saw what happened next. The double doors creaked open and someone cut loose with an automatic weapon. The bullets whanged into the metal tank of the sprayer and exploded one of the tires. As loud as that sounded with my cheek mashed into the concrete just inches away, it was nothing compared to the pipe bomb. It exploded with a deep kettledrum rumble that accelerated into higher registers as the shock wave spread. The whole world seemed to go tumbling over a cliff.

By the time I gathered my wits enough to pry myself off the ground, most everything that had gone up with the explosion had come down. But there was still a fine particulate suspended in the air, and as much as I wanted to, I couldn't ignore the detached human arm hanging by the crook of the elbow at the top of one of the ruined doors. My guess was the owner of the arm had mistaken the thud of the bouncing bomb for an attempt to force the door and had decided to give the besieger a surprise.

I heard the crash of falling timbers from the conflagration behind me and the sirens of approaching fire trucks in the distance. Sulfur and the tang of hot metal filled the air. The Winemaker's Rome was burning. This was the time to charge boldly into the wine cave and take the fight directly to him. This was the showdown that Winnie, Ray, and I had sacrificed so much for—but as I stood on the threshold of the final confrontation, the thought of simply walking away came to me unbidden.

I had been running on adrenaline and several stiff jolts from a flask I'd hidden on the backhoe. Now I was out of gas. I was feeling my fifty-plus years and all the injuries I had sustained in the crazy run-up to the assault. In fact, I realized that I had never expected to get this far. I figured that I would be killed before I got through the fence or certainly before I blew up the generator. I never expected that there would be an opportunity to reconsider.

I shook my head, as if to dislodge these thoughts. I owed it to the women at the Bridle Bit, to the countless others the Winemaker might enslave, and, most of all, to Winnie to leverage my good fortune as long as it lasted. I checked my cell phone for status messages, but I wasn't really surprised to find a blank display. I followed protocol anyway and texted about entering the cave. Winnie was supposed to be coming through the rear entrance, and the idea was to join forces in the middle.

The doors to the wine cave dangled open like elephant ears. I slipped in from the right, stepping over the ruined corpse of the shooter and the body of another man who must have been standing behind him. It didn't take long for someone else to join the party. A pistol shot erupted from a hallway at the back of the cave's front room.

I dove to the floor like I was going to swim on it, thrusting the P90 out in front of me. I aimed at the dim shape crouching in the hallway and pressed the trigger. The snub-nosed barrel vomited slugs, drowning out the cough of a second answering round. It missed by a mile. In the strobelike muzzle flash from the P90, I saw a man in fatigues slide herky-jerky down the rough Gunite walls. I rolled to the side in case he had any fight left in him, but it was wasted motion. The pistol slipped from his hands, and then slowly, ever so slowly, he bent forward to press his forehead to the floor as if he were doing a yoga stretch.

I got to my feet and sidled up to the hallway entrance. Shielding the bulk of my torso behind the wall, I thrust the assault rifle into the yawning darkness and hosed it down. The unmistakable sound of champagne bottles disgorging followed the crystalline ting of bullets hitting glass. That didn't leave much doubt about what was stored in the next room.

I rushed through the opening, dodging through a pinched hallway into a larger space. In a scooped-out section along the left, hundreds of champagne bottles were stacked for aging. Bubbling liquid from the ones I'd shattered pooled below and in front. Beyond that, filling up the remainder of the cavernous space like giant shark's teeth, were rows upon rows of wooden A-shaped racks. I knew that they were riddling racks, used to hold bottles while they were methodically hand turned to position the dregs of the wine for disgorging.

But there was more than champagne and champagne paraphernalia. There was also a white-haired man with an automatic weapon in the far corner of the room—and just to make things really bizarre—two more men were turning bottles as if this were just another day at the office. Zombies.

Riddling is a task that requires precise repetitive movements—and was therefore the perfect operation to be "automated" by the Winemaker's electronic slaves. On that score, I shouldn't have been surprised. But their presence suggested something else. Ray was supposed to have jammed the signal controlling the zombie workers by now. There was also the question of how the Winemaker had the power to transmit the controlling signal.

All this thinking took too long. The guy at the other end of the room used the time to level his weapon in my direction. Slugs nickered overhead and slammed into the racks between us. I ducked behind the nearest one. He continued firing as he dodged to my right, trying—I assumed—to bring the zombie workers into the line of fire and hamper my defense.

I wasn't going to let that happen. I scampered left and then forward into the maze, cutting the distance between us. When I got to within a few rows of him, I took a knee to change the magazine on the P90.

"Riordan" boomed a voice that sounded uncomfortably close. "Your girl is dead. We evacuated the Winemaker. Reinforcements are coming. There's no percentage in this."

I couldn't let myself believe it. He was playing head games. "Donovan?" I guessed.

He chuckled. "My reputation precedes me."

"Yeah, as a murderer of civilians."

"We do what it takes."

I crept forward, trying to hold my voice level as I answered. "So the girls at the Bridle Bit were freedom fighters?"

A boot scraped nearby. "All progress comes at a cost," he said, and I knew we were crouching behind racks mere feet apart.

We both made our move. He popped up with his M4 carbine on auto and began raining a stream of fire over the tops of the racks. If I had stood—or even squirted out from the side—I would have been cut in half. Instead, I put my shoulder to the rack in front of me and launched forward. It was hinged at the top like a sandwich board, and the force snapped it closed and toppled it into the next rack. I kept driving with my legs until that rack toppled, too, pinning Donovan at the waist under oak boards, broken wine bottles, and fizzing champagne.

I struggled over the protruding wine bottles on the uppermost rack to get at him only to realize that the P90 had slipped from my grasp. As Donovan strained to retrieve his own rifle where it had landed by his head, I reached to pull the last weapon I carried: the knife on my ankle. I flopped onto him, my body splayed across his upper torso. He located his rifle and was attempting to pummel me with the stock, but my blade had already found its way between his ribs. We were chin to chin, the light fading from his eyes, when I hissed, "How's that for progress?"

I rolled off him, yanking the knife from him as I stood. I wiped the blade on his shirt and put it back in the harness. I should have been jaded by all the killing, but this seemed like a new low. I glanced over my shoulder, shamed by what I'd done and what the riddlers must think of me. I needn't have worried. They continued blithely with their task, grasping bottles, giving them a slight shake and turn, and then moving on to the next one.

I retrieved the P90 and then hurried to the rear of the chamber and the corridor leading farther into the hillside. The next room was much like the last, containing wine barrels instead of champagne—and no people. The third and fourth rooms were just like the second. When I exited the final one, I stepped into a long corridor with an amber light glowing in the distance. I found the source of the light fifty yards down: an emergency LED powered by batteries. To the left of the lamp was a sliding steel door and a corpse with shotgun wounds lying in front of it. Winnie's calling card.

I searched along the edge of the door, looking for a knob or a handle or some way to open it. Nothing. I yanked out my phone and pressed the button in the contacts list to call her—a breach of plan protocol that was to be used only in case of extreme emergency. It was a waste of time. The phone showed no signal bars this far underground. Foolishly, I pounded on the door and then called her name. All I heard in response was the echo of my pounding reverberating down the corridor.

Maybe she had fought her way in, found the same locked door, and had decided to pull out. Or maybe the Winemaker had sent reinforcements down after her, and she'd been forced to retreat. I turned away from the door and hurried along the corridor toward the back door Ray had spotted during the reconnaissance flight. The hallway climbed steeply, and when I reached the crest of the rise, I spotted the inverted U-shape of the door and beyond that the darker shade of the night sky.

I was sprinting by the time I hurtled through the portal to the gravel turnaround beyond. I was convinced I would find a firefight in progress, but there was no one left to fight it. The door swung freely on its hinges, undamaged in any way from the pipe bomb Ray had given Winnie to open it. The shotgunned body of one man was slumped in the driver's seat of a white van. A second lay in a bag-of-bones position by a ramp extending from the back. Off to one side, in the shadow of a granite outcropping, lay a backpack—the backpack Winnie was supposed to have carried.

I pressed the button on my phone to call hers and was not surprised—and very depressed—to hear it ring from within the pack. There was only one more thing that could go wrong, and I soon confirmed it.

Twenty yards off, at the base of an aluminum transmission tower, was the wreckage of a second drone. A drone Ray was meant to be piloting.

CHAPTER 31

Ray

THIRTY MINUTES BEFORE ZERO HOUR, Ray pulled his Dodge Aries to a stop in front of the gate to the fire road that ran to the top of Mount Saint Helena. When he got out to open the padlock he and Riordan had attached during their previous visit, he was surprised to find it was gone. There was no lock of any sort.

Ray decided that the park ranger—or someone else in authority—had discovered their lock and had removed it. It didn't seem like a good omen. It didn't seem like a good omen at all for an enterprise decidedly lacking in good omens. He spat out a fragment of cellophane from the wrapper of the Little Debbie cake he'd been opening with his teeth and watched as it fluttered through the light from the Aries's headlamp. Then he heard Riordan's voice in his head nagging him about someone of his advanced age having Little Debbie cakes.

Screw him, thought Ray. Riordan's favorite food was SpaghettiOs—

often eaten cold right from the can. That was a healthy mix of MSG, rat excreta, and bug antennae if there ever was one.

He flung the gate open and lowered himself gingerly back into the car. It was hard now to sit comfortably, much less take a piss. His prostate was acting up again. What someone of his advanced age shouldn't have was an enlarged organ the size of a rutabaga. That's what someone of his age shouldn't have. If he ever got into a debate with a proponent of intelligent design, all he would have to do is cite the prostate to win hands down. Any engineer with half a brain could have come up with a better design to inject a little fluid into a pipe than to wrap the blasted injector around the pipeline and risk cutting off the stream.

The old Luger digging into his backside didn't help matters any. Riordan had insisted he take it for protection, and Ray had shoved it in his waistband like he'd seen the detective do. *Probably shoot my butt cheek off if I'm not careful,* Ray thought. He knew how to work the gun, though. He'd shot it many years before. It came from Riordan's father, who was an old friend of Ray's. Ray and he had plunked cans with it in the desert behind the trailer park when Ray was about the age of Riordan and Riordan's father was living alone in the trailer where the detective lived now.

Ray shook his head. *A lot of history in* that *family.*

He nudged the car into gear and pulled through the gate. Then he got out to close it and once more went through the painful ritual of reestablishing himself behind the wheel. *Were the Little Debbie cakes somehow making his prostate worse?* They *were* chock-full of Yellow Dye No. 5, and he'd read that the dye messed with men's reproductive systems. He hated to think that Riordan could be right.

He knocked the box of cakes from the seat to the floor and urged the car up the winding fire road toward the summit. He drove slowly, carefully, hugging the mountainside away from the cliff. He didn't want to repeat the near derailment he'd experienced when Riordan and he had last gone to the top.

Ray promised himself that if anyone was going to execute his part of the assault properly it would be him. He didn't have much faith in Winnie. When he had presented ten single-spaced pages of his carefully researched, thoroughly timed, and meticulously described master plan, she had swept the stack of legal sheets from the coffee table, labeling it "OCD" and "fucked-in-the-head." Fucked-in-the-head Ray understood. Only later, when he had a chance to look up OCD, did he realize it stood for obsessive-compulsive disorder, which still didn't make much sense to him in this context. What was clear was that Winnie wasn't going to follow any plan but her own.

Riordan, never much of a planner himself, was clearly upset. "This isn't sandlot football where the quarterback can say, 'Go long' and hope for the best," he shouted. "Ray may have gone a bit overboard, but we have to plan."

"Kill the Winemaker," snapped Winnie. "That's my plan. And you're right—this isn't football, sandlot or otherwise, because we're not a team and neither of you is the quarterback of me."

"Jesus," said Riordan, as Winnie stormed out.

Ray and Riordan salvaged what they could from the ten yellow legal sheets. It boiled down to a grand diversion to give Winnie the best chance to do whatever it was she was going to do. In the end, she at least agreed to carry a cell phone and take one of Ray's improvised explosives to blow the back door. It was something, but it wasn't much.

The headlights from the Aires found one of the blocky buildings that lined the road to the top and then the other. A minute later, Ray pulled off the rutted fire road onto the football-field-size patch of asphalt at the summit. He parked where he had parked the last time and cut the motor, leaving the lights on to work by. He glanced at his watch. It was ten minutes to zero hour, 1:50 in the morning. Riordan would be cutting the power cable to the Winemaker's property soon and then trying to breach the fence. If he managed all of that, he would move to blow the generator. Ray needed to have the kamikaze plane ready to launch once he received the signal from Riordan.

He levered himself out of the car and half jogged to the trailer, suddenly anxious that everything he'd worked and planned for over the last few days was actually happening. He fumbled open the door to the trailer and pulled out the disassembled wings and fuselage of the Piper Cub. He carried them to a spot between the beams of the car's headlights and used a pair of crisscrossing rubber bands to attach the wings to the top of the plane. Then he hurried back to the trailer to grab the Styrofoam cooler containing the Molotov cock-tails. The cocktails were actually two 500-watt lightbulbs from which Ray had carefully removed the screw caps and filaments, filled with a self-igniting accelerant, and sealed airtight with special epoxy. He chose the lightbulbs to ensure that they would shatter when the plane crashed-landed into its target, but their fragility made them dodgy to handle and transport, to say nothing of the difficulty of attaching them securely to the plane.

He'd settled on a padded cradle under each wing, again relying on rubber bands to actually affix the bulbs to the cradles. When he managed to strap them onto the Piper Cub without lighting himself or the plane on fire, he sighed with relief. In many ways, this was the most dangerous thing he had to do that night. The feeling of relief faded as he squatted by the plane and pondered the question that had plagued him since he had conceived the plan: Would the stupid thing actually fly? With the bulbous appendages under each wing, the store-bought model hardly looked airworthy. Ray had wanted to construct a purpose-built plane to carry the cocktails, but Riordan had nixed that. He didn't think Winnie would sit still for it, and Riordan was probably right. It was just one more example of how Winnie had stampeded their plans.

Ray returned to the trailer and wheeled out his flight caddy, a rolling metal chest containing all the paraphernalia he needed to gas up, start, and pilot his planes. He did everything on his checklist to prep for takeoff and then returned to the Aires to sprawl in the backseat, which felt more comfortable than sitting, given his rutabaga of a prostate. He clutched his Walmart cell phone in his hand. Even if everything went like clockwork, Riordan wouldn't be texting him for another thirty minutes. He watched the minutes click by on the digital display of the phone, listening to the crickets chirp in the tall grass surrounding the asphalt. He'd read that you could estimate the temperature by the frequency of their chirping. You counted the number of chirps in fifteen seconds and added thirty-seven. He figured it to be about 80 degrees.

When the phone buzzed, he jolted awake, impaling the back of his head on the spiky door lock of the Aires. Drool had puddled on the front of his shirt. Ray held the phone close to his face to read the text. Riordan had kept his message short and to the point. "I'm in & the power's out" was all he wrote.

Ray was relieved again—and immensely embarrassed that he'd fallen asleep during what must have been a difficult time for Riordan. He chided himself to do better. He pushed himself off the seat and slithered out of the car. He grabbed the starter motor from the flight caddy, flicked on the juice to heat the engine's glow plug, and then pressed the starter to the nose cone of the prop. The motor caught almost immediately and Ray hurried to snag the plane by the tail so it didn't start down the runway before he was ready. After disconnecting the glow-plug wire, he took the radio controller from the caddy and shoved the throttle open. The engine screamed. Ray let go of the tail and watched as the Piper Cub trundled across the asphalt. He'd seen video of albatross takeoffs that looked more graceful. Just when it seemed the plane would go skittering over the side, it bounced off the runway and wallowed into the air, clearing the branch of a scrub oak by inches.

Ray let go of a breath he didn't know he'd been holding and hurried back to the caddy. He powered on a tablet computer to monitor the GPS tracking and video feed from the plane. The darkened Alexander Valley yawned beneath the aircraft, dotted only by a few distant lights now that Riordan had severed the power main. Without many landmarks to go by, Ray steered almost exclusively by GPS until the outline of the buildings on the Winemaker's property became visible on the video. He made for the L-shaped building that housed the tasting room and pushed the elevator down to put the plane in a power dive. The last things he saw were the rapidly approaching shake tiles of the roof followed by a sudden flare of light. Then the screen went dark.

The flare seemed to indicate that the Molotov cocktails had ignited as planned, but Ray had no way to be certain. It didn't matter. He knew what he had to do next. He called the county fire department to report a blaze on the Winemaker's property. Even if there was no fire, Ray and Riordan hoped the hubbub from the arriving fire trucks would serve as an additional diversion for the assault.

Ray set the phone and the controller down, and paused to blot the sweat on his forehead with the back of his arm. The hardest part was done. He had one more craft to launch, but it was more of a Hail Mary than a serious attempt to influence the outcome of the attack. The aircraft was a four-bladed electric helicopter, light, nimble, and capable of flying indoors as well as out. It was intended as a mobile jamming platform to interfere with the signals controlling the Winemaker's electronic zombies. In particular, it was intended to jam the signals controlling the Winemaker's zombies *inside* the wine cellar.

The theory was that Ray would pilot it through the back door of the cave after Winnie blew it open. Ray would no longer be able to control it once it got inside the cave, but it was programmed to navigate corridors automatically, seeking any transmitters it detected in the area, sort of a flying Roomba. It was also programmed to detect the frequencies the Winemaker was using to control his slaves and then automatically adjust to them. Ray doubted a single-frequency jamming device like Winnie and Ray had employed at the brothel would ever work again. The Winemaker would adapt.

Ray knew there were too many variables, too many factors outside his control for the device to have a serious chance of working. The biggest variable was Winnie herself. Who knew if she would even block the door open? When Ray and Riordan had explained what they wanted, she just laughed and walked from the room. Ray then tried to interest Riordan in flying the craft through the front door, the one that he was assigned to blow.

Riordan had looked down. "What sort of chances do you give me for making it that far?" he asked. "You better stick with the unguarded back door—and hope that she leaves it open."

Ray had nodded mutely.

Now Ray walked back to the trailer and pulled the quadcopter down from its shelf. It was about three feet across with four variable-pitch blades on pods emanating from a central hub. Compared to the gas-driven airplanes, it was simplicity itself to fly. He walked it out to a place in front of the Aires, set it on the ground, and flicked on the power. Then he returned to the flight caddy, retrieved the radio controller, and tuned it to the quadcopter's frequency. He pushed the throttle forward, and the craft rose as smoothly as a dragonfly, barely making a sound compared to the noisy gas engine of the Piper Cub. He caused it to pitch slightly forward and then zipped it across the asphalt and over the edge of the summit.

The flashing red dot representing the craft on the display of the tablet computer was less than a half a mile from the wine cave when he first heard the sound: a motorcycle with a small displacement engine. At first, he thought the sound came all the way from the highway, but then he realized that wasn't possible. The sound grew louder and Ray struggled to pilot the quadcopter while he scanned the darkness for the bike and tried to decide what its presence meant. At last, a lone headlight materialized in the only place it could—the dirt track leading to the summit—jumping and flashing as the rider flew over the rutted road at tremendous speed.

Ray vowed to stand his ground, but his resolution quickly dissolved and he soon found himself windmilling across the asphalt toward the edge of the summit. He heard the wheels of the bike chirp as they found the blacktop, and the headlamp of the motorcycle bored into his back, projecting the shadow of his elongated form off the cliff. Just as the bike came upon him, he dove to one side, flinging the controller into the bushes.

CHAPTER 32

Winnie

WINNIE PARKED THE SUV on a spur of the dirt road behind Marionette Vineyards. The dashboard clock read 2:20 a.m. when she got out to walk the remaining half mile or so to the back door of the wine caves. She was late—at least according to Ray's master plan.

Shadows from the transmission towers lining the road fell across her like jail bars as she walked. The aroma of sickly sweet wildflowers mingling with the acrid tang of dust filled the night. She thought about Riordan, and then she tried not to think about him. Winnie knew she'd treated him badly. She might've at least said good-bye.

She followed a tight curve around a granite outcropping and came abruptly to the road's end. There, at the far side of a turnaround, was the hill with the Winemaker's cave. Set into the hillside, sheathed in concrete but lacking markings or any other sort of adornment, was a single steel door. It gleamed dully in the moonlight—almost tauntingly, it seemed to Winnie. She wondered if the pipe bomb Ray had made for her would even dent it.

She crouched in the shadow of the outcropping and removed her backpack. She had to assume there was a video camera monitoring the door, so she wanted to be ready with the bomb and the detonator before she approached it. But before she had even unzipped the pack, the sound of wheels moving quickly over gravel boiled up behind her. Headlights stabbed past the corner, pivoted, and shone on the door. A white van just like all the other Winemaker's white vans skidded to a stop less than ten feet away. She dropped to her haunches and brought up her sawed-off.

One man tumbled out from the passenger side and another from the rear. The man on the far side hurried to the wine cave and waved at an unseen camera or window. The door swung open and he went inside. The guy at the back of the van wrestled a ramp of some sort from the interior. He was brawny and stupid looking—more pecs than brains—but when he happened to glance up and see Winnie squatting by the outcropping, she knew there was no way to avoid bringing the fight to them now, however much she would have preferred to wait.

The boom of the shotgun startled her even though she had caused it. The spread caught the beefy guy square in the chest and he dropped to the ramp, slumping and twisting to the ground as Winnie turned her attention to the driver.

She pumped the shotgun slide with one hand while she reached for the side door with the other. She yanked the door open and shoved the muzzle in the gap between the headrest and the seat. The driver was pinned, the seat belt tensioner locked by his urgent attempt to face her. He was fumbling for a gun in a shoulder holster when she pulled the trigger. The front windshield fractured like a mosaic; a viscous coating of blood and flesh stained the center in a bull's-eye pattern. The seat belt unspooled slowly, lowering the driver's ruined head to the steering wheel. Winnie shoved him aside to yank the keys from the ignition and sent them hurtling into the night.

She ran in a crouch toward the wine caves. She laminated herself along the door jamb and poked the barrel of the shotgun through the opening, doing the same with her head for a two-second peep. Winnie saw a long corridor, narrow and sloping downward, lit by banks of fluorescent lights. A sliding steel door stood open on the left near where the slope flattened out. She couldn't see inside. There was no one visible in the corridor, no one running to investigate the gunshots.

Winnie dodged across the threshold, sprinting at full speed. Five steps into the corridor, she heard a tremendous boom, and the lights overhead flickered out. She smiled and then felt herself tear up. The crazy bastard had done it—with a pressure cooker no less. She prayed that meant he was still alive.

A yellow emergency light came on above the sliding door just in time for her to see the last guy from the van cross the threshold. He skidded to a stop with a terrified look on his face, and she pulled the trigger. His head jerked back. He tottered for a moment and then went down in a heap. Winnie hurried past his sprawled body to crouch along the wall on the far side of the door.

A long minute went by—and then another. She peered anxiously behind her, worried that someone would sneak up from farther down the tunnel. She seemed to have lost her momentum, hesitating for the first time in a long time. Winnie had caught a brief glimpse of the space beyond the door, and it looked to be a lab or a physical therapy room. It, too, was lit by emergency lighting, and she'd noticed parallel bars of the sort used to do ambulation and gait training. She hadn't seen anyone else in the room, but multiple hallways fed into it.

It seemed obvious that the men in the van had come to pick up someone, someone who needed a wheelchair—if the ramp in the back meant anything. It could only be the Winemaker bolting for safety. This was the chance she'd been waiting for. She knew she should charge into the lab to find him. But she didn't.

A second explosion interrupted her ruminations. It was smaller, and it seemed to come from farther down the cave. Riordan blowing the front door. It dawned on her why she was waiting, what she hadn't been able to admit to herself. She was worried about Riordan—and she realized that she wanted his help after all. Winnie was waiting for him.

Others were not. As she watched, the body of the dead guy jerked and he gave a galvanic heave forward. Someone was trying to throw him out of the doorway. It was now or never. In another moment, they would close the door and she would lose the opportunity.

Winnie dove to a spot near the body, twisting to the right to bring her gun to bear on whomever was thrusting the corpse out of the way. It was a mistake. The two giants she had faced at the gym and the PG&E truck were waiting for her with shotguns of their own. As she brought her sawed-off up to fire, the quicker of the two—the one Riordan had beaned on the head—took a galumphing step onto the barrel of her gun. Her shot scorched the floor. Stray pellets might have nicked the other foot of the giant, but it didn't matter. He was like her—he felt no pain.

She released the gun and tried to roll away. It was no good. The giant was slow, but he didn't waste time reaching for her. He simply fell on top of her, gripping her around the ribs so tightly that she had trouble breathing. He tottered to his feet, hoisting her up like some kind of wildlife trophy. She beat on his legs with her hands and kicked back with her feet. He didn't feel any of her blows below the waist, and she couldn't reach his head.

The other giant—the one she had tangled with at the gym—came around to grin at her as she dangled upside down. He was still smiling when he clubbed her in the mouth with the butt of his shotgun. Searing white pain radiated across her jaw and spots swam in front of her eyes. She felt herself being thrown to the floor, kicked, and then hoisted back to her feet.

With her head lolling, her eyes pressed tightly in pain and blood dripping from her mouth, she heard rubber wheels squeegeeing over concrete.

"Close the door," said a voice she knew and dreaded. "And bring her over here by the light."

The door clanged closed as she was dragged across the floor like a wet mop.

"Hold her head up," said the voice. "Look at me, bitch."

The giant behind her clamped his hand under her bruised jaw and yanked it up. She grimaced with pain, closing her eyes even tighter.

"I said look at me!"

More pressure was applied to her damaged jaw. She yelped and pried her eyes open.

The Winemaker stared at her from his perch on an elaborate electric wheelchair. "What did you mention on our Skype call?" he asked. "Something about not winning?" He worked his mouth into a fissurelike smile.

That same mouth clamped into an angry line when a pounding from the other side of the sliding door intruded. Winnie thought she heard Riordan calling her name and felt a stirring of hope.

The Winemaker snatched it away. "Ignore it," he said to the giants. "No one can get through, and Donovan will deal with it shortly. We have more important things now." Seemingly on its own accord, the motor of his wheelchair kicked in and ran him to within inches of her. "Nothing to say now?"

Winnie licked blood from her lips and swallowed, but she found no words.

"Did you recognize something of yourself in these two?"

"W-Why?" Winnie managed to croak.

"You mean why did I use the technology to help them?"

"Yes, why?"

"That's Sergy behind you, and Anatoly over there. They are not from the same family, but they both come from a remote area in Ukraine where a certain genetic mutation is common. It's the cause of a growth disorder known as Banning-Billheimer syndrome. BB syndrome for short. Its victims grow to unusual size and height, but lack coordination. They often suffer from partial paralysis when the bones in the spine grow faster than the spinal cord, stretching and damaging it. That was the case with Sergy and Anatoly."

"Lots of people could benefit. It's why Ted built our company. But that's not—"

"Not my style?" The Winemaker smiled grimly. "You misunderstand me. I'm happy to restore their mobility. I'm happy to restore the mobility of thousands of young men like them—and any others who volunteer—to build a superior army. Think of it—immensely strong troops who don't feel pain or fatigue. No force of jihadists, however fanatical, will be able to stop them."

Winnie realized that her jaw must be broken. It was intensely painful to talk. "Selfless," she muttered nonetheless.

"Patriotism is selfless by definition. But I'll acknowledge a personal motivation. There's no denying that you, your precious Ted, and that idiot detective put me in a position to benefit. I have the same version of the technology as Sergy and Anatoly. It's of limited use to me—directly. The muscles in my legs were damaged in prison. But I can use it to move other things. This wheelchair, for instance. And more interestingly, Sergy and Anatoly. That's my other reason for helping them. In exchange for receiving the technology, they also give up control of their bodies when I want. Instead of an old damaged body, I now have two immensely big and powerful ones to direct."

"That's sick."

The Winemaker dismissed the comment with a head shake. "But as you must have realized by now, our version of the technology is lacking in some way. We lost some small but vital piece of the puzzle when we took the designs and the software from your husband's company. I need it back—and you're going to give it to me."

The Winemaker kicked the footrests from the wheelchair out of the way and stood on his wobbly legs just in front of it. He nodded to Anatoly. "Get a knife and cut off her clothing. She must be wearing the transceiver under the tracksuit. Don't damage it."

The moment the Winemaker mentioned the word *knife*, Winnie twisted to free herself from Sergy's grip. It was futile. He was immensely strong, and no advantage she had in agility was going to let her slip out of his iron embrace.

The Winemaker laughed. "When I was in prison, I was brutalized and raped many times. I owe you for that. After we recover the transceiver, we're going to pull the battery from it and paralyze you. Then I will use my Ukrainian friends to repay the debt."

CHAPTER 33

Riordan

I TURNED AWAY from the transmission tower and the wreckage of Ray's second drone to retrieve Winnie's backpack. As far as I could tell, everything she packed before she left—phone, shotgun shells, and pipe bomb—was still there. I couldn't think of a reason for her to leave it behind. I couldn't think of a reason, that is, other than the Winemaker had captured her.

I pressed the button on her phone to retrieve her call history. There wasn't any. On a whim, I speed dialed Ray's number. Maybe he knew where she was even if they hadn't talked.

The phone had only rung three times when I dropped it to the ground and bolted for the cave. I was suddenly convinced that she was behind the sliding steel door in the corridor. I dodged through the cave door, desperately rummaging in the backpack for the pipe bomb Ray had made to blow it open. I hoped the explosive would do as good a job on my new target as it had on my old one.

Ray had affixed a magnet to one side of the bomb to hold it in place. I slapped it against the stainless steel near the jamb and pushed the detonation switch forward. It didn't take long for me to decide that I should have given the whole exercise a little more thought. This bomb was bigger than the one I'd used at the other end of the cave, and what was worse, there was not much space in the narrow corridor for the explosion to dissipate.

I ran back a few feet the way I had come and crouched by the near wall. The next thing I knew, I was splayed out across the floor, my head whirling and a piercing ringing filling my ears. Dust choked the air, and two wavering light beams projected from the emergency lights that had been blown from the wall. The door itself was now a twisted ribbon of metal lolling out from the threshold like a gigantic tongue.

Blam came the first shotgun blast. It sounded dull and muffled over the ringing in my ears, but I felt the vibrations through the ground. Many more followed in quick succession, and I next heard a tearing, scraping sound as someone wrestled with the remains of the door. I struggled to my feet in time to see the most macabre vision of my life. It wasn't exactly Washington Irving's headless horseman, but it was as close as I ever care to get.

Racing down the corridor at full tilt was a man—a man very much like the Frankenstein monster I'd hit with the golf club. It was hard to identify him, though, because his face and part of his skull were missing. It didn't stop him from threading the debris with ease— or from putting a stiff arm out to block me. The explanation for his dexterity might have been the passenger on his back. There, with arms locked around the giant's neck like a jockey urging his mount forward, was the Winemaker.

I could have easily dodged the giant's outstretched hand, but I stood rooted, transfixed by the gruesome spectacle. He knocked me over, the Winemaker cackling and cursing as they passed.

I'd lost track of the assault rifle after the explosion. I was back to my standby weapon, my knife. I scrambled to my knees and flung it at the retreating pair. They kept on running.

I got to my feet to chase after them, but I was distracted by more scraping behind me. Another Frankenstein—this one with his head intact—emerged and rumbled my way.

I dove at his knees. He ran through my tackle, leaving me clutching one of his size-sixteen clodhoppers. I clamped on to it with everything I had, tugging him back. He wobbled like a mast on a rocking ship, heeled over into the Gunite wall, and then crashed to the floor. Two things happened next. I got a facefull of waffle sole for my trouble—and Winnie shouted my name.

In spite of being loopy from the kick, I laughed at the sheer joy of hearing her voice. She came dancing up, wearing nothing but her underwear and the high-collared RF shield Ray had made for her.

"Are you okay?" she demanded.

There were so many things that I wanted to ask, but I knew this wasn't the time. "Yes. Go. The Winemaker and the other one went out the back door."

She hesitated for a moment, clearly worried about me handling *this* Frankenstein, who was now gaining his feet.

"Go," I insisted.

She nodded and shot the gap between the monster's outstretched hand and the far wall. I used the distraction to locate the assault rifle, which lay two paces in front of the giant's lumbering form.

I jumped forward, hugging the far wall as Winnie had done and then reached for the gun. The smarter thing would have been to kick it down the corridor. My opponent, slow as he was, was too close.

He piled into my midsection. I flopped over like a shooting-gallery target, something snapping in my ankle. But I held on to the gun. I snaked my finger through the trigger hole and trained the stubby barrel down my torso at the heavy-boned face of the monster crawling up my body.

The garlic on his breath reached me before I pulled the trigger. The rounds decimated his uppers and went straight down his gullet. He coughed up a bubble of blood and slumped on my chest, his hand falling dead at my throat.

I let the gun slide out of my grasp and lowered my head to the floor. In spite of the hot July night and the smothering insulation of his body, I shivered.

I was done. I had nothing more for the fight.

CHAPTER 34

Ray

RAY ROLLED INTO THE SCRUB at the end of the asphalt, trying to avoid the motorcyclist. Rocks and branches bruised and jabbed him as he went, but the most painful intrusion came from Riordan's Luger at the small of his back.

The motorcyclist dumped his bike, hopping off with his handgun drawn. He strode to within a few feet of Ray and fired. The bullet bit into Ray's left shoulder. It hurt less than he expected, but he imagined the real pain would come soon enough. Ray groaned and lay still, playing dead.

The headlamp of the downed motorbike shone off to the side, providing ambient light but no direct illumination. Ray heard the cyclist flip his helmet visor up and then the creaking of his leathers as he bent down to get a better look.

Ray already had his right hand around the butt of the Luger. He snicked the safety forward and whipped the gun out from behind his back. It seemed to fire of its own accord, but the slug sailed well over the cyclist's head. The cyclist jerked back, raising his arms involuntarily. Ray willed himself to level the shaking pistol at the man's midsection. He put two shots into his gut and watched with a galloping heart as the cyclist tottered backward to collapse at the edge of the parking lot.

Ray rolled onto his right elbow and struggled to his feet. Pain radiated down his left arm and across his chest, making him think that the bullet had clipped his collarbone. At least the bleeding wasn't bad. He gingerly patted the wound. It seemed the bullet had gone clean through his trapezius.

He walked over to the motorcyclist and kicked the man's gun farther from his body. He was unconscious but not dead—at least not yet. In his place, Ray knew that Winnie would finish him, but now that the danger had passed, he didn't see the point. In fact, Ray couldn't see the point of much of anything. His arms and legs were trembling, and he wondered if this was due to the shock from the wound or the rush of adrenaline. Probably both.

Think, he told himself. *What should I do now? The quadcopter had surely crashed. Should I stay? Should I go straight to the hospital?*

He took a few listless steps into the scrub, searching for the controller he had thrown to the side when the motorcyclist approached. It was too dark to locate it easily, and Ray gave up looking for it.

He shuffled back to the light thrown from the Aries's headlamps and stepped behind the flight caddy he'd parked by the bumper. He glanced at the tablet computer and wasn't surprised to find that the video feed from the quadcopter had gone dead. On the other hand, he was still receiving data from the craft, and that data told him that the drone—wherever it had landed—was detecting transmissions on one of the frequencies the Winemaker used to control his slaves.

Ray looked down at the computer for a long moment, his hand poised over the touchscreen. *What in the hell could* that *mean?* He knew the drone had crashed outside the cave.

He shook himself. He needed to get his head back into the game. If there was any way he could possibly help Riordan and Winnie, he should do it.

He put his finger to the screen and activated the jamming.

CHAPTER 35

Winnie

Winnie felt light-headed from despair, the pain in her jaw, and a lack of oxygen from Sergy's crushing embrace. Her face was tingly and numb, her field of view narrow and murky. She wasn't dreading what the Winemaker and his Ukrainian slaves were poised to do to her as much as she feared being paralyzed again. Paralyzed and then dead, with the Winemaker in possession of the stimulator technology. He would win, and she would lose.

She must have blacked out for a moment because the next thing she knew, Anatoly was slicing off her tracksuit with a box cutter. He made a hash of the job. Desire and innate clumsiness causing him to fumble and score the skin of her legs. When at last he was finished, he dropped the knife and reached for her panties.

With Sergy's arms still clamped around her torso, she brought her legs up to kick at Anatoly's face, but even a crushing shot to his nose didn't stop him from yanking them to her ankles.

"Idiot," snapped the Winemaker, who remained by the wheelchair. "The transceiver first. It's got to be under the vest."

Anatoly seemed not to hear him. His stared at the place her panties had been and reached to insinuate a hand between her legs.

"Damn you," said the Winemaker. He lowered himself into the chair and fumbled beneath his jacket.

Winnie was too busy kicking to see exactly what the Winemaker did next, but a blank look came over Anatoly's face and he moved purposefully, almost robotically, beyond her reach. It was clear the Winemaker had taken control.

Anatoly picked up the box cutter and approached from the side. Sergy clamped a paw over her face and pulled her head back to make it easier to get to the fabric of her vest. The renewed pressure on her jaw was excruciating, and she felt herself losing consciousness once more. She wished she would pass out and never wake up.

She had just caught a sickening whiff of garlic on Anatoly's breath—and felt the steely cold of his knife against her throat—when something stood the room on its ear.

A shock wave threw her and Sergy to the ground. Metal fragments and other debris ricocheted off the walls. Hot air roiled over them. She was woozy and nauseous, and wanted nothing more than to press her face to the cool floor, but she knew she had to move.

She half turned in Sergy's embrace and fired an elbow into his eye. He stiffened and twisted away. She scrambled to her feet, finding her underwear still wrapped around one of her lug-soled boots. She yanked them up.

The lights in the room were out, but a dim orange glow came from a connecting corridor. Sergy lay at her feet, squirming and coughing. The Winemaker's wheelchair was blown over and he lay in a fetal position on the ground beside it. Anatoly, a few feet behind Sergy, mimicked the Winemaker's pose.

Winnie realized how lucky she'd been with the explosion. The Winemaker had been killed or knocked unconscious while in control of Anatoly's movements, so both of them were out of commission. Sergy was her main problem now.

As if to reinforce the point, he lunged at her ankle. She dodged out of his reach and skipped past him to the spot Anatoly had discarded his shotgun. She had no idea where her own weapon lay, but Anatoly's gun was still there, half covered by a piece of the sliding steel door. It was then she understood that the blast had come from the exterior hallway. Riordan was bringing the cavalry.

She fished the gun out by its barrel, reversed it, and seated the butt in her shoulder. The long barrel required more aiming than her sawed-off, but she had to make the best of it. With the stock gritty against her cheek, she advanced on Sergy, aligning the sights on a point between his eyes.

She pumped off a round to no effect. She held down the trigger, slam firing four more in quick succession. The first missed again, but as she closed her distance, angry swarms of buckshot decimated Sergy's face and skull. He reeled and fell backward.

Anatoly was next. She straddled his body, putting the muzzle inches from his ear. She pumped the action, but it jammed midstroke. The spent shell was stuck, almost certainly from the way she'd abused the gun earlier. In frustration, she leaned down to swing the butt into his jaw, returning the favor he'd paid her.

This seemed to have the opposite effect than she had intended. He shook his head, blinking his eyes open. He now moved of his own accord. She cocked her arm to take another swing, but he rolled into her thigh, tipping her onto the floor. Winnie scrambled on her hands and knees away from him. She couldn't afford to let one of these bastards get hold of her again.

She pivoted into an outside sweep kick, catching Anatoy hard in the shoulder. He snarled and struggled to his feet. Winnie had a brief opening for another kick, but what she saw then completely derailed her. Incredibly, Sergy—or the corpse of Sergy—was also lumbering to his feet. He ape walked to where the Winemaker lay, slung him over his shoulder, and bolted for the door.

Anatoly spied his fellow Ukrainian on the move. He snarled again and charged. Winnie jumped out of his path, barely managing to hook his boot with hers. He fell but quickly gained a knee. He stumbled to his feet and tore headlong through the exploded door, following on the heels of Sergy and the Winemaker.

She thought through what had happened. Yes, she had blasted Sergy and his frontal lobes to kingdom come, but his reptilian brain—and his motor function—remained. The Winemaker had regained consciousness and realized that it was time to cut and run. He had switched horses to his faceless but functioning mount, leaving Anatoly to delay pursuit.

He didn't delay it much. Winnie threaded her way through the debris of the sliding door and injected herself into the hallway. There, stretched out on the ground, was Riordan. He seemed to have tripped Anatoly yet again.

She shouted his name, completely forgetting the injury to her jaw. A bubbling warmth flooded over her, and she imagined for a moment that she'd regained sensation.

"Are you okay?" she asked, sorry that it came out more angry than concerned.

"Yes," he said. "Go. The Winemaker and the other one went out the back door."

She hesitated for a moment. He didn't look okay. He looked spent and drawn.

"Go," he shouted.

She dipped her head in acknowledgement and slipped past Anatoly. She flew up the corridor and through the exterior door, expecting to see Sergy and the Winemaker hoofing it down the road or struggling with the keyless van. She was disappointed. The corpse of the driver lay smeared across the gravel and the van was on the move. Sergy's ruined visage mocked her from the driver's seat as he swept by. Apparently, there was more than one set of keys.

Winnie took a half step after the van but checked up when she heard shooting from the cave. She thought about going back to help Riordan, but she was diverted again by the sound of a crash. Rather than turning with the road, the van had gone straight into the transmission tower at the base of the neighboring hill. She glanced into the cave again, feeling an almost gravitational pull of guilt. But she couldn't help herself. She picked the van and the Winemaker over helping Riordan.

She came up to the driver's side and jerked the door open. Sergy's head lay against the steering wheel in nearly the same position as the original driver's had. The handle of a knife she recognized protruded from his shoulder, blood weeping from the wound. But the knife hadn't killed Sergy and it hadn't caused the crash. Somehow, the Winemaker had lost control. He lolled in his seat across the way—conscious, the first hint of fear clouding his eyes, but paralyzed.

Winnie didn't know why they couldn't move and she didn't care. She yanked the knife out of Sergy's shoulder and pulled his head up by his hair. She slit his throat from ear to ear, finishing the job she had begun with the shotgun. She could actually see white from a vertebra when she released him, his head hinging open like a gruesome Pez dispenser.

She walked purposefully to the other side of the car, flinging excess blood from the knife as she strode. There was a certain irony in what she was going to do next. The knife, she knew, was Riordan's. He must have thrown it at the retreating pair. But more to the point, it was the same weapon he'd used in his very first encounter with the Winemaker. She would gut the Winemaker with it now. She would let him watch as his intestines spilled into his lap, and then she would cut his throat exactly as she had cut Sergy's.

She unlatched the passenger door, pulling it open slowly in an almost courtly fashion, as if she were a doorman at an expensive hotel. She knew the Winemaker's ears still worked. She would say the last words he would hear on this earth.

What issued from her mouth surprised her. "See you in hell," she screamed.

But it was too late. She sensed immediately that he was dead. Heart failure or a stroke had finished him before she could take her revenge.

She stepped away—the blade in her hand still dripping—and looked back to the cave. Riordan was there, dead or alive, no thanks to her. She had made her choice, both in what she had done and what she had said—even if no one living would be able to recount it.

•

Riordan came limping up before she could go to find him. They embraced and kissed in spite of her broken jaw. When she explained what had happened, he seemed not to question—or even consider—

her decision to pursue the Winemaker. It didn't make her feel any less guilty.

They compared notes on their injuries, and then Riordan called Ray on one of the burner phones. "He's been shot," he relayed to her with his palm over the receiver. "Sit tight," he told Ray. "And put some pressure on the wound. We'll be there in fifteen minutes."

Winnie hurried to retrieve her rental car so Riordan wouldn't have to walk on his injured ankle. On the way back, she heard a short burst of automatic-weapons fire and accelerated into the turnaround, ready to ram whatever new threat had arisen.

She found Riordan limping from the van to the car, the assault rifle slung over his shoulder.

"What was that about?"

"You said he had a heart attack. I wanted to be absolutely sure it was fatal."

She nodded, paradoxically relieved that she hadn't been the one to do it and that it *had* been done. It wasn't smart to be anything less than 100 percent certain now.

They found Ray on top of the mountain, sitting against the bumper of his old car with a wad of paper towels duct taped to his shoulder. He looked pale and shaken but, considering his age and the story he had to tell, surprisingly collected. When Winnie let him know how important jamming the Winemaker's signals had turned out to be— that he had stopped the Winemaker from making his escape—he became downright frisky.

They agreed to split up. Ray's injury was a gunshot and any attempt to get professional treatment would be reported to the police. Since Ray seemed to have controlled the bleeding with his garage mechanic's dressing, he and Riordan would drive south and find an emergency room far enough away that no one would connect the "accidental" shooting of an eighty-year-old man with the Marionette Vineyards gun battle.

Winnie would go to the nearby Queen of the Valley hospital in Napa for treatment of her jaw. She'd blame it on a car accident and refuse to check into the hospital overnight. They would meet again in Palm Springs in five days' time.

Winnie watched as Riordan helped Ray into the passenger seat of the Dodge and then limped around to where she stood by the other car.

"You did it," he said, smiling his crooked smile.

"*We* did it," she said. "All of us. You, Ray, me—and your crazy plan."

"Our OCD, fucked-in-the-head plan?"

"I still say it's OCD, but I withdraw the fucked part."

She put her hands on his shoulders and leaned over to graze his forehead with her lips. "Take care of yourself, old man," she said. "I love you."

Even in the dim light, she could see Riordan was surprised. Surprised and pleased. "I—I love you, too."

She found his hand and squeezed it. "Good-bye."

"Good-bye. See you soon."

Winnie nodded as if she meant it, but she knew she wouldn't see him. She got into her car and caravanned with them to Napa, exiting at the turnoff for the hospital but doubling back after waiting on a side street to be sure they had passed.

Winnie drove to Marionette Vineyards, slowing only a little to rubberneck the armada of police and fire vehicles on the property before continuing north.

When she crossed the Oregon border, Winnie told herself that their personalities were not compatible, that there was too much difference in their ages, and that eventually he would miss being with a woman who could feel.

As she pulled away from the hospital in Seattle, she confessed to the empty passenger seat that she had been motivated by vengeance—not just at the cave, but always—while Riordan's sole motivation had been a desire to help and protect her.

When Winnie arrived in British Columbia, she parked at a cove along the Sea to Sky Highway. She sat on a driftwood log at the end of a rocky beach far away from everyone. The tide was rising and the air was heavy with the dank smell of kelp. She rattled a clutch of pebbles in her palm and then tossed them one by one into the lapping waves. Funny orange-beaked birds rushed to peck at the splashes.

She didn't deserve August Riordan's love, however much she craved it. The best she could do now was spare him the inevitable heartbreak.

AUTHOR'S NOTE

The technology to restore mobility in spinal cord injury patients described in this book is real—as are many of the headlines on related research cited by the Winemaker—but it is not as mature as portrayed. To learn more about the technology's current capabilities and promise for the future, read the Functional Electronic Stimulation (FES) page on the Christopher and Dana Reeve Foundation website (www.christopherreeve.org).

Many of the scene-setting photographs are also "real" in the sense that they were taken in the California and Nevada locations described in the book. Some, however, were included not because they are literal illustrations of a particular place, but because they suggest a mood or an atmosphere that is *en rapport* with the text.

Two things in the novel that are decidedly not real are the characters and the plot. Names, characters, businesses, events and incidents are either the products of the author's imagination or used in a fictitious manner. Any resemblance to actual persons or events is purely coincidental.

I would like to thank my fellow writers Sheila Scobba Banning, John Billheimer, Ann Hillesland, Donna Levin and Russ Wyllie for helping me to make *No Hard Feelings* the best I can make it. Thanks are also due to David Hough for his superlative editing and Michael Kellner for his evocative cover and interior design.

Finally, I would like to thank my wife Linda for keeping the faith—and the leopard-skin hot pants!

CPSIA information can be obtained at www.ICGtesting.com
Printed in the USA
LVOW07s2332090816

499677LV00002BA/149/P